Jenna's Submission

THE SHADOWDANCE CLUB 2

AVERY GALE®

DEDICATION

Mom,

You always told me I could do anything, and you were right.

Your unconditional love and support have always seen me through.

Thank you for a lifetime of lessons in love.

Chapter 1

J ENNA LAMONT PULLED her baby-blue 1967 Triumph Spitfire off the side of the drive leading to the Shadow-Dance mansion where she'd grown up. For several long minutes, she simply tried to steel herself for what she knew would be a very long few days with her family. Oh, she loved them all more than life itself, but there was a lot about her they didn't know, and keeping secrets was exhausting when your older twin brothers were former Navy SEALs and Dominants. And virtually impossible when their best friend and chief of security was the only man to ever completely unnerve the unflappable and independent woman she'd always considered herself to be.

Running her hands absently over the soft, white leather interior of her little pride and joy, Jenna admired the details of the imposing steel gates blocking her entrance. She had to admit, her brothers' recent overhaul of the entrance was truly jaw-dropping. Looking to the left, Jenna felt tears sting the back of her eyes as she saw her brothers, Alex and Zach had done the one thing she'd asked of them when they had broached the subject of a major renovation of the entire property at a Lamont Holdings, Inc. Board of Directors meeting three years earlier.

Membership on the Lamont Industries Board of Directors was a bit of a family joke since the entire conglomerate was still entirely privately held. Her parents, Daniel and Catherine Lamont, her brothers along with their new wife, Katarina, and Jenna made up the entire board. And although technically her father was still CEO, he stepped back further each year, allowing his children to each head different areas of the Holdings Co., as it was affectionately dubbed. Since they all had different interests, his system seemed to be working well.

Jenna had often wondered whether she and her brothers had become interested in *their areas* as Dad called them, or if her parents had created those *areas* based on their individual abilities and interests. Shaking off her mental meanderings, Jenna stepped out of the small classic car she treated more like a child than a mode of transportation. When they had said they planned to remodel everything, including the front entrance, Jenna had asked her brothers to leave Henry's Gatehouse intact.

Henry Lott's wife, Sherry, had been her father's secretary for over forty years before her passing when Jenna was in high school. Sherry and Henry had moved with her parents to the mountain when her brothers were first born. Daniel hadn't wanted his children to be raised in the city and had subsequently built what he'd called a mountain retreat on ShadowDance Mountain. The mountain had been a part of local folklore for more than a hundred years. Tribal elders had always claimed it was a place for spiritual rejuvenation where the Great Spirit came down to Earth to celebrate and dance in the shadows of the mountain splendor.

Legend or not, Jenna knew to the bottom of her heart this would always be her home. This was the one place she could return to renew her tired soul. That didn't mean the place didn't have its thorns, namely Colt Matthews. When her brothers first brought their team leader home the Christmas of Jenna's junior year of high school, she developed a crush to end all crushes on the tall, dark, and handsome stranger. In the seven short days he'd spent with her family, she'd seen him as mysterious and dangerous, every teenage girl's dream.

Colt had to have known because she'd followed him around like a damned puppy. For his part, Colt had treated her like an annoying kid sister, teasing her even more than her brothers had… and that was saying a lot.

Jenna had always been close to both of her brothers. She'd always been the one who insisted that, even though they were mirror images of each other, their personalities were very different, and her relationship with each of them was unique as a result. Alex had always been the more alpha of the two very alpha brothers. He was the thinker, the planner, the rule maker, and rule follower. There had always been very little in Alex's world that wasn't either clearly black or clearly white. When someone had a problem needing a well-thought-out solution, they went to Alex first.

Zach, on the other hand, was the more reflective of the twins. Zach often judged a situation or person with his heart. Anyone needing to talk it out or a shoulder to cry on went to Zach. Now that they were both married to her best friend, Kat, Jenna wondered how the other woman navigated the stormy waters that often surrounded the two brothers. Smiling to herself, Jenna had every confidence in her fiery friend. Hell, Kat had practically grown up at ShadowDance, she'd spent so much time here, so it wasn't like she hadn't known what she was getting into marrying those two yahoos!

Jenna's thinking turned back to Henry. The sweet man

had always been the caretaker of the grounds, but after Sherry lost her battle with cancer, his own health had also started to fail. Henry and Sherry had become a part of the Lamonts' extended family, living in a small house Daniel and Catherine built for them behind the main house.

When Henry got to the point where he wasn't able to maintain the grounds any longer, he had told Jenna's parents he felt he should "probably just move to that old folks' home in town." Catherine Lamont had stalled while Daniel built a small gatehouse beside the entrance at the base of the long, winding drive leading to ShadowDance. Within weeks her parents were suddenly *very concerned* with "security" and installed huge steel gates which could be opened from inside the small gatehouse, and begged Henry to man the newly created post.

Deep down, Jenna had always known the threats to their security had either been completely manufactured or grossly exaggerated by her parents in order to keep Henry close to the only family he had left. Henry had faithfully driven his enclosed ATV to the gatehouse to protect "his peoples" every day until his death three years ago. Her brothers had waited until after Henry's passing to install all the electronic surveillance equipment now used to make sure their family and Club members were safe.

Jenna was thrilled to see her brothers had honored her request and Henry's Gatehouse, as it was known to everyone, sat beside the drive just as it had for so many years. Looking into the large window, Jenna felt tears roll down her cheeks when she saw a large picture of a smiling Henry hung inside the small building. The picture was one she had taken late one summer afternoon when she'd been home from college. She'd been out walking and had stopped to spend a few minutes with her beloved friend, taking a few posed and several candid shots while they'd talked about all sorts of nothing.

There was also a large bronze plaque mounted to the small stone building, the words *Henry's Gatehouse* boldly paying homage to the man they had all loved. Jenna knew her dad had a picture of Sherry hanging in what had been his office and that he'd put a similar plaque on Sherry's desk. That beautiful oak desk was now being used by Kat, who had been given the solarium just off Alex and Zach's office.

Jenna and Kat's friendship had survived Kat's run from Alex and Zach years earlier, and they'd been none too happy with their little sister when they discovered she'd known where Kat was and had been communicating with her for several years. But that communication had set the stage for Kat's return to ShadowDance after a terrifying experience with a crazed sadist, so Jenna didn't think they had too much to bitch about, and she'd be more than happy to explain it to them in excruciating detail.

Jenna was enormously proud of Kat's success as a web designer. Her friend's business was a wonderful creative outlet and allowed her to work from home. And God knew the Brothers Grimm as Jenna often referred to them, weren't going to let their pregnant wife venture far from their loving care.

Shaking her head, Jenna already felt sorry for her future niece or nephew. Having two daddies who never missed a trick and worked from home was going to suck. Poor kid was never going to get away with a thing! Sighing softly to herself, she moved back toward her car. Might as well head on up to the mansion on the hill and find out what could be so important she'd been called home from halfway around the world. The telegram she'd received from Alex had only said that it was imperative she attend the next board meeting followed by the details of travel arrangements he'd already made for her. She still bristled at the message's last word—it was so typical of Alex...*non-negotiable*.

COLT STOOD WITH his muscular arms crossed over his massive chest, watching the wall of monitors on the top floor of the ShadowDance Club housing what was known as the Crow's Nest. The area was the security and electronics hub for the entire ShadowDance property. Every hidden camera, every security device used funneled directly into this central monitoring location. The Eye in the Sky, as it was sometimes referred to because of their link to numerous military satellites, was always staffed by at least two men, and during Club events, at least one additional "watcher" helped keep an eye on the dozens of monitors wirelessly connected to the hundreds of cameras covering every inch of the property both inside and out.

The only place not monitored full time was the area known as the mistress suite. It was actually a group of rooms at one end of the mansion's second floor which was the private area used by Alex and Zach, The Club's owners, and their wife, Katarina. The men had designed and built the area for Kat, but a recent incident involving a man stalking her had exposed security weaknesses they'd made certain had been corrected while the trio was on their honeymoon.

Colt Matthews held the title Chief of Security, but the Crow's Nest was Mitch Grayson's domain. Grayson had also been a part of the "teams" and he'd been recruited by the Lamonts as soon as they learned he hadn't re-upped with Uncle Sam after his last tour.

Knowing Jenna Lamont was due anytime, he made sure he was in the Crow's Nest, so he'd have a chance to observe her before she made it up to the "house." He'd always found it amusing the Lamont family members all referred to their sprawling mansion as just a house. His team referred to it by the much more accurate term "mansion." Good Lord, the place was enormous. The master suite alone was larger than most single-family residences in Climax.

Colt was brought out of his musings when he saw Jenna's classic sports car pull up and park off to the side of the front gate. What the hell was the little hellion up to now?

Chapter 2

COLT PULLED UP a chair and watched the screen as Jenna sat in her car, looking lost in thought for so long he was beginning to wonder if she wasn't going to turn around and go right back down the way she'd come. When she finally got out of her car, he used the joystick to zoom in on her face and was shocked to see dark circles marring the smooth skin under her beautiful green eyes and the tiny strain lines around her mouth.

Christ, what was she thinking not taking care of herself any better than this? Colt knew when she'd bolted before dawn the morning after Alex and Zach's wedding, he'd pushed her too hard, but the woman would try the patience of St. Peter himself. Jenna's wistful expression as she approached the recently refurbished stone structure known as Henry's Gatehouse made Colt lean toward the monitor as if that might get him closer to the woman herself. Even with her tired expression and melancholy demeanor, she was stunning.

Jenna Lamont was one of those women who walked into a room and conversations between men and often women stopped. And amazingly, Jenna never seemed to realize the effect she had on people. He'd seen her work a room during one of her family's many social functions completely oblivious to the ripple effect her presence had in the room. She had always just gone about her business, never aware of the way men walked into walls and tripped over themselves vying for her attention.

Colt met Jenna when she was only seventeen years old. He'd been twenty-six and had agreed to spend Christmas with his friends after they'd discovered he didn't have family of his own to spend the holidays with. Colt had walked into Daniel and Catherine Lamont's beautiful home and watched as Alex and Zach Lamont's tiny bit of a sister launched herself into each of their arms. She'd wrapped her slender legs around each of her brothers, in turn, hugging them hard enough they'd both let out groans and told her to lighten up or they were going to expire from oxygen deprivation.

Colt had chuckled, but they'd quickly assured him years of ballet had left their little sister deceptively strong and sporting leg muscles that could squeeze you like a python. There had been an innocence about Jenna during that first visit that was conspicuously absent during his next visit to ShadowDance a year later.

During his second visit, he became aware of Jenna's newfound interest in kickboxing and any form of street fighting she could con someone into teaching her. Colt often wondered what had happened to prompt her interest in self-defense and what had stolen the innocence that had surrounded her the first time they'd met. He'd never mentioned it to Alex or Zach until they'd been drinking late one night, not long before they married Katarina.

At Colt's question, both brothers had leaned back in their over-sized chairs, lost in their memories for several minutes before they'd finally conceded she had seemed distant that second year Colt had spent Christmas with them. They said at the time they had chalked it up to stress over college selections and what they'd so bluntly referred to as "girl stuff." Colt knew he'd sparked their curiosity, and knowing the two of them as well as he did, he didn't doubt for a minute they planned to address it with Jenna at some point.

Colt had asked Jenna about the change himself during a rather intimate encounter after the wedding and had felt her completely shut down, both physically and emotionally at the inquiry. He'd also made the observation she was a natural submissive. The two things combined had been like dropping a match in a gas can. After she had unloaded on him, she'd promptly returned to her own suite. By the time he'd checked the next morning, he'd been told she had left the mansion before dawn. Jenna had not only run, but she'd been all but out of touch with everyone except Katarina during the past eight months.

"She looks sad." Grayson's soft observation spoken from over his shoulder was likely based as much on what he "felt" as on what he was seeing. Mitch Grayson's sixth sense was legendary among team members. As spooky as it was, his "spidey sense," as he called it, had never been wrong as far as Colt knew.

"Indeed, she does," was all Colt managed to say as he punched the button to swing open the steel gates so Jenna could proceed up the mountain drive. Colt knew Grayson had let both Alex and Zach know as soon as they'd seen Jenna drive up. Even though Katarina had begged them to call her as well, Alex had said they had just gotten her settled and threatened to do them both bodily harm if they notified the very pregnant Mrs. Lamont of her sister-in-law's arrival.

God, it was fun watching Alex and Zach try to corral the tiny blip of a woman they'd married. Katarina was just a little over five feet tall, and right now, she looked like she was hiding an over-inflated basketball under her shirt. She was convinced she "waddled like a duck," but Colt was personally impressed by how graceful her movements seemed to be considering she looked like she could topple forward at any moment. Just for the briefest second, Colt wondered what Jenna would look like round with his child, but he quickly shook off the thought.

His first order of business with Ms. Lamont was to regain her trust. He'd enlisted Alex and Zach's help when they'd made it clear they were not only aware of the sparks between their best friend and sister, but they would help him in any way that kept them from seeing her naked and stayed within the bounds of the "Safe, Sane, and Consensual" motto they all followed as part of their BDSM lifestyle.

As Colt made his way toward the door, he noticed Mitch cringe as he dropped his phone back onto his desk. Evidently, Alex was standing by his earlier admonishment to not call Katarina's cell phone when Jenna arrived. Kat might be little, but she was hell on wheels when she was angry, and even though every man on the security staff towered over her, there was no doubt in any of their minds who'd win in a throw down. Smiling to himself, Colt was glad she'd cornered Grayson with her request and not him.

"Sure, smile, you bastard. You know she's gonna be five kinds of pissed off, and it won't matter I'm only following my bosses' orders... Fuck!" Grayson continued muttering to himself something about tiny, round blonde fairies who could throw fireballs as Colt laughed and left him to his ramblings.

Alex, Zach, and Colt had brainstormed and strategized for months on what they had jokingly started referring to as "Project Jenna." They'd tried to anticipate all possible outcomes, but hadn't planned on having her stay away so fucking long. The brothers had finally enlisted their parents' help. Well, *help* wasn't really an accurate term since the elder Lamonts had only agreed to be unavailable to answer questions about the "emergency meeting" Jenna was being called home for. Apparently, refusing to answer was as close as either Daniel or Catherine were willing to get to actually lying to their beloved daughter. Colt was smiling as he descended the stairs. Hell, he felt lighter than he had in months. Project Jenna was now officially a go.

Chapter 3

NEARING THE BOTTOM of the stairs at the other end of the hall, Colt could hear Jenna's outraged, "What the fuck do you mean the meeting has been postponed? You called me home from fucking Egypt! Do you know what a nightmare air travel in the Middle East is like for a woman traveling alone? Of course, you don't. You two asshats are just too fucking unbelievable for words."

"Language, Jenna Beth," was all he heard Zach say. Colt knew without even entering the room both brothers were leaning against the stone mantle of the fireplace dominating an entire wall of their office as they watched their sister in full rant. He knew she was pacing the room because she could never sit still when she was mad, and her brothers had given her plenty of opportunities to exercise her pacing skills. Colt had positioned himself in a doorway behind a small alcove just outside the office. He wasn't exactly hidden, but he wouldn't be obvious to Jenna either. He planned to let her brothers lay it all out for her before he made his presence known.

"Don't you 'Jenna Beth' me, you big galoot. Boy oh boy, you two take the damned cake, you know that? If I'd pulled this shit when you were working Special Forces, you would have skinned me alive. But, oh, that's different... because, of course, your work was ever so much more important than the financial future of Lamont Oil. I swear to you, if I didn't care that my future niece or nephew actually *had* his or her daddies, I'd kick you both off a cliff. Hell, maybe I'll still kick you off a small one, yeah, not enough to kill you... just enough to hurt you bad! Damn, I'm too tired to deal with you two assholes right now. Shit, and now I'm too wound up to sleep... fuck a duck.... I'll be in the gym kicking the ass of whichever unlucky jerk is the first one to walk through the door. Damn and double damn..."

Alex's voice was calm but laced with steel. "Calm your ass down and sit, Jenna. We have some questions for you before you go off all GI Jane on some poor unsuspecting former soldier in our employ. And just so you know, they've all been briefed about you. After you cleaned the clocks of several of my best recruits last fall, word spread fast. They all knew you'd snookered them and none of them were thrilled about the pile of cash they lost when you laid them all out flat."

Colt could tell Alex was having trouble hiding his smile. Both brothers had been equally annoyed and proud of their diminutive sister when she'd taken down four of their security team's biggest members. When the men had heard she was headed their way again, they'd quickly warned the newest among them to not be fooled by her small stature and willowy appearance. Shifting his attention to Zach, Colt could tell he was biting the inside of his mouth to keep from laughing out loud.

Jenna plopped down in the nearest chair but was still muttering to herself. All he caught was "blabbermouth pussies," but he decided to let it go. Choosing his battles was going to be key when dealing with the spirited woman currently fuming as the three of them looked on. Once she ran out of steam, they'd get down to the business of finding out just what had happened between those two visits. Whatever it was, it had obviously changed Jenna forever.

After they'd compared notes, they realized that during their visit when she'd been a senior, she'd told them she'd been taking kickboxing lessons, and when she'd asked them to teach her street fighting, they hadn't thought to question her. In hindsight, that should have been a huge red flag because mixing those skills would have been unacceptable to any legitimate instructor. But they'd only asked her about the kickboxing, and she'd hedged with an excuse about wanting to be ready for college. They'd been young and distracted with their own lives and hadn't pressed the issue. It was a mistake they regretted and didn't plan to repeat.

Gaining Jenna's trust would be enough of a challenge on a good day, but to earn it while she protected secrets she'd been keeping for years would be impossible. All three of them knew if they were going to help Jenna recognize and accept her attraction to Colt, they were first going to have to find out what had happened to her.

SINCE ZACH WAS usually considered more sensitive than his brother, Alex, he'd been elected to take point in their "interview" of their sister.

"Jenna, it's come to our attention that your sudden interest in kickboxing your senior year might have been a little more significant than we were led to believe." He saw Jenna's posture become stiff and defensive, and quickly added, "Now don't go getting all pissy, we'd just like to make sure there wasn't some other reason for your sudden interest in self-defense. We're concerned we might have had some kind of trouble we missed at the time." *Something that might still be causing you a lot of pain.*

Zach paused for a few seconds, but she remained silent, so he continued. "As I recall, you also expressed an interest in street-fighting skills. Alex and I have spent a lot of time trying to remember things that happened during that time. The only thing we could come up with, that stood out as being out of the ordinary, was one of the guys from our unit spent a few weeks here that fall while he was recovering from a broken wrist."

Both Alex and Zach watched her closely for any reaction, and there it was. Her jaw tightened, and her fingers clenched into fists for just a split second before she caught and corrected her reaction. *Bingo.* To her credit, Jenna hadn't looked away from him, but at Zach's raised eyebrow, she said, "I don't know what you're talking about," in a chilled, detached voice so out of character for her, Zach was astonished she'd even consider they might believe her.

"Jenna, don't lie to us, ever. You're too strong a woman to feel you need to hide anything from us. Honey, you know we love you, nothing will ever change that, but please, don't disrespect our relationship by trying to deceive us." Alex had spoken quietly, hoping to get her to spill it without them having to pry for each piece of what was no doubt a painful memory.

SUDDENLY JENNA FELT like she was five years old again. Her

parents had always seen nothing but good in their darling daughter. Anytime she'd been 'busted,' it had been her big brothers who had called her out. And now, she felt like the walls were closing in on her as the memories of the night her whole world changed came bubbling back to the surface like scalding hot lava. Jenna knew she was breathing too fast. *Oh shit, this is so not happening. I am not discussing this with my brothers, ever!* Jenna heard Alex and Zach talking, but they sounded so far away. she couldn't make out what they were saying, and it didn't matter because she was too busy trying to clear the little black spots from her vision to really care what they were yammering on about.

COLT HAD SEEN enough to know Jenna was two beats from a full-blown panic attack. He'd heard the signs in her vocal pattern several seconds before he'd seen the rapid increase in the rise and fall of her rounded breasts. God Almighty, the woman's body was a fucking work of art. Stepping fully into the room, he'd shaken his head slightly to get her brothers to step back before he sat on the ottoman directly in front of Jenna and took her hands in his own.

"Breathe with me, Jenna. Let's slow it down a bit, shall we? In two, three, four, and out, two, three, four… Again, in… now out… That's it… No, look at me, don't look anywhere but right here." Gesturing two fingers to his eyes, he wanted Jenna to focus on him rather than her brothers and the information they were demanding.

During his special ops training, Colt had discovered he had a talent for interrogation, and it hadn't seemed to matter if he was prying information from terrorists, petty criminals, witnesses, or victims. He had always been able to slide through the cracks of their protective walls to bring confessions and memories to the surface with equal ease.

Right now, all Colt cared about was calming down the beautiful woman in front of him. They had obviously triggered something very powerful, and the memory was clearly traumatic for her to fall over the edge that easily. When Alex had recalled Ted Scott had stayed with their family for a week or so before returning to active duty, they'd all had a sinking feeling they knew what had taken place. After Scott had been killed during a cave explosion in a damned Afghan hellhole, they found out he'd been transferred to their unit because he'd been accused of sexually inappropriate behavior by several women at the base where he'd been previously stationed. As they'd mourned the loss of a fellow soldier, it had never occurred to either Alex or Zach to make sure their sister hadn't also been a victim of the man they'd allowed to stay in her home. Christ, just thinking about it had made Colt almost physically ill. Zach had spent hours in the gym beating the bag until he'd barely had the energy to remain upright and Alex hadn't been able to do anything but stare out the huge picture windows into The Club's gardens for hours on end.

Colt saw her coloring was finally returning to something much closer to normal, and even though they seemed to always push each other's buttons in a bad way, the look in her eyes told him she was grateful for his help.

"I think your sister has had enough of that particular discussion for the moment. Let's move on to something else, shall we?" Colt sat back a bit, but kept her hands held in his as he watched Alex shift position.

"Jenna, Zach and I are concerned whatever has happened in the past may be the reason you seem determined to work yourself into an early grave." When she'd opened her mouth to protest, he raised his hand to still her words. "No, hear me out. Mom and Dad have voiced similar concerns more than once. We've discussed it at the past several board meetings—all of which you've managed to be too busy to attend. So, as of this moment, you are on an indeterminate leave of absence."

Colt lost his grip on her hands when Jenna shot to her feet and shouted, "*What?* You can't just take upon yourself to decide what's best for me, King Alex. Goddamn it, you are so not the boss of me!" Colt struggled to not smile at what was obviously a well-used response to her older brother.

The minute the words left her mouth, Colt saw her wince. She probably knew she sounded like a whining child, but to her credit, she didn't hesitate, Jenna just forged ahead. "Zach, don't you see how wrong this is? Can't you do something with your asinine brother?" She looked at Zach with pleading eyes before letting loose on him. "What am I supposed to *do*? I can't just lounge around here until Mr. King-of-All-He-Surveys-Alex decides I'm good to go... Damn, you guys are taking this alpha male thing out on me because Kat's pregnant, aren't you? You can't wail on her ass, so you're going to make my life miserable. Shit, it's going to be months before she can go The Club and play. You can't possibly think you'll be able to keep me captive at ShadowDance that long. Does Kat know about this? Boy, she is going to kick your asses when I tell her what you two have gotten up to."

Colt stood and watched as Jenna paced. She had to know she was rambling as she stalked from one side of the room to the other. Colt looked on as she muttered,

"Fucking hell, they've got a lot of nerve. What was God thinking giving me two Neanderthal, knuckle-dragging brothers, anyway? If this didn't just about frost my cookies, I don't know what does."

Colt could almost feel the tension radiating from Alex as he watched Jenna wage an internal battle, and he wondered if her brothers had ever seen her this angry. So far, she had followed Colt's predictions down to the last curses, and she was playing right into their hands. Now that she was solidly pissed about their edict, they would present their counteroffer, which, even though it was going to sound like a compromise, was actually their original plan.

Smiling to himself, Colt stood back and watched Alex straighten and do his best to look contrite.

"Well, clearly we've gone over the line by trying to look after sister dearest's best interests. Perhaps we need to rethink this. Any ideas for an alternate plan? Zach? Colt? At this point, I'm open to suggestions."

Zach looked up into space trying to appear as though he was really giving Alex's words careful consideration. Colt thought, at that moment, his friend might have missed his calling. Zach could make a fortune in Hollywood as an actor. Finally shaking his head, he turned to Colt.

"Well, I don't know. Any ideas Colt? You seem to have reached Jenna a few minutes ago when we weren't doing such a bang-up job." Zach had just set the trap, all Colt had to do was bait it and they'd sit back and wait for Jenna to bite.

"Well, if it's R & R she needs, I'm headed to the cabin this week. I'd be happy to take her along and see to it she engages in some stress-reduction activities." Colt wanted to pat himself on the back for the double meaning of his words. Damn, this was almost too easy.

"What? I can't spend a week with you in some flippin' mountain cabin! Christ, you don't even like me. Why would you want to help, let alone spend the week with me?" Colt knew Jenna was giving herself a mental head slap. She would know she was giving the enemy too much information. She was nobody's fool and had lived with two Dominant brothers her entire life, but he'd still been surprised by her comment.

Colt stepped forward until his face was just inches from hers and growled, "What makes you think I don't like you, Jenna?"

"Um, well, you are always picking on me about everything, and then after the wedding, well, that didn't go so good for either of us, so naturally I just thought you'd want to stay as far from me as possible, ya know?" Jenna kept looking at him, but she wasn't looking him directly in the eye anymore—she'd taken a step back and shifted her gaze just to his left. *Interesting tell, sweet cheeks. Hope you don't play poker.*

"It seems you have been misinformed, Jenna. I do like you, maybe more than I should. But I'm not sure you are capable of following directives for a week, so perhaps you'd like to rethink that lounging-by-the-pool-for-a-few-months plan your brothers mentioned earlier." *Bait and challenge laid on the table—now we to wait her out.*

Colt knew they were taking a big gamble, but so far, she'd only surprised him twice. The first time was the intensity of her response to her brothers' questions. Then again when she blurted out she didn't think he liked her. *Damn, she has no idea how wrong she is.*

Zach leaned forward to draw Jenna's attention before asking, "What's it going to be, Jenna? We'll let the questions about Ted Scott go *if* you can make your case to Colt that Scott had nothing to do with the changes we all noted in you." He paused for several beats to let his words work through her anger before continuing. "You know exactly what Colt is offering. You spend the week with him and prove that his belief you are a sexual submissive isn't what caused you to run from your own home in the middle of the night like a scared rabbit after our wedding. More importantly, prove it to yourself. Spend a week exploring the obvious attraction between the two of you. If you come back at the end of the week and want to return to your old life, we'll leave you to it."

All three of them knew Zach stood a better chance of throwing down the challenge than Alex did. Zach had always been her champion. He'd once told Colt, Jenna had held his heart in her hand from the moment their mom had brought her home from the hospital.

Jenna stood staring into the fireplace for so long, Colt was beginning to wonder if he'd overplayed his hand... again. Finally, after several long minutes, she turned to him and glared.

"Fine. I know you don't think I can do this that I won't be able to walk away when the week is over. But I can. And I will. I told you once before, I'm not a sub, and I meant it. I'm too damned independent to take orders from a Dom who just wants to use my body to get his rocks off. Bring it, Matthews. Give it your best shot."

Even though Colt wanted to strip her and paddle her ass for her defiant attitude and belligerent words, he just slowly let out the breath he hadn't even realized he'd been holding during her little double-edged compliance speech. Oh, he was definitely going to enjoy training Jenna. The fire inside her was exactly what he found impossible to walk away from, and God knows, he'd tried.

"Very well, Jenna. But, I'm going to caution you now—from this moment forward, you'd best check the attitude and hold your tongue, because as of right now, I'll be keeping track, and rest assured, you'll get every single punishment you earn. I need to make some adjustments to the supplies I've already put together since I'll be feeding an additional person, and I believe Katarina has spa appointments scheduled for both of you first thing tomorrow morning."

He gave her a few seconds to process his words before continuing. "Why don't you spend the morning with Katarina, have lunch together, and enjoy some girl time before I pick you up at 3:00 p.m.? Don't pack anything except any medications you might need. I'll provide the clothes I'll want you to wear and everything you'll need during your time with me." Colt knew she would notice the change in his voice. She might as well become familiar with his Dom tone now. It would save them time tomorrow.

The play of emotions crossing her pretty face told Colt Jenna felt like she'd just made a deal with the devil himself, but she reined in whatever response had been dancing on the tip of her tongue. After several seconds, she took a deep breath before closing her eyes and nodding.

GREAT JOB, JENNA, way to walk straight into it. As her brothers were so fond of saying, her life was officially FUBAR, but even "fucked up beyond all recognition" didn't begin to cover it. Rubbing her forehead, trying to stave off the raging migraine she felt coming on, Jenna wanted nothing more than to fall face first into her bed and stay there for the next week. Maybe then she'd feel more prepared for what she'd just agreed to.

As a successful businesswoman, Jenna rarely came out on the short end of negotiation, but she had the feeling she'd given the three men standing in front of her every damned thing they'd wanted. *Fucking hell.*

STANDING JUST DOWN the hall, Kat had heard the power play taking place in her husbands' office. She smiled to herself... Oh, sister mine... you have just been played by the best of them. If she hadn't been so selfish in her desire to have her best friend and sister-in-law living closer, Kat would have stepped in and made sure Jenna was forewarned about the scheme Kat had known for a week the three men had been hatching.

They always waited until they thought she was asleep, then they'd sit in the office and strategize. Yeah, right. Strategize because that sounded much better than "plot and scheme." Soldiers were always so fond of snazzy terms for behaviors any seventh-grade girl had down to a science.

Katarina rubbed her rounded tummy and spoke quietly to her unborn child, "We want Auntie Jenna close, don't we? And, if this is what it takes for her to find happiness with the man who obviously adores her, well then, we'll just let your daddies think they have gotten away with this one." With that, she pushed away from the wall where she'd been leaning and headed in to greet the woman who was her sister in every way that had ever mattered... and then she was going to look for Mitch Grayson.

Chapter 4

J ENNA AND KAT went to Rissa's first thing the next morning. Sometimes, having the mini-spa right next door was a to-die-for blessing if you were to ask Kat, but then, waddling like a duck tended to make a woman appreciate being primped and pampered. Jenna was on her third mimosa and seemed to finally be unwinding while Kat sipped her orange smoothie and tried to hide her disappointment. Even though she didn't drink often, Kat was envious of Jenna's bubbly orange concoction.

They'd both had facials, been waxed, buffed, and massaged until Kat's legs had barely held her up. Rissa apologized for not letting them choose the services they'd wanted, but it seemed their favorite esthetician had been given strict instructions she'd followed to the letter because she really wanted to keep her job. Now Jenna and Kat were reclining in the comfortable overstuffed chairs in the salon while they waited for their Barely There Pink and Sex on a Bus Red nail polish to dry. Indeed, there was nothing like a complete overhaul to make a woman sweet and mellow. Lying back listening to the soothing music, chatting with Rissa as she got things ready for her afternoon appointments, Jenna turned to Kat and asked how she was adjusting to married life.

"Well, your brothers are usually fairly easy to deal

with, or at least, they were before I got knocked up." Then laughing, she added, "I'm still not convinced them forgetting my birth control pills when they packed my things for the honeymoon was entirely accidental. They didn't seem very surprised when I told them I was pregnant, but, holy shit, were they ever thrilled! And for God's sake, how many men buy EPTs to take along on their honeymoon 'just in case'? I mean really, they're not exactly super sneaky for guys who did black ops for so many years. If they aren't any better than that, it's a miracle they survived."

Rolling her eyes, Jenna had to agree, and knowing her brothers, leaving the pills behind hadn't been an accident. Her brothers did not do accidental… *ever*. Jenna knew they had been overjoyed to have Katarina back in their lives and hadn't made any secret of their desire to start a family with her. Kat had told her the two of them had confessed they'd known for years about her dream to have a large family. I seemed they planned to make that dream a reality at their earliest opportunity. Knowing those two masterminds, they wouldn't have wanted to leave anything to chance, so they'd happily created the opportunity.

Jenna could practically predict how Alex and Zach justified their decision to leave Kat's birth control behind… *Why trust the future to chance when you can direct it?* Oh yeah, she was sure Kat's suspicions were dead-on, but her new sister-in-law didn't seem to mind, except being pregnant meant her brothers were keeping Kat from playing at The Club like she wanted to.

One of the reasons Jenna didn't usually drink around men was alcohol was what she called *straight-up truth serum*. Even a small drink made her say what was really on her mind, and for some reason, her social filters didn't seem to work well when they were pickled.

Smiling to herself at her own joke, Jenna turned to Kat. "What's it like being a submissive to two of the bossiest men on the planet?" If she'd shocked Kat, her pal didn't let it show.

"Well, I'm not sure you really want me to answer that. Even though we've always shared everything, it seems a little weird to tell you about sex with your brothers."

"*Eww.* I didn't think about it like that… Damn, how am I gonna get the lowdown on this thing before I have to deal with Colt Matthews for a whole fracking week? Hey, Rissa, wanna tell me about sub sex?" Jenna's crude question sent her into a fit of giggles, and it didn't take long for Kat and Rissa to join in.

Kat closed her eyes and Jenna could practically hear the wheels of her friend's quick mind scheming up ways to keep her close. Jenna had overheard Kat telling Rissa she hoped Chief Snoop, as she'd dubbed Colt, could manage to behave himself long enough to convince Jenna to stay.

ALEX AND ZACH had assured Kat even though she saw Colt as an *arrogant buttinski*—her words, not theirs—he was actually a very popular and sought-after Dom at The Club. They insisted the unattached subs at The ShadowDance Club loved him. Submissives he'd played with swore he was as intuitive as they came, and his aftercare skills were "to die for." When she'd raised her brow in amusement, they'd waved off her snark and insisted they were just repeating what they'd heard subs say for years.

Alex and Zach told her Colt had actually trained both

of them years earlier, and they wouldn't be entrusting their sister to him if they didn't have every faith in his ability to show Jenna a side of herself they doubted she'd ever taken the time to explore. *Blah... Blah... Blah. I still think he's an arrogant buttinski, but if he can get my bestie to stick around, I'll cut him some slack.*

COLT WAS STANDING in the hall outside the spa listening to the women telling Jenna all about how to "get around a Dom's rules." Looking up at Alex and Zach, he raised his eyebrow.

"You going to deal with your woman?" At their nods, he added, "Give a heads-up to Grayson about Rissa. I know he's topped her a few times, and I'm sure he'll be interested in this as well."

Shaking his head, Colt added, "Hell, I might need to hold another Dom class for you pussies." The grin spreading across his face softened his words, but he also knew Alex and Zach would spend hours torturing their little sub. And even though they wouldn't spank her until after the baby was born, Colt knew the Lamont twins would find plenty of creative punishments for their little spitfire. He also knew Rissa would be putting in some time over The Club's spanking bench with her rounded ass a lovely fire-engine red displayed for all to see. Knowing Grayson's penchant for giving the other Dom's a chance to add a couple of swats for good measure, Rissa wasn't going to be sitting comfortably for at least a week.

"Well, gentlemen, I believe it's time I ended their little gab session and took your drunk little sister off your hands for a few days." Colt turned and pushed through the doors, carrying a bag containing the clothes he planned to dress Jenna in for their trip to his cabin. Oh, she was not going to appreciate his fashion sense at all. *Let the games begin.*

"YOU WANT ME to wear *that*? In a vehicle? Going down a public highway? Are you out of your fucking mind?" Jenna's voice had climbed the scale, ending up shrill enough, she wondered how many dogs would show up from the neighboring county.

Colt crossed his arms over his massive chest and looked down at her with an air of arrogance she'd come to recognize as his 'this is not a fucking discussion look.'

"I do indeed expect exactly that. Now, you can either wear what I have provided, or you can wear nothing. It's your choice."

That's not a choice, asshat... that's manipulation at its most basic.

With his bulging arms still crossed over his massive chest, Jenna's focus blurred as she wondered what he would look like without his snug fitting shirt. *I'll bet it's a fucking sight to behold. Damn, the man is sex on a stick. Yep, a two-alarm panty-melt coming right up!* Jenna started to giggle at her own musings, but went instantly quiet at the thunderous look on his face. Pretty obvious he didn't see anything at all amusing about this conversation. *Go figure.*

Damn, those mimosas are gonna get me in a lot of trouble... but right now, I'm having a little trouble working up to give a rat's ass. Turning the small bag he'd handed her upside down for dramatic effect, Jenna said, "Um, you probably didn't notice, but there aren't any panties in this bag. And well, this dress is completely sheer, so I'm going to need a strapless bra, too." Shaking the up-ended bag, she added, "See? Nothing resembling undergarments in this bag. Hey! I need shoes, too."

"Jenna, you are holding in your hand exactly what I want you to wear. Now, either put the dress on, or I will lead you out to the truck just like you are. And I have to tell you, sweetheart, that will be no hardship for me because you look mighty fine standing there completely exposed to my view." Colt's words had exactly the effect he'd know they would. Jenna had dropped the bright-red dress over her head before he'd finished speaking. She hadn't even remembered she was standing in front of him stark naked. Chuckling to himself, he took her by the hand, said their goodbyes to Rissa, reminding her to send him the bill for this morning's services for Jenna, and walked out to his truck.

Chapter 5

A S THEY NEARED The Club's outside door, Jenna discovered she was having trouble walking in a straight line, even with Colt's hand firmly locked around her upper arm, she felt like a willow in a strong breeze. *Damn, what did Rissa put in my drinks, anyway? Wow!* She looked down at her bare feet and groaned.

"I need shoes. Look at my snazzy pedicure, it's going to be wrecked by the cobblestone walk."

COLT DIDN'T BOTHER to answer, he just looked down at her and raised an eyebrow. When they reached the front entrance, he picked her up into his arms, pushed through the heavy wooden doors, and headed to the passenger side of his truck. Opening the pickup door, Colt set her inside, then reached across her to secure her seat belt. When Jenna started to lean forward, his growled "Stay where I put you, Jenna" made her freeze in place.

She watched with wide eyes as he closed the door, then moved around the front of the truck. When he was seated behind the steering wheel, Colt turned to face her.

"When I place you somewhere, I will expect you to

stay exactly there. When I set you in or help you into any vehicle, I will always see to your safety belt, and you will remain in the vehicle when we arrive at our destination until I come around and open the door for you. Do you understand this?" Colt knew the ever-analytical Ms. Lamont would need a continuous flow of information at the beginning of her training. Her mind was so sharp, her insatiable thirst for knowledge would be a constant distraction unless it was fed.

"Yes, that's pretty basic and straightforward. I do believe I can remember that, but thanks for checking." Jenna knew her voice was dripping with sarcasm, but damn, what did he think she was, some kind of freaking dimwit? Well, okay, so she was a bit toasted and not firing on all cylinders, but geez.

"Watch your tone, princess. You have already earned a punishment for becoming inebriated this afternoon. I'm fairly certain you don't want to go for another before we even leave the parking lot—or do you?" His arrogant tone grated on her last nerve, but she didn't think it would be in her best interest to mention it.

"Inebriated? I'm just tipsy, that's all, geez you don't need to be such a drama queen, Matthews. Damn, I just had a couple of mimosas. Orange juice is good for you, ya know." Jenna knew she was poking the bear, but just couldn't seem to help herself. She really was going to have to find out what was in those drinks.

"You had three, and you skipped breakfast and lunch. And... that's two." Colt started the truck and headed down the drive. "Not taking proper care of your body is a punishable offense in D/s relationships, pet, as is lying about how many drinks you had."

"Wait, how do you know how many drinks I had?

Were you spying on us?" Jenna had a sinking feeling she already knew the answer. Neither Colt nor her brothers would see a thing wrong with monitoring every inch of the ShadowDance property, and God knew, they would consider the inside of The Club fair game.

Just fucking dandy, I don't even want to think about the peep show they got this morning with the full wax job I got. Bet they were thrilled with the conversations, too. Jenna just wished she could remember what all was said, but the warm sunshine streaming in through the window, the gentle movement of the truck as Colt maneuvered his way down the curving highway, and the soft leather seats, on top of too much alcohol were combining to make her too sleepy to worry about it right at that moment.

COLT HADN'T BOTHERED to respond her questions. She already knew the answers even if she hadn't liked thinking about all they might have given away during their discussions. Right now, he'd let silence work in his favor. She was fading fast and with any luck, she'd sleep all the way to the cabin. He'd get a chance to mentally prepare for the week to come, and she wouldn't know exactly where they were when she woke up. Not knowing where he'd taken her might make it a little less tempting for her to try to bolt when the going got tough. It was going to have to get pretty fucking intense if he had any hope of bringing down all the barriers his little princess had spent years erecting to protect her tender heart.

There had been several years he'd been as adamant in denying their mutual attraction as she still appeared to be.

For the past couple years, he'd known she was the one he'd been searching for, but he wasn't foolish enough to believe convincing her of that fact was going to be anything but the biggest challenge he'd ever faced.

Pausing when he reached the highway, Colt looked over at the woman sitting next to him. He'd never been one to back away from a good fight, and he wouldn't start now. Reaching over the sleeping beauty next to him, Colt reclined her seat, then pulled the soft throw from behind his seat to cover her. The dark circles under her eyes made him curse silently under his breath. *Damn woman doesn't take care of herself worth a damn.* Shaking his head, Colt pulled away from the stop sign at the bottom of the ShadowDance drive and headed west on the highway.

Even though the cabin he shared with Mitch Grayson and Bryant Davis was still on ShadowDance Mountain, the only vehicle access was from the opposite side of the river, so they'd need to make the twenty-minute drive which would take them to one of the few bridges spanning the fast-moving water flowing at near capacity from last winter's record snowfalls.

Colt couldn't wait to show Jenna how crystal clear the water flowing beneath their overhanging deck and how the rocks lining the riverbed formed a natural mural displaying the beautiful local geology. And it was going to be fun to see her shock when he dropped her into the frigid water the first time she got out of hand. *Yes indeed, it's going to be an interesting week for sure.*

Chapter 6

J ENNA'S EYES FLUTTERED open when Colt opened her door. Her sweet smile as he leaned across her to unfasten her safety belt was full of innocent wonder. Colt struggled to hold back his laughter at how misleading that look was because Jenna Lamont was no one's shrinking violet, that was for certain. But, then again, where would be the fun in life with a doormat? Colt slid his arms behind her back and under her knees, then turned to walk to the cabin. Jenna finally found her voice, and turning to look all around her, asked, "Where is your cabin?"

Colt smiled. "Hard to spot, isn't it? It's above you. The entrance is hidden in the rocks, see the staircase straight ahead of us?"

"Wow, you've taken great care to ensure the place blends into the environment, haven't you? Is the entire residence inside the rock walls?" Colt could tell Jenna was finally coming fully awake, and that she seemed genuinely interested in the place Colt Matthews considered a soul-restoring hideaway.

COLT MATTHEWS AND Mitch Grayson had spent many

nights in locations Colt was certain God himself had forsaken, talking late into bleak nights, brainstorming details of what would become their dream retreat. The entire structure was built into the side of a canyon wall overlooking the river running through the lower part of ShadowDance Mountain. When Grayson had suggested including his friend, Bryant Davis, Colt had readily agreed. The man was a world-renowned engineer, and on the occasions they'd met, he had seemed like a stand-up kind of guy.

A rock shelf about halfway up the canyon wall effectively hid the largest part of the cabin's exterior from view when passing below along the river's edge. The front of the residence was entirely glass enclosed and faced the south, so the interior was bathed in warm sunshine during the long winter months. They'd all laughed that even during the longest winter months, none of them would ever suffer from seasonal affective disorder because they'd be getting plenty of nature's golden energy booster.

As they approached the bottom of the staircase, Jenna wasn't surprised to see well-hidden surveillance equipment and a high-tech security panel Colt proceeded to punch a long series of numbers into.

"The codes change at irregular intervals and are totally random, and so far, we have never had a security breach. Like your brothers, Grayson and I have both made a number of enemies over the years, so we make every attempt to see to the safety of our surroundings." Colt's statement of the obvious made Jenna smile.

"Indeed, you do. But do you really think international terrorists would travel halfway around the globe just to rob you?" Jenna had always felt her brothers' obsession with security was, at times, completely over-the-top. She understood they or their families might become the targets of domestic crimes, kidnapping, etcetera. But satellite and infrared technology seemed a bit too close to paranoia for her comfort.

Colt wasn't sure how much Alex and Zach had shared with their family regarding their team's continued black ops work, so he knew he needed to keep his comments in general terms.

"It isn't like any of us are completely out of the business, Jenna. We still contract for Uncle Sam as I'm sure you're aware. And you need to see it from a criminal's mindset. If someone is trying to bring you down, and they are relentless in their efforts, you want to distract them, right?" He waited for her to nod her assent, then continued, "What better way to distract your enemies than to target someone or something they love, be it a person or place?" When she didn't look convinced, he added, "Okay, think of it this way, if you wanted to *really* hurt your brothers, what would you do?"

"Hurt Kat," Jenna's softly spoken words told him understanding had dawned. Everyone has a weak point, and for most people, it was the person they loved.

"Absolutely. There have been vast techno improvements to the ShadowDance security network since Katarina's arrival. Most aren't visible to the naked eye, but I assure you, they are in place. Your little whirlwind of a friend doesn't make a move at least three people besides your brothers aren't aware of. Alex and Zach have made sure each member of the security team knows her safety takes precedence even above theirs. Something our superiors at NSA routinely balk at."

Smiling as he leaned against the deck railing where they had stopped to talk, he looked over and studied her profile. She was breathtakingly beautiful, and in the fading light of the late afternoon, the reddish-golden rays of sunshine highlighted her grass-green, wide-set eyes and lush, deep red lips that always looked bee-stung.

Jenna had inherited the best of her mother's soft beauty in addition to her father's dark hair and skin tones, but while both of her parents were statuesque, Jenna was diminutive. Colt was sure she couldn't be over five foot two. He remembered his friends always cautioning visitors to not be fooled by her size, reminding anyone coming home for a holiday or to visit with them to beware of the *Warrior Fairy*.

After Jenna had taken up kickboxing while still in high school, she continued into college and had even been accomplished enough to be competitive on a national level. Now, after she'd spent the past several years avoiding close physical relationships, her recent mention of self-defense was being looked at speculatively. Colt intended to find out exactly what had happened to prompt Jenna's sudden need to feel capable of defending herself from a physical attack. That, along with his desire to finally put an end to her denial of their mutual attraction, was the basis for this trip to *Pomola*.

"What does *Pomola* mean?" Jenna asked, looking toward the front door. "I know you well enough to know there is a story behind the name." She was smiling and relaxed, and Colt couldn't remember the last time he'd spoken to Jenna for this long without some sort of snarky remark crossing those sweet lips. He honestly enjoyed her company; she was bright, intuitive, and loved her family deeply. He'd always known she held an explosive passion in check, simmering just below the surface.

"Native American legend calls the bird spirit associated

with winter winds and storms *Pomola*. The bird spirit *Pomola* was supposed to be large enough to carry off a moose. So, since there are moose in this area, and God knows, we experience the ferocity of the winter's storms and wind, it seemed appropriate." He smiled down at her look of wonder and knew her mind was always processing every bit of information it took in. She analyzed, categorized, and stored information with astonishing speed. Teaching her to shut down her constant over-thinking was going to be one of his biggest challenges.

He had no doubt she used those same analytical skills to build and maintain the glass walls around her heart she'd spent years erecting and polishing to a gleaming shine. She didn't realize while she'd put all those protections in place to keep out the pain, they also kept her from experiencing life's gifts of passion and joy. If everything went according to plan, he'd be changing that, and this week would give him a good head start.

Chapter 7

A FTER KEYING ANOTHER long series of numbers into a second security pad, Colt opened the door and stepped forward to block Jenna's entrance.

"Let's review why we're here and exactly what my expectations will be during this week." The timbre of Colt's voice didn't give any indication he was speaking about anything more interesting than next Thursday's weather prediction. His gaze was steady and held her captive with an intensity that was a stark contradiction to his matter-of-fact tone. Jenna found herself so focused on Colt, she wasn't even aware of any of her surroundings, and she had a fleeting thought about how odd that seemed, but it was gone just as quickly.

"First rule, you'll do exactly—that means no less, no more—as you're instructed. You are expected to obey commands without hesitation. Disobeying and hesitation will both be punished. For the rest of today only, if you have a question about a command, I'll allow you to ask. I may or may not explain my reasoning. Do you understand this rule, pet?" When Jenna simply nodded her head, Colt added, "Jenna, I believe you know enough about the lifestyle your brothers have chosen to know that response is not good enough. Try again."

"Yes, Sir, I understand the rule," Jenna's voice sounded

soft and airy even to her own ears.

"Very good, princess. Now, the second rule is no one else touches your body other than me or someone I have given permission. Grayson and I do sometimes enjoy a ménage if it works in everyone's best interest, so don't be surprised to see him at some point during this week. I'll assess our progress, and he and I will decide what will work the best for your training." As he'd been explaining this rule, he'd run his hand under her dress and was tracing his fingers through her rapidly damping folds. "I see you are not completely opposed to that idea, are you, pet?"

Colt's grin was sexy and entirely too cocky for Jenna's liking. She stiffened and started to shift subtly away from his touch until she saw his brow raise in challenge.

"I'm not sure I want to do that, I'll have to let you know after I have a chance to think it through." Jenna started to fidget against his touch, arousal bursting through her system at warp speed. At this rate, she was going to come standing right here on the damned front deck. *Damn, I have no fracking self-control at all.*

"WOULD YOU LIKE to rephrase that, or should I just add another punishment to what you've already earned this morning?" Colt's fingers never stopped moving as she trembled. The flooding of her sweet cream over his fingers told him all he needed to know. Sweet Jesus, but his little Jenna was going to be a joy to take in hand.

"I understand, but I still think—"

"Another punishment it is then," Colt cut off Jenna's protest with a stern voice. "Now, on to rule three. You are not allowed to come without permission." He watched as her pupils dilated and her breathing hitched. God damn, he loved her responsiveness. *Note to self. Remind her she isn't allowed to play poker with the security team. They'll fleece my little lamb in a heartbeat!*

"But how am I supposed to stop something like that? I can't make my body not react to—Oh my God!" Colt halted her protest by plunging his fingers deep inside her sopping depths. He was shocked at how little progress he actually made inside. Christ, but she was tight. He was instantly hard. *Damn it all to hell, how long has it been since she's had sex?* He'd always assumed the globe-trotting oil executive would have been at least somewhat sexually active, but now he was fairly certain that wasn't the case.

Leaning forward to brush a soft kiss over her lips, he felt her tremble against his fingers. "Oh, my beautiful Jenna, you will learn to control your release. Remember, your pleasure belongs to me, and you'll have it when I say you can. No self-stimulation unless you are instructed to do so by myself or Grayson. We often like to watch how a woman gives herself pleasure. It's not only informative, but hotter than hell. Understand?"

"Y–yes, I u–u–understand." Jenna was nearly panting and added a softly moaned, "Please."

"Please what, princess? What do you want? You'll be allowed to ask for what you want. But keep in mind, I may or not agree it's what you *need*. And providing a sub with everything she needs is every Dom's obligation and pleasure. I'm going to push you, don't doubt that for a moment, I'll try to shove aside every wall you try to hide behind. I'll take every ounce of your resistance and shatter it with pleasures you haven't even dreamt possible. Come now, Jenna."

Colt's voice had been growing in intensity and volume until the last sentence was so sternly spoken, it left no doubt it was a command. He'd deliberately increased the intimacy by speaking directly against the sensitive shell of her ear to begin binding her body and pleasure to his own.

It was important that a sub's body reacted to the Master's voice without the brain's involvement being required. The best way he'd ever been able to explain it was the sub's reactions should be almost reflexive. His words had barely crossed his lips when she exploded in orgasm. Her knees collapsed, but Colt had been ready and caught her easily around the waist. His fingers moved through her swollen tissues until he was convinced he'd wrung every bit of orgasm he could from his sweet sub.

She was absolutely stunning, all flushed with her sated expression and soft, unfocused gaze. Once she was able to stand again, Colt steadied her and watched until she seemed to come back to the present. Once her eyes seemed focused on his, he simply said, "Strip, princess."

It took a couple of seconds for Jenna to realize what he'd said. "Out here? What if someone sees?"

"First, it was an order, not a suggestion, so that's another punishment. You're already at four. That's a lot of swats, pet, best strip, *now*," Colt's last word left little question about his frustration. Grasping the hem of her dress, she hurriedly pulled it over her head.

"Better. Now, I intend to keep you just like this for most of the week. You'll be either inside the house or with me at all times, so the only people besides me who will be seeing that gorgeous body of yours will be those I chose to allow the privilege." With that, he stepped aside and ushered her inside.

"CABIN" WAS A ridiculous term for the beautifully designed and exquisitely furnished structure Colt escorted her into. Even as off-balance as she felt from both the mind-blowing orgasm and her own nudity, Jenna was positively stunned at Colt, Mitch, and Bryant's retreat. The glass front offered a panoramic view of the river, mountains, and the canyon the house sat in stole her breath. It flashed through Jenna's mind how the view would be ever changing with the changing seasons, each one with its own elements of splendor.

One wall of the living room had been left as the natural rock the room had been carved from. The mantle over the fireplace was a smooth slab of stone they'd obviously taken great care to shape and smooth to glossy perfection. And while it was obvious it was a man's home as evidenced by amazing photos, paintings, and prints showcasing a love of nature and wildlife, it still showed evidence of a designer's eye. Jenna couldn't help but assume that was Bryant's influence. As she looked down the hall, she could see it was particularly wide and wondered if they had utilized an old mine within their design.

Colt stood back and watched her as she took in everything around her. She supposed most women would be intimidated by his intensity, but she was somewhat immune after dealing with her brothers her entire life. When he saw her eyes widen at the hallway, he nodded.

"Yes, we did use parts of an existing mine. It helped save some time with the carving and blasting, but it made for a whole lot of paperwork, I assure you. Seems the

Bureau of Mining isn't inclined to be pushed, no matter which Pentagon hotshot we asked to call them. The only person who was even remotely influential was your father."

His hollow chuckle told her they'd probably pulled every trick out of their respective repertoires to get the mining hard hats to conform to their timetable. She knew too well how her brothers operated, and she couldn't see Colt being any different. Her dad, on the other hand, was a diplomat to the bone. No doubt, he would have used his considerable negotiating skills and charm to help when he could. It surprised her Colt had seemed to know exactly what she was thinking, and it was equally unnerving. Kat had warned her it was a 'Dom thing,' so she shouldn't have been surprised, but it was still a bit creepy. She suppressed the smile threatening to surface at the thought of all the helpful hints for all things Dom-related she'd gotten this morning. Kat and Rissa were probably paying dearly for all their advice.

COLT STOOD WATCHING Jenna for long moments. It was amazing to watch her expression change in small increments as thoughts worked through her razor-sharp mind. Finally, he straightened from the wall he'd been leaning against, drawing her attention.

"Come on, let's get your punishments out of the way, so we can put the supplies into the freight elevator and get everything put away. I'm hungry, but I don't want this hanging over your head during dinner."

He led Jenna to the bar and stood her in front of one of

the tall barstools. He moved around the bar, and when he returned, he carried a large, leather-covered paddle. Jenna's eyes went impossibly wide, and her breathing hitched when her gaze locked on what he held. Colt simply waited until she stilled as arousal replaced the temporary panic that had first filled her expression.

Aww, the eyes are always the windows to the soul, my love. I do so appreciate how your body broadcasts its desire even when your words and actions try to deny it. When Jenna started to step back, his one-word command "Don't" was all it took for her to freeze in place, her gaze dropping immediately to the floor. *You, my lovely pet, are a true natural submissive. Now, let's see what we can do about helping you acknowledge all that hidden passion.*

Chapter 8

"LEAN FORWARD AND place your forearms on the stool, pet." When she was in position, he asked, "Can you tell me why you are being punished?" Colt's tone was cool and detached as if having a naked woman bent over in front of him was everyday business. It suddenly occurred to her, this was everyday business to him. Why was that such a depressing thought? Next week, she'd be gone, and he would simply replace her with someone new.

"Jenna? I asked you a question." Colt's voice was much sharper this time, but it didn't matter because the realization she wasn't anything special made her sad enough to be unaffected by the change in his tone.

"Well, I drank too much this afternoon while you were spying on me, and I didn't want to wear just that skimpy little dress you gave me, and I don't answer or strip as fast as the other women you obviously do this to, so no doubt you'll be looking forward to being rid of me at the end of this week." Damn, and here she thought she'd slept off all the alcohol. Just as she finished speaking, she heard a whoosh a split second before her ass felt like it had been set on fire. The force rocked her up onto her toes as she screeched, "Holy shit! What the fuck! That hurt!"

"Language, Jenna! And good, it was damned well supposed to hurt. Check the attitude, or we'll be at this a very long time, princess." *Whoosh, smack.* "Now, those two won't even count toward the five you had coming for the drinking, and the five you had coming for hesitating with the dress, stripping, and the answers. Those two are for your snarky answers just now. I suggest you try again."

Tears had started to burn Jenna's eyes, but they weren't entirely due to the searing heat radiating through her ass cheeks. She knew her reaction was because she hated knowing she had disappointed him although she wasn't sure why on earth his approval suddenly mattered so much to her. Her voice was shaky, but her tone much more respectful when she answered. "I'm being punished because I drank too much, and I didn't want to wear the dress you gave me, and hesitated in my answers and stripping when told to, Sir."

While her tone wasn't exactly repentant, it must have been close enough, Colt decided to move on. "Since this is your first time, I'll not make you count the strikes. We begin."

Jenna didn't even realize he'd spoken before he began landing stinging swats on her already-burning backside. He varied the timing and placement of the strikes, and she found the anticipation of the next one almost as arousing as the strike itself. *Arousing? Oh, hell no! I am so not getting hot from this... Oh, my heavenly God. I will not come, I will not come. Geez, come on, get done already. I know if I come, he'll be seven kinds of pissed off.*

COLT COULD TELL Jenna was edging closer and closer to subspace. How interesting, it seemed his little princess was totally turned-on by having her ass paddled. Smiling to himself, he picked up the pace, well aware of how close she was to climax. He had no intention of punishing her again so soon, so immediately after landing the last blow, he plunged his fingers into her soaking-wet heat and said, "Come for me, Jenna." He kept his fingers working in and out of her tight pussy as she went liquid around him. Her body stiffened, then began trembling as her orgasm seemed to erupt from her very core.

The rapidly building waves of her release made her vaginal muscles ripple around his fingers, and he was forced to drop the paddle to the floor so he could catch her as her knees folded. He was going to have to remember to always have a good hold on her when he fucked her standing up. He smiled to himself when he realized the strength of her climax and its connection to her leg muscles wasn't something he even wanted to attempt to curb with training. Knowing he could bring her that level of pleasure was enormously satisfying.

Jenna didn't even remember Colt picking her up and moving her to the sofa where he sat and held her on his lap. He'd wrapped a soft blanket around her and was softly praising how well she had taken her punishment and how proud he was of her. She felt like she was floating slowly back to earth, and when she looked up at him, the disquiet must have shown on her face because he asked, "Confused, pet?" Without waiting for her to respond, he continued, "It's called subspace. It's a kind of endorphin-driven mind trip that some submissives are able to attain. Most subs require quite a lot more pushing."

He chuckled and then added, "I can't begin to tell you how very pleased I am to know you were able to achieve that so quickly. I want you to know, I'm not a sadist by any means, Jenna. I like many intense D/s elements, but I don't particularly like handing out pain for pain's sake. I'm going to enjoy teaching you the joys of erotic spanking."

She felt her brows pull together at the suggestion a spanking could ever be considered erotic.

"Oh, don't frown, sweetness, you're a natural. You enjoyed this spanking, so I know you'll really enjoy an erotic session with my hand on your perfect ass." His palm continued the soothing strokes up and down the outside of her thigh for several seconds before she felt the subtle shift in him. "Up you go, let's get the truck unloaded. And before you even ask, yes, I expect you to go outside just as you are."

COLT WOULDN'T TELL her that he'd know if anyone was within a mile of the cabin because their infrared sensor security system was state-of-the-art. The entire perimeter of their property was monitored by various cameras, and Grayson would be the only one other than him seeing her sweet body. They'd made sure he would be the only person with access to those feeds tonight. Colt wasn't ready for the rest of the team to be ogling his woman yet. *And baby, you are so very much mine!*

Chapter 9

J ENNA'S LEGS FELT like they were made of rubber as she carefully made her way down the stairs. She'd declined Colt's help because she really needed to put some distance between them. If she wasn't careful, she was going to fall for him, and that was a sure way to get her heart broken. *Remember what happened the last time you thought you were in love? Don't forget how much it hurt and how devastated you felt. Keep in mind how soul-crushing the betrayal was... and that was one of your brother's friends, too. If Ted could hurt your brothers, Colt sure as hell would be able to as well.*

She needed to remember it wasn't safe to let Colt into her heart. She had kept quiet about what had happened the last time because the bastard her brothers trusted to stay in their home had promised her they wouldn't make it home from their next mission if she told anyone what he'd done. Jenna had believed him, so she'd hidden the bruises from everyone, including Kat. Then she'd spent years trying to bury the memories of the night everything she thought she knew about love was shredded by a wolf in sheep's clothing.

"You're very quiet, princess. Care to share the thoughts making you so melancholy?" Colt had watched as Jenna became so lost in a dark abyss of thought, she hadn't even realized they'd stopped near his truck. He'd studied her as she'd worried her bottom lip until it looked bee-stung, and he was tempted to press his own against hers to see if they were as sweet as they looked.

It seemed Jenna was a bit like her sister-in-law, Katarina in that she also mumbled aloud when she was thinking intently. He'd only caught bits and pieces; "betrayal," "hurt," "brothers," and "bruises" were the only words he'd been able to make out. Everything he was seeing was pushing him closer to the troubling conclusion he'd tentatively drawn earlier.

"Jenna? I'd like to know what you were just thinking. I could make it a demand, but I'd rather you would trust me enough to share." Colt just waited for her response.

"Um… rain check? Let's get this stuff moved up top. I know how hungry you said you were." She gave him one of her patently brilliant smiles. God, she was radiant when she smiled. *Well, at least she didn't shut you completely out. Give her time, she'll come around.*

They'd made quick work of unloading the truck and were putting the supplies away when Jenna suddenly realized she hadn't even considered she was naked, and he was still fully dressed.

"Can I ask you a question, Colt?" She didn't know exactly how all this D/s stuff worked and hoped a polite question wouldn't be considered too unreasonable.

"Sure. While I appreciate your efforts at protocol, I want you to understand, I will be very, very strict if we're in a scene or in the bedroom, but the rest of the time, basic courtesy and respect will be fine. Also remember, I told you that for the rest of today, questions were fine." Smiling at the relief she knew showed on her face, he asked, "So, princess, what's your question?"

"Why do I have to be naked and you get to have on all your clothes? Doesn't quite seem fair to me." She was confused about how it made her feel. The sense that she belonged to him or something else that would be equally disastrous. She'd feel better if they could level the playing field.

He stopped working and leaned against the black marble countertop. Colt crossed his arms over his massive chest and repeated the move by crossing his ankles drawing attention to his bare feet. God in heaven, the worn, faded jeans, and the tight white t-shirt stretched across pecs that looked as if they were rope-covered steel had her dying to see what he looked like without anything hiding all that male perfection. His hair appeared wind-tousled, and his lips were quirked up just enough to show amusement. Oh, he was certainly eye candy of the finest quality.

"Like what you see, sweetness?" Even though his voice held a note of humor, it was also thick with arousal.

Jerking her eyes up to his, Jenna knew her face was flushing crimson with embarrassment at being caught lusting after the gorgeous man standing in front of her.

"Um, well, of course. You're a good-looking man, but you already know that. Oh damn, this is so embarrassing…" She couldn't believe the mess she'd gotten herself into. Her damned body was giving her away even when she'd finally managed to shut down the words. She knew without even looking down, her nipples were drawn up into tight buds, and her pussy was already wetting the insides of her thighs.

IT HAD TAKEN all of Colt's self-control to remain still as Jenna's eyes moved over him in a slow perusal that had his cock standing up begging for attention. *Talk about feeling like a piece of meat. Holy fuck, woman, give me a break, or I'm going to fuck you on the kitchen floor and we'll worry about dinner in a few hours!*

Pulling himself out of his fantasy of laying her out and working up a ravenous appetite, Colt smiled. "Well, for obvious reasons, I like to look at what's mine. You are stunning, Jenna, and I want to have both visual and physical access to you without having to worry about clothing barring my way. And, your body tells me even more than your words most of the time. Doms like to think of it as Mother Nature's lie detector. Let's hope you don't ever lie to me, so I'm able to show you how effectively it works. You don't want to test how serious an offense I consider lying, and that includes lying by omission, princess, just so we're clear."

He paused briefly, watching the play of her expressions as she processed everything he'd said before continuing. "Your body will tell me more about what it wants than your words can ever hope to convey or hide. I'll measure your breathing and pulse as easily as I read the need in the soft sighs and breathy moans you make when I touch you. There won't be anything about your body I won't know, I promise you."

Satisfied when he heard her soft intake of breath, he pushed away from the counter. He'd put their dinner in to warm, and now it was time to relieve some of the sexual tension between them.

"Let's go out on the deck and begin. I'm anxious to start your training." When she opened her mouth to protest, he silenced her with his finger to her lips. "Think before you speak, pet. Is what you were about to say worth the consequence you are likely to suffer?" When she kept silent and slowly shook her head, he nodded his head toward the door. "I didn't think so. Now shall we?" Placing his hand against the sensitive area just below the small of her back, he led her out onto the large deck.

Thinking to himself about all the little things he'd do to make her feel special and cherished, he had to admit a gentle hand laid along the low point of a woman's back— that sweet erogenous zone just above her ass—was going to be one of his favorites. He'd known subs who would begin to cream from that gesture alone, and he'd met very few women who didn't move at a deliberate pace which kept his hand firmly in place.

Stroking the side of a submissive's face, light touches to the very tender spot just behind the ear, and soft caresses on the back of the neck were calculated moves. He didn't use touch to manipulate women, rather it was intended to ensure she knew how special she was and how much he valued her trust. Gaining a submissive's trust was a gift to be cherished. He was looking forward to spending the next five or six decades enjoying each and every facet of his chosen lifestyle with Jenna.

Chapter 10

S TANDING AT THE railing looking down at the meander-
ing river, Jenna was grateful for the accent lights below
the deck that made the crystal-clear water visible. Taking a
deep breath of mountain air, she marveled at the beauty
surrounding her. Turning around, she was surprised to see
Colt studying her rather than enjoying the view. She was
further shocked by the fierce look on his face… there was a
hunger in his expression that made her think he wanted to
consume her. *Wow!*

She started to take an unconscious step back, but his
hand wrapped around her upper arm, stopping her.

"Don't move. You never step away from a Dom who is
speaking to you or studying you without his or her express
permission. Doing so with me or at The Club will most
certainly end in punishment. Remember, you are the sister
of the owners of one of the most respected kink clubs in
the country,"—*and will be my submissive, and as such you'll
also be a target*—"so there will be Doms and subs alike who
will take great pleasure in trying to trip you up. They'll
relish the idea of showing you how little you know; and
then they will delight in your humiliation at the punishment they'll be justified in seeing meted out. Hell, many of
the Doms will demand the opportunity to punish you
themselves.

Club rules are tricky in this regard, and we'll only be able to protect you so much. If you interfere in another couple's scene, are offensive to a Dom or insult his sub, then the Dom would be within his or her rights to demand your punishment. Most don't want to personally see to the punishment, but some do. I'm going to try to teach you not only my personal rules, but also The ShadowDance Club rules as we go along this week. Now, I assume you are on some form of birth control?"

Jenna had been so lost in his words, it took a few seconds for her to realize he'd ended with a question. "Yes. I also have annual physicals, so I know I am disease free. Because, um, well, I haven't actually had sex in a long time. I can provide proof of my health."

COLT STRAINED TO hear her last words, they'd been uttered so softly, and wondered just how long it had been since she'd had sex. Proceeding in the all-business manner he'd adopted, he stated.

"I'm also clean, I have paperwork for you inside. I trust you about yours, but you will have to provide copies to The Club before you'll be allowed to actively participate in any type of play. Now, tell me about your sexual history." *Bingo!* Jenna's eyes went wild, her muscles all seemed to contract at once, and she took two steps away from him before she even realized what she'd done.

"Well... oh, my God, I can't do this. I have to go... I can't, it wouldn't be safe. I can't go on, this just isn't going to happen. I'll just get my things and call my brothers to pick me up if you'll just show me where you put my bag.

I'm really sorry, but this is just too… No, I just can't." Her words were stuttered, and he could see she was quickly edging into panic. She was almost frantic and looking everywhere but at him. *Wow, talk about finding a hot button…*

"Jenna, stop. Look at me. Now!" When she finally fell silent and looked up at his face, he could see the first tears start to slowly slide down over her pale cheeks, and he was lost to her in that moment. He'd wanted her for years, but this was something so much more. This was a soul-deep yearning to love and protect that he was certain would only become stronger over time.

He pulled her close and enveloped her in his tight embrace. For long moments, he just held her while she sobbed against his chest. When the tidal wave of emotion didn't abate, he leaned down, scooped her up into his arms, and moved to one of the lounge chairs. Easing down, he pulled a soft blanket from the nearby cabinet and wrapped it around her. Even though he was sure she wasn't chilled, her shaking was beginning to concern him.

"Jenna, honey, you need to stop before you make yourself sick. I don't know what about my question triggered this reaction, but as your Dom, this isn't something I can let go. We're going to have to talk this out. Anything that affects you either physically or emotionally is of interest and concern to me. This is clearly something that's having a profound effect on you in both of those areas. Now, look at me, I want to see those beautiful green eyes while we talk. Come on, princess, that was an order, not a request."

Slowly Jenna raised her tear-stained face to his, her expression so filled with pain and sadness that, for several heartbeats, he was rendered speechless. *Holy Jesus, what did*

that bastard do to you? And why are you still afraid of him?
Suddenly, he knew her brothers hadn't told her Scott had
not made it out of their last mission alive. Likely they
would have believed she would have made friends with
and become attached to the man who'd stayed in their
family's home. They'd probably hoped she wouldn't ask
and they'd be able to spare her the pain of knowing they'd
lost a teammate and she'd lost a friend.

Families of team members were often profoundly af-
fected by the loss of any team member because they knew
it so easily could have been their own loved one. Before he
could take this burden from her, she was going to have to
confirm his suspicions about Scott. Colt would bet his
prized flogger, he'd just figured out a large part of the
puzzle that was Jenna Lamont, but he'd have to proceed
carefully or risk causing her further harm.

When Jenna's teary emerald eyes met his, he gave her
a small, encouraging smile and then, leaning forward,
whispered softly against her lips, "Good girl."

JUST THOSE TWO words worked wonders to calm Jenna.
Even though she knew she was going up against a wall and
that she didn't have any choice but to explain her melt-
down, she hoped she'd be able to convince Colt not to tell
her brothers. It didn't matter they weren't still active
Special Forces team members, it was likely they still
worked with the teams in the course of their 'contract
work' as she'd heard them refer to it, and that would give
Ted Scott the access he'd need to destroy her family.
Personally, she was hoping they'd give up that life entirely

now they were married and soon-to-be fathers.

"Now, pet, I want you to explain to me what just happened here. I think I have a fairly good idea, but I need to hear it from you." Colt's voice was laced with compassion, but she knew she'd just been given an order.

COLT WATCHED JENNA gather herself up as if preparing for battle. He could almost hear the wheels spinning in her head as she rolled the satin edging of the blanket back and forth as if finding comfort in caressing its slick texture between her small fingers. He simply watched and waited, letting her pull herself together. He smiled, thinking he could almost see her drawing her courage around her into a protective cloak. After several long minutes, she finally spoke.

"Do you remember when Ted Scott came to recuperate at ShadowDance?" Colt stiffened, and Jenna looked up in alarm.

"Sorry, pet, I didn't mean to scare you. Yes, I remember when that happened. I'm afraid I wasn't exactly his biggest fan, so I tend to react to any mention of his name. Please continue." Colt hoped he'd been able to explain away his reaction, and she would continue to tell him a story he was dreading with every fiber of his being.

"Um, yeah, well, that makes two of us… about the not liking him thing. Anyway, when he first arrived, I was really kind of, well, I had a crush on him, I guess you'd say. Well, I, oh God, I really don't want to go into all the details, okay? But…" Colt watched as Jenna stopped to take several deep breaths before she was able to continue.

"One night my mom and dad were going to be gone overnight. They didn't worry about leaving me alone with Ted because Selita was always at the house. But... then Selita was called to town to help a sick friend, and well, he overheard me assuring her I'd be fine and not to worry. I really didn't feel threatened by him, we'd sat and watched movies late into the night several times, and he had never done any more than kiss me." This time her pause was filled with more tension, and he could see her pulse pounding at the base of her neck.

"Construction had started on The ShadowDance Club, and Ted had made some comments about its intended use. I blew off answering because I was too embarrassed to talk to him about that stuff, you know? I was so young, and even though looking back now I realize he wasn't really that much older than I was, he seemed a lot older... and a lot stronger, too."

Jenna's gaze dropped with her last comment, and truthfully, Colt was grateful because he knew at the mention of Scott being stronger than she was, pure rage had swept through him like a storm surge. There wouldn't have been a chance in hell she'd have missed seeing on his face.

"Later that night, he tried again to get me to talk to him about The Club. That's when I figured out he must not be that close to my brothers or he'd already know the answers to the questions he kept asking me. So, I started making excuses for why I needed to get back to my room. You know, homework and getting things ready for homecoming, etcetera. I wanted to retreat back into my room because I knew the door locked. Now that I think back on how violent he became, I'm pretty sure that wouldn't have kept him out, but at the time, it seemed like my only hope.

I was afraid to call Kat because I knew she would be frustrated with me for being alone with him. She'd taken an instant dislike to him when he'd first arrived and was always reminding me to never let my guard down."

After taking a few deep breaths, Jenna continued. "I know it seems like I'm stalling, but I just wanted you to know why I didn't do anything at the time. Anyway, long story short, he wanted to have sex with me, and when I refused him, he beat me and raped me." She lifted her gaze to his and Colt felt like someone had just driven a sword through his heart. The shame and sorrow in her eyes made him want to howl at the injustice. "Oh my God, I can't believe I've actually finally told someone about this."

Colt watched her turn to stare off into the distance as she started hyperventilating. For a few seconds, he was so stunned by her admission she'd never told another living soul this story, he didn't move to get her back in hand. Finally, he snapped back to his senses and began gently shaking her shoulders until she looked up at him.

"Jenna, breathe with me, princess. Come on, pet. Nice and slow… in… out… again… in… now, out." Colt kept her breathing in time with him until he felt the muscles in her arms relax beneath his fingers.

"Okay, can you tell me the rest? You have been so very brave, pet. I'm very proud of you." Colt had never been more sincere in his entire life. Hell, he couldn't imagine the strength it had taken for a young woman to weather that emotional storm alone.

Nodding her head, she spoke quietly, but now, she seemed emotionally detached from what she was relating. It was almost as if she was telling this part of the story about someone else, a behavior Colt recognized as a PTSD symptom. Jenna may have believed she'd overcome this violation, but it was clear to Colt she hadn't. The fact she was easily sent reeling headlong into the emotional quagmire victims often struggled to pull themselves out of for years was all the evidence he needed to know she had not even really begun to process this trauma.

"After he'd finished with me, he spit in my face and told me if I ever told anyone what had happened, he would tell everyone I'd come on to him and that he… Oh, God, please, swear to me you will never tell anyone, because he said he'd make sure neither of my brothers made it back alive from their next mission. And, I know they aren't really on the teams anymore, but they probably work with those men, and I'd never forgive myself if they got hurt or worse because of me. I mean it, Colt, I just couldn't stand to live another minute if that happened. Promise me, please, I'm begging you. Promise me."

Jenna was lost in racking sobs again. Colt pulled her against his chest and tried to calm her down, but he doubted she was even hearing the words. He knew if he didn't pull her back from the emotional ledge she was falling over, she'd likely need to be hospitalized in order to get the meds required to settle her. He knew that was the last thing she'd want. Standing up and keeping her in his arms, he quickly descended the stairs and walked straight out into the cold river until the water was up to his knees, then he sat down, which put them both chest deep in the frigid water. When Jenna started gasping and struggling to get out of his hold, he just tightened his arms around her. "Jenna, stop moving. I need you to calm down. I want to help, but you have to be willing to listen. Believe me, I'm anxious to get out of this fucking freezing water, too, but this was the only way I knew to shock you out of that pain-filled memory.

"Now, look at me. I need to know you are back in the present with me. That's it, look right at me. Are you going to be able to listen and *hear* what I'm going to tell you?" At her jerky nod, he said, "Ted Scott is dead. He can't hurt you anymore, and he can't hurt your brothers either. Do you understand? I wish to hell your brothers had told you the son of a bitch was sent to hell. The bastard died several years ago, and I promise you, if he weren't already dead, I'd kill him with my bare hands, but he's already gone, sweetness. He can't hurt you ever again."

Colt watched Jenna's eyes go wide then watched as emotion swamped her again, but these were cries of relief, so he slowly got to his feet and made his way back up the stairs. He wrapped them both in the blanket he'd discarded earlier before making his way down the hall. They were both going to warm up with a nice warm shower, and then after he was sure Jenna was safely tucked in and sleeping in his bed, he had a phone call to make.

Chapter 11

S TANDING UNDER THE pulsing spray of warm water, Jenna looked around her, admiring the innovative ways they'd used the natural rock walls whenever possible throughout the cabin, even in the shower. Multiple showerheads that looked like waterfalls and garden sprays massaged her tired muscles from every direction. The entire length of one shower wall had a built-in bench, and the glass front gave a clear view of the rest of the enormous bathroom which also held a hot tub big enough for five large people.

The entire space had the feel of a tropical paradise hidden away in some river canyon in Central America, complete with beautiful palms and hanging baskets of trailing vines. Considering where the men had likely spent time, her tropical paradise comparison might not be that far off base.

Jenna was just reaching for the shampoo when Colt finished stripping out of his wet T-shirt and jeans and joined her.

"Here, let me," he said, taking the shampoo from her hands. "Another important element in successful Dominant/submissive relationships is that the Dom is not just obligated to care for his submissive partner, but he is honored and privileged to do so. And, I want to be clear on this point. Jenna, because I know you are a bright, savvy businesswoman, and it's important that you know being submissive does not take anything away from that part of you. As a matter of fact, you will likely find learning to let go of control in one facet of your life will make you more effective in other areas."

At her confused expression, he continued. "I know it doesn't make sense to you now. But if you will truly submit, honestly let go during these next few days, you'll come to understand what I'm telling you."

"I don't for a minute think you are going to let go easily," he chuckled. "Your mind is going to fight it all the way because you have had to maintain control in so many ways for so very long. But, my beautiful pet, if you will just try, you'll find a freedom you have never imagined possible. You'll love the exhilaration of being liberated from all those pesky responsibilities and decisions. Most subs love the freedom they experience when they don't have to make the decisions or worry whether they're doing things right or wrong during a scene. There's no question about what their partner wants because it's been negotiated, and the sub's only responsibility is to let go and trust... knowing their Master will take care of them and provide everything they need."

Jenna was listening, but if she was honest, she wasn't really absorbing the words. She was drained, both physically and emotionally. Hell, she felt as if someone had just leached every bit of energy right out of her. Colt's words sounded like they were being spoken from a great distance and didn't really pertain to her.

His strong hands worked the shampoo through the long strands of her hair, massaging her scalp. It felt so incredible, she was having trouble focusing on anything but how wonderful his touch felt. She suddenly realized he'd stopped talking and was just watching her. She was sure her dazed expression had given away that she hadn't exactly been completely cognizant of everything he'd said. When he smiled and just pulled her into his arms, she went willingly.

COLT WAS CERTAIN he was giving Jenna information she wasn't going to be able to fully grasp, but he hadn't realized just how 'not with him' she was until he'd stepped in front of her and seen she was practically catatonic. God, if he could just get her to let go like that during a scene, she would be floating in the upper atmosphere of subspace in no time at all.

He quickly finished washing them both and then gently dried her. He took great pleasure in helping her comb her long, silky black hair, then left her in the bathroom for a couple of minutes of private time while he pulled the sheets back on the bed. When she opened the door, he stepped forward and took her hand. Leading her to the bed, he settled her in before lying down beside her. She completely blindsided him when she pulled him close.

"Please make love to me," she whispered. "Chase away the awful memories and replace them with something beautiful. I haven't been with a man since that night."

It took Colt a few seconds to get his emotions under control enough to respond. "Are you sure, princess? You've had a very difficult evening, and I want you to be very sure this is what you want. Believe me, there is nothing I'd like more than to sink inside your soft body, but I don't want this to be about hiding. You are too precious to me to me to risk you'll regret this decision in the morning."

Jenna's eyes were tear-filled, but he was certain they weren't tears of sadness. He recognized her need to find a connection with someone who wouldn't just be fucking her, but someone who would be loving her. It was a fundamental difference—between having something stolen from you and giving it freely.

"I need you. I need you to show me how it can be, how it should have been the first time. Please help me sweep those dark shadows out of my mind." Colt was sure Jenna worried about appearing needy and weak. He'd have never used either of those words to describe her, but he was also absolutely convinced she needed to feel the warmth of a man holding her and the peace of knowing the connection between them was genuine.

"I'd like nothing more than to show you how beautiful I can make you feel, my beautiful pet. It won't always be like this, I won't always make love to you. There will be times when I will just fuck you. There will be times when it will only be about what I want and my pleasure will be the only thing I seek. But tonight, oh my precious Jenna, tonight I plan to love you. I'm not just going to make love to you, sweetheart, I am going to *love* you. I want you to remember this moment for the rest of your life because I assure you, it's going to be burned into my soul."

All the time he'd been talking, he'd been running his fingers from her clit back through her wet folds, making sure she was wet enough to let him slide into her tight sheath. As he rose over her, he slowly pushed her legs wide apart and leaned on one forearm as he parted the soft, swollen petals of her pussy and guided the tip of his cock into her opening. When he started to enter her, she gasped, and he saw her eyes glaze with heated desire.

Pushing his way inside so slowly he thought he might well lose his mind, Colt wanted to savor the clench of her body wrapping itself around him. He didn't want to hurt her, but holding back was testing his control like nothing else ever had. Reminding himself this was about her pleasure, about making sure she understood he would always take care of her, Colt fought the urge to take her in a way that would leave her no doubt who she belonged to. *You are mine, Jenna. Mine!*

"Oh, my fucking God, Jenna, you feel like heaven," Colt rasped out when he was finally fully seated inside her. "You're already tightening around my cock in rhythmic pulses that are threatening my control. Please, love, I'm begging you, hold still, or this is going to be over long before either of us wants it to end."

Colt heard the rough sound of his own voice and took several deep, steadying breaths as he struggled to hold back and not rut into her like an out-of-control animal. He felt beads of sweat popping out on his forehead at the effort it was taking to stay in control.

"Relax your vaginal muscles, pet. This is not the time to tighten them, because I'm holding on by a thread, and it's quickly unraveling."

"Move. I need you to move. Please. Oh, God, please move. It feels amazing. All those ripples and bumps caressing me."

Jesus, Joseph, and Mary, he was going to have a fucking aneurysm trying to hold on to his control. Colt felt her try to ease the grip she had on his cock, but as soon as he began sliding out, her body overrode her mind and clamped down in an effort to keep him inside.

Colt didn't usually allow anything even vaguely resembling topping from the bottom, but her desperate pleas were so sincere, he let it go. *Remember, this isn't a scene. You're supposed to be showing her how pleasurable sex can be.*

He was so large when she'd first seen him in the shower, she'd been sure he would never fit inside her. She was clutching his shoulders and heard herself moan his name. "I didn't think you'd fit. When I saw you in the shower, I… I just couldn't imagine you'd actually be able to…"

When Colt heard her breathe out his name, he couldn't hold back any longer.

"Hold on to me, princess, and just let me love you." He started long strokes in and out of her tight passage, making sure her hips were tilted, so the ridge of his cock slid over her G-spot each time he entered her, and the coarse hairs at the base of his penis tickled her clit at the same time. She was fluttering around him, and he could tell by her breathing she was quickly spiraling toward her release, and Colt was grateful because he knew he wouldn't be able to last long, she felt so un-fucking-believable.

He whispered sweet words into her ear, telling her how perfect she felt, how tightly she was squeezing his cock, and what a wondrous gift she was giving him by trusting him to replace the memories for her. And when he finally said, "Come for me, Jenna," just before sealing his lips to hers in a mind-stealing kiss, he felt her explode in his arms. The strength of her orgasm was staggering. The squeeze of her internal muscles was just shy of painful.

He'd never experienced anything like the rapture of making love to Jenna. She took him right over the edge, plunging them both into a deep pool of pleasure. Hell, he hadn't come during a woman's first orgasm since he was a kid. Christ, what she did to him was incredible. He'd never experienced a release that powerful, it had truly rocked him all the way to the depths of his soul. Gasping for breath, Colt rolled to his side, taking Jenna with him.

"Oh my God, woman, you just stole my soul. I have never felt anything like that, you are amazing."

Jenna's eyes filled with tears. "Thank you for showing me how heart-stopping it's supposed to be. I had no idea it could feel so wonderful. You made me come earlier... and it felt really good, but nothing like this... this was, oh my, I just don't really know how to describe it. I'll never forget how you chased away all the shadows with light and filled my heart with hope."

She'd been stroking the side of his face as she spoke, and Colt was speechless at her soulful words. In that moment, the decision was irrevocable, he'd never let her go. It didn't matter what he had to do, he'd never be able to let her walk away. His life's mission was now to win the heart and soul of this woman.

Colt kissed her, tucked her against his chest, and stroked her back softly until he felt her relax. When he heard her breathing even out, he knew she'd finally fallen asleep. Slowly, he eased away from her and quickly returned with a warm cloth and cleaned his seed from between her legs. She grumbled a protest, but he easily shushed her back to sleep. As much as he loved seeing his cum marking her in the most primal way, he knew she'd rest much better now. Tucking the blankets around her to ward off a chill from the air-conditioning, Colt settled a chaste kiss on her soft lips before dimming the lights, slipping on a pair of gym shorts, and making his way into his office.

Lifting the handset of the com device that would connect him directly to Grayson, he waited until the other man answered.

"Did you get it?"

"Yeah, but—"

Colt stopped him. "If you can't scrub it enough so her brothers won't be tortured forever, delete it all. I'll deal with the fallout. Get a call in to General Franklin. I'm going to hold his feet to the fire over this. I'll never forgive the bastard for not telling us about Scott's history before he joined our team. Jenna has paid a huge price for his negligence. I'm not letting this go… not ever."

"I totally understand and agree. I'll try to clean the tape, but honestly, I don't think it's possible. The whole thing gutted me, and I wasn't even there. You okay, man?" Grayson's ability to absorb and identify the feelings of those around him was just one of the man's amazing gifts. Colt knew his friend was a full-blown psychic, but few others did. Most of their team knew he had an amazing sixth sense, but Colt and Bryant Davis were the only ones who knew the full extent of Mitch Grayson's gifts.

"I won't even try to lie to you." Chuckling, he added, "Wouldn't fucking work, anyway. I'll be okay, but I'm shaken. Seeing the woman I love in that kind of pain was the hardest thing I've ever had to do. But she's going to be okay. I'm not stupid enough to think this is over; this is just the first layer of blocks she's built around her heart, but I knew I had to blow up this wall in order to reach the rest. And, I still don't know why she mentioned resuming her martial arts training."

When Colt had begun to suspect Scott's involvement, he'd enlisted Grayson's help setting up equipment, so they could record his conversations with Jenna. He'd hoped to get something they would be able to let Alex and Zach hear. Her brothers were both worried sick thinking about how they might have endangered their sister and what damage had been done to her. But what had transpired was not a conversation he wanted his friends to have to sit through. The guilt of not only the sexual assault, but the added burden of her years of suffering in silence to protect them as well would be too much for them to handle. He knew it would break them in ways they would struggle forever to overcome. Sometimes, you had to protect your friends from themselves, and this was shaping up to be one of those situations.

Chapter 12

KATARINA LAMONT WAS sitting in Alex and Zach's spacious office, answering Sheriff Dylan Marshall's questions. She watched his expression go from interest to disbelief in a heartbeat when she shared the details of her last night in Las Vegas. Kat knew Alex and Zach had sent men to try to track down the woman who had helped her escape Cal Robertson the night he'd almost killed her in a BDSM dungeon club several months earlier. She also knew they hadn't had any luck locating the woman who had no doubt saved Kat's life.

Being the honorable men they were, her husbands still hadn't given up. Mia had risked her own safety to help her, and Kat was sure they'd leave no stone unturned in their attempt to locate her. Finally, Alex broke the silence filling the room after she'd tried to describe Mia.

"Katarina, it's important that you give Dylan every detail you can remember. Can you be more specific than she made you think of an Inca princess?" Aha, so that was the comment that had Dylan sitting up in his seat like his spine had suddenly become a steel rod.

"Okay, I'm sorry, I didn't mean to be vague, but it's kind of hard to put into words. She was kind of regal acting, like she didn't really fit in there, you know? She was poised, and her eyes were bright with intelligence and insight. I'd also seen her at a few of the different clubs Cal had taken me to. She always seemed to be around, now that I think about it. But I never saw her scene with anyone, and even though she was dressed in clubwear, it was never anything over-the-top."

Scooting back so she was leaning against the back of the soft leather, she relaxed and leaned her head back and closed her eyes as she continued sifting through her tortured memories. Zach moved closer to slowly lift her feet up onto the low table in front of the sofa, and she smiled her thanks. She opened her eyes and moved her gaze from one to the next, making certain she focused on each of the men watching her before continuing. She wanted them to know she appreciated what they were doing.

"She was always friendly to me. Truthfully, she acted kind of like a sympathetic, older and wiser sister. She gave me the impression she thought I was being naïve hanging out with Cal and his minions." *Turns out she was oh so right!*

"Kat, can you give Dylan a detailed physical description as well? Dylan seems to think Mia might be someone he knows." Zach's words surprised her, and when she turned to Dylan, she was sure her shock was probably easy to see. She had always liked and admired the sheriff, he seemed honorable. Kat started to stand, but Zach settled her back.

"No, kitten, please sit back and let's get these swollen feet elevated again, shall we? You'll be able to think much better if you're comfortable."

Looking first at Zach then quickly turning her attention to Dylan, Kat said, "Okay... But do you really think you might know her? How can that be? I'll do anything to help you find her. I owe her my life, I'd really like to be able to thank her and make sure she's all right." Kat paused and lifted her eyes to Alex's and smiled.

Alex was the more alpha of the twins and was her 'paper husband' as she teasingly called him because she was legally married to him. Since he was the eldest of the twins—by two whole minutes, he laughingly reminded everyone—she'd married Alex in a very private civil ceremony, but Kat had been 'bound' to both men in a beautiful celebration and considered them both her husbands, equally.

Even though Alex was known to everyone who knew both brothers as the tougher of the two to deal with, Kat knew she and the child she carried were his one true weakness. His smile of support and love warmed her, and she continued.

"Mia was taller than me... Hey, don't give me that look, I know that covers just about everybody. I guess I should say she was *a lot* taller, she was probably five seven or five eight. She's slender but muscular; she obviously kept in great physical condition. Oh, and she had a really interesting accent, too." She stopped to ponder for a minute.

Dylan leaned forward, his formerly relaxed pose now tight. He reminded Kat of a jungle cat ready to pounce on some unsuspecting prey.

"Spanish or Portuguese residual linguistics, perhaps?"

Kat was surprised to hear Dylan's question, not only because it was startlingly accurate, but also the wording was pure seasoned investigator rather than the small-town sheriff's role which was the only one she'd ever seen him in. Even though they had both grown up in Climax, Dylan was almost a decade older than she was, so he'd been gone from the community by the time she was leaving grammar school.

She'd heard Alex and Zach make references to his former career in the DEA, but she hadn't known him during that time, so she often forgot his training and expertise far exceeded his current position.

"Yes, I think Portuguese is closer than Spanish, though. Do you think this might be the woman you know? Do you think you can help us find her? I'm really worried about her, and I'd like to thank her for her kindness." Kat was excited by the possibility Dylan might have a way to contact Mia.

Dylan sighed and pulled an envelope out of his shirt pocket, running it between his fingers as if he was considering whether or not to share the contents. He sighed and looked up.

"Katarina, do you think you'd recognize a picture of the woman who helped you?" The stark pain in his eyes startled her, and she wondered yet again what it was everyone in the room but she seemed to know.

"Well, sure, I think so." Kat looked from Zach, who gave her a small, encouraging smile to Alex who merely nodded.

Dylan pulled a photograph from the envelope and handed it to Kat. Even though Katarina was certain her immediate reaction had been answer enough, he needed her confirmation.

"Is that the woman who helped you?" Dylan knew in his heart it was *his* Mia, it had to be. *Christ, what was the woman thinking, going after Cal Robertson without backup?* And what had Robertson done with her before he'd come to ShadowDance Mountain? Since the bastard was now six feet under, there was no way to ask the asshole any questions. *Fuck, what a mess!*

Springing to her feet before Zach could stop her, Kat's

excited words bounced around the room.

"Yes, this is Mia. Why do you have her picture? Are you going to tell me what's going on?" Then looking at Alex, she continued, "Alex, this isn't fair. You all know what this is about, and you aren't telling me. I don't like it. I don't like it at all." She was getting well and truly pissed off, and the longer she talked, the more agitated she was becoming. She knew her doctor had cautioned her against becoming overly distraught because her blood pressure was hovering close to what was considered too high, but she was really frustrated. They were keeping something really important from her, and she didn't understand why.

ZACH MOVED TO stand in front of their sweet wife and cupped his hands gently along the underside of her jaw, so his fingers threaded into the pale strands of her hair. Using his thumbs, he brushed soothing strokes over her heated cheeks. He looked straight into the most unusual blue eyes he'd ever seen, watching as they quickly turned from their usual Caribbean blue to a deep sapphire. That change only occurred when she was deep in the throes of passion or when she was off the chart angry, and he didn't have any question about which was the cause now.

"Kitten, Mia is a nickname Dylan used to call his DEA partner, um, and well, she is also his ex-wife. Her real name is Melita Sanchez. Now, let's get you upstairs to rest, okay? You're getting too wound up, and I'm worried about your blood pressure. We don't want anything happening to you or the baby, now do we?" Zach watched lightning flash in her eyes, knowing Kat had instantly become boiling mad at his patronizing tone.

"Damned dominant men are going to be the death of me yet. Are you really going to go there? Of course, I don't want anything to happen to the baby, and I'm only mad because you are treating me like a fragile piece of glass, and it's damned annoying, I'll tell you. Now stop patronizing me, and tell me what the fuck this is about." Boy, she was on a full roll now, and Zach caught himself wincing at her ire.

ALEX PUSHED OFF the front of his ornately carved mahogany desk and stepped toward her. "Katarina, language. That's one, love. Now, we will catch you up at dinner. Go upstairs now and get some rest." At her narrowed eyes, he added, "Don't defy me on this, Katarina, you won't like the results, I promise you. Let Zach take you upstairs, and perhaps you can sweet-talk him into one of his foot massages you are so fond of." He leaned forward as he was speaking, pressing a kiss to the very tip of her nose, then placed his hands on each side of her heart-shaped face and smoothed his thumbs over her soft cheeks. Taking just a second to look at her again, his expression softened, and he brushed a soft blonde curl behind her ear before he ran his hands down her arms and enfolded her small hands in his. He raised them both and kissed the backs of her hands, a sensual caress of his lips, his eyes full of lust and promise, before handing her off to his brother. As Zach led her from the room, Alex had to stifle a chuckle at her mutterings. *Oh yeah, dinner is going to be a fiery occasion this evening.*

Kat had always 'processed out loud' or at least loud

enough to get her into trouble on many an occasion. On the way out of the room, she was muttering to herself about blasted men and their over-inflated egos and senses of entitlement. Zach looked over his shoulder at his brother, grinning. Alex knew it was going to take Zach quite a while to settle her back down, and he obviously intended to enjoy every minute of the process.

Chapter 13

A LEX TURNED TO Dylan and asked, "When is the last time you saw her?" He knew his friend had never gotten over losing Melita. Even though the other man had never explained what had precipitated their breakup, it was obvious it hadn't been something Dylan had wanted. Alex watched as stark pain reflected in the sheriff's eyes, and Alex knew he was working to swallow down the emotion before he answered.

"The night before I moved back to Climax, we had dinner and were sitting on the terrace talking as we often did. Suddenly, she slid divorce papers over to me and told me she just couldn't give up her career 'at this point'. I knew she was working on a case involving a suspected sex trade ring. She'd lost a good friend in college when the woman answered an ad about living abroad. The ad sounded a lot like those many traffickers set up. You know the script—*Live in exciting places for free, all you have to do is perform light household duties or be a nanny, etcetera*. Her friend was found a few weeks later in an alley behind a brothel in Paris." Sighing, he added, "She'd been beaten and raped to death. Mia never got over the anguish or her anger at the injustice she'd felt when the crime was basically swept under the rug and overlooked by authorities both here and in France.

"Christ, Alex, I tried everything I knew to talk her out of the divorce. I told her to keep working, and when she was ready, I'd always be here waiting for her. She insisted that wasn't fair to me, I was too good to be left waiting like that, and she knew I wouldn't touch another woman unless I was really free to do so. I finally signed the paper, I was sick about it, but in the end, she really didn't leave me any other choice."

Alex watched stark pain move through his friend's eyes as he paused to reel in his emotions once again. The stark pain in his friend's expression made Alex's heart clench in sympathy. "She never would look me in the eye and tell me she didn't love me. She just kept saying it wasn't right to keep me tied to her, always trying to emphasize that it wasn't fair to me. Fuck, you know I haven't taken a sub anytime I've been at The Club. Hell, I can count on one hand the number of times I've even taken a woman out for a meal, and I haven't fucked one since that last night with my wife. I always wondered if she wasn't trying to protect me from something, you know, like if we weren't married, the bastards she was chasing wouldn't be able to use me as leverage against her."

Leaning back in his chair, Dylan sighed. "I'll contact my old boss at the DEA and see what he knows. Even though he knows we aren't still legally married, he knows how it ended, so I'm hoping he'll share whatever he's heard. Christ, this is my worst nightmare come to life. I wanted her to be happy and fulfilled, but I wanted her safe, too. Was that so wrong?" Pushing his hand through his shaggy, dark-brown hair, he looked to Alex like a man whose heart hadn't even come close to healing, and now, it was being battered again.

"I'm sorry, my friend. Of course, you know everything

we have is at your disposal. Is there any chance she would try to contact mutual friends or try to make her way to you if she was in trouble?" Alex thought there had been plenty of time for her to make contact, but he felt he needed to ask.

"I don't know. Maybe. But this feels darker to me. I'm going to head back into town and make some calls. Can you let Grayson know I might be asking for his help? I know he has computer skills and access to resources I can't utilize."

Alex smiled because they both knew the other man could hack into just about any computer in the world in a matter of hours. Hell, Alex and Zach had laughed about how the damned geek had broken into the Pentagon's top-secret levels in under an hour just to prove to their commander it could be done.

They made their way to the front door of the house, and Alex patted his friend on the shoulder as he spoke. "Absolutely, I'll let him know to expect your call and to help you in any way he can." Just then, Alex's phone rang with the tone assigned to Colt Matthews. "I need to take this. Keep me posted on what you find out." Dylan turned to leave just as Alex opened his phone and said, "Talk to me."

Smiling to himself, Dylan murmured, "You can take a man out of the forces, but you'll never erase their soldier mindset."

"I WANT TO talk to you face-to-face about this, but I don't want you coming out here, and I'm not going to leave

Jenna alone here, so it'll have to wait a few days. She's okay, it was a tough afternoon for her, but I've gotten through her first layer of defense, so that's something, anyway. I know you want details, but right now, you're just going to have to trust me and be patient." Colt felt guilty for stalling Alex when he knew both Jenna's brothers were worried about what might have happened to her and what part they'd played.

Even if their actions had been unwitting, they'd still put a sexual predator in the house with their teenage sister. When they found out all the details, they were going to be completely guilt-ridden, and Colt wanted every bit of information he could gather before he had to tell them everything she'd endured.

"Fuck this, Matthews, tell me what's happened. And what do you mean by 'a tough afternoon'? Tell me what's going on, right now!" Alex was nearly shouting as he finished speaking.

"It was an emotional afternoon for her. You know how it is with subs when you break through a barrier—there's always an emotional catharsis that accompanies that, and it's exhausting. She's fine, she's resting now. I'll call you back in a day or so when I have all the details. Christ, Alex, for a Dom who is always preaching patience to the subs he's trained as well as all the Doms he's mentored, you sure don't practice what you preach. I've got to go, I'll be in touch."

SELITA WATCHED ALEX stare at his phone, dumbstruck after Colt had disconnected.

"Goddamn it! Doesn't being the boss mean anything to people anymore? Shit, he's not the team leader anymore! I can't even call him back, I know it'll go directly to voicemail." He stomped back to his office, threw himself into his oversized leather chair and stared out the floor-to-ceiling window. He was so lost in thought, he didn't even hear her step into the room.

Selita watched Alex stare outside and smiled to herself. People so often forgot about their household staff being around all the time. They didn't worry about things they said making it down the hallways and around corners. While her 'two boys', as she considered Alex and Zach, were always careful to make sure they sheltered their wife, they weren't nearly as careful about ensuring Selita was out of earshot.

She finally cleared her throat to draw his attention. When he turned to her, she asked, "Alex, I can talk to you for a few minutes, yes?" When he nodded and started to get to his feet, she held up her hand to stop him. "I just wanted you to know that I be worried about your sister for a long time as well. She not the same after I had to be gone and that soldier boy who think he an ocean rider was here alone with her. She only would wear long sleeves and high turtles for weeks, very strange. And she not her usually popping self. I'm glad you are having Mr. Colt try to get the story, I tried to ask her questions then, but she think my body too busy and tell me no more questions."

WHILE SELITA WAS talking, Colt was scrambling to figure out the messed-up slang and still listen to what she was telling him. Damn, it was like trying to decode the message as it was coming in. *Let's see, "ocean rider," shit, surfer? "Turtles" probably meant turtlenecks. "Popping?"*

"Selita, I think I was with you up to 'her usually popping self.' Umm think you can help me out with that one?" Smiling at the older woman, he remembered how Jenna and Kat had always loved listening to her butcher common American expressions and slang. Trying to decipher it all was a game for them, but honestly, it had never seemed worth the effort to him or Zach. They'd been happy to just let her rant, nodding or shaking their heads based on her tone and called it good.

"You know, popping, like in soda? Those little things that tickle your nose!" She looked at him like he was a dimwit.

"Aha… you mean she wasn't her usual bubbly self?"

"That's what I say, right? Were you even listening to me?" Uh-oh, now she was beginning to sound indignant, and that never ended well for him.

"I appreciate you telling me. And I agree, we've been worried about Jenna for a while. Did Mom and Dad ever know she'd been alone with Ted Scott?"

"I tell them I had to be gone that night, but not until after they got home later that week. And by that time, he was gone." She had started twisting her hands together, clearly worried she'd somehow caused whatever had happened to his sister.

"Not to worry, we'll get it all worked out. Please don't let it trouble you. Jenna will be fine. As I'm sure you've figured out, Colt Matthews has some pretty strong feelings for our little sister, and you can rest assured he plans to take very good care of her, okay?" She nodded, clearly relieved, and when she would have turned to leave the room, he stood and walked around the desk and hugged her. "Please don't ever doubt how important you are to each and every one of us, Selita. You are a valued member of this family, don't ever forget that, keep it etched in your heart, all right?"

She looked up at him and smiled, big tears pooling in her dark eyes. She wrapped her arms around his waist and hugged him tightly before turning on her heel and scurrying from the room.

Alex walked slowly up the stairs. He was undecided about how to proceed with the questions about Jenna. On the one hand, he felt he owed it to his parents to let them know what he and Zach suspected and make sure they were aware there might be a lot of fallout headed their little sister's way. On the other hand, he trusted Colt completely, and if he said he was handling it, then he was, it was that simple. He'd talk it over with his brother in the morning, and they'd decide what all their options were. But for now, he needed to get upstairs to his wife. It humbled him that holding her could bring such peace to his soul, and besides, why should Zach be getting all of her attention? Smiling to himself, he turned and started taking the stairs two a time.

Chapter 14

J ENNA WOKE UP and saw Colt had turned on the small
bedside lamp, so she wouldn't awaken in the dark. She
wondered how long she'd slept, but before she could move
to see the clock, she heard him say, "Come to me, pet."
Startled, Jenna turned to see him sitting in a wing-backed
chair in the corner of the room.

"You scared me. Why are you sitting over there? Were
you watching me sleep?" Jenna still didn't move, she had
gone to sleep knowing she needed to work harder to
maintain some distance between them. Her fear was her
heart was going to be shattered beyond repair when she
had to leave ShadowDance Mountain and Colt went back
to all the other women she knew were available to him at
The ShadowDance Club.

"I gave you an instruction, pet, and I expect you to follow it. Come here, *now*."

The authority in Colt's voice sent a zing of arousal
through her as she scrambled to get out of the bed and pad,
completely naked, to stand directly in front of him.

"You are so very beautiful, pet, but you must learn to
obey immediately and without hesitation. A slip like that at
The Club will most certainly get you punished." He was
running his hands up and down along her sides from her
waist to her knees. The distracted touch wasn't inherently

sexual, but it was intimate and sensual beyond measure. "And I don't want you at another man's mercy. You belong to me and only me, love. Don't forget that." Colt's words sent a shiver through Jenna she didn't even try to hide.

"But just for this week, then I'll go back to work, and you'll go back to The Club, and I'll be..." Jenna couldn't even finish her sentence, it was just too sad to think about right now, and she was determined to not let worries about things she couldn't change cloud the chance she had to make great memories right now. She was standing naked in front of the man whose touch she'd craved for years, and she wasn't going to spoil a single minute of it.

COLT LOOKED DEEP in Jenna's eyes as she spoke about having to leave and could see it was clearly not something she was looking forward to, but she seemed determined to limit their time together to a week. He wondered if she really thought he was that much of a player. Did she really believe he'd bring her here to fuck for a week and then just turn her back to her old life as if he'd had his fill of her?

Christ, he didn't even want to entertain the idea. Realizing she might have that low of an opinion of him was damned humbling. Shaking off the negative track of his thinking, Colt wondered what else he could do to assure her where he felt they stood with each other. Apparently, it was time to step things up a bit.

"We'll discuss your week deadline more later, princess. But right now, I'm in the mood to play, and I believe Mitch would like to get to know you a bit better before we teach you more about our lifestyle." With those words, he looked past her to his friend who was leaning against the doorframe where he'd been since Jenna had moved to stand before Colt.

Jenna jerked her gaze to the other man and immediately began moving her hands, trying to cover her breasts and bare sex. "Oh, my God, Colt, I don't have any clothes on, please, let me go get something to wear. Oh shit, this is so embarrassing. I didn't even hear him come to the door. How long has he been standing there?"

Turning to Mitch, she asked, "How long have you been standing there Mitch? When did you get to the cabin? Jesus, this is so weird, please, can you step outside into the hall for just a minute, so I can get dressed?" She knew her face was flame red, she felt like an inept teenager rather than a highly trained geologist and accomplished oil company executive.

"No can do, darlin'." Mitch pushed himself from his casual pose in the doorway and moved toward her in slow, measured steps. "I'm here to help with your training. No need to be embarrassed about your beautiful body, Jenna, you are a smokin'-hot babe. If you belonged to me, I'd keep you naked every single chance I got." He stepped close and smoothed the backs of the fingers of one hand from her temple, along the side of her face and neck, over her shoulder to trace a line down the entire length of her arm until his fingers encircled her wrist. His hold wasn't tight, but it communicated clearly that she wasn't going anywhere.

MITCH WATCHED THE base of Jenna's throat and smiled to

himself when her pulse increased to match the acceleration in her breathing. *Well, well, I think Colt's little sub is going to enjoy a ménage more than she believes she will. Seems she is more like her older brothers than we might have believed.* Mitch kept his hand around her wrist, it was just enough restraint to give them an indication of how she was going to handle bondage. *So far, so good, sweet thing. God, I can't wait to sink my throbbing cock into your hot body. Jesus, how did Matthews get so lucky? Fuck, if I could just get Rissa to react like this, I would think I'd died and gone straight to heaven.*

Mitch slowly pulled Jenna so her tightly peaked nipples were just inches from his chest. He knew she'd be able to feel the heat radiating from his body. He gave her a teasing grin when he saw goosebumps wash over her skin. If this sent a tidal wave of sensation through her, she was in for a real treat during their ménage.

"I want to touch you, Jenna. I want to get you accustomed to my hands stroking this magnificent body before Colt and I shoot you into the stratosphere. I can smell your arousal, you know. You can't deny the attraction and allure of having two men catering to your pleasure. Move your legs shoulder-width apart."

When she complied, he continued in a low, compelling voice that held her in its velvet grip. Colt moved to stand directly behind her, and Mitch had a clear view of his friend in the mirror Jenna didn't seem to have noticed, giving the two men a three hundred and sixty view of her lovely body. Colt was skimming his callused fingertips softly over her lower back and the rounded cheeks of her ass. When his fingers circled the dimples at the top of her curved ass, pressing slightly on the erogenous zone, he smiled over her shoulder letting Mitch know that was a hot spot for her.

"You're loving our touch, aren't you, darlin'? I love

watching your eyes dilate and cloud with lust. Having a front row seat to a woman's pleasure is a huge turn-on. I can't wait to run my tongue through that sweet nectar I know is coating your sweet cunt." Mitch knew some women considered that word crude and demeaning, but he hoped Jenna realized he hadn't meant any disrespect. Slipping his fingers through her soft folds, Jenna shuddered, and he felt her flood his fingers.

Looking over Jenna's shoulder at Colt, Mitch told the other man, "Your woman is amazing, brother. Hope you are appreciating this gift from God. Christ, she is so beautiful, responsive, and intelligent. It's a privilege to be able to help you introduce her to the pleasures of ménage."

"She is all that and more, but don't think we don't have our work cut out for us. Seems my little sub thinks all I want is a week's worth of fucking. I'm going to be working hard to help her see that isn't the case. I have every intention of making her my own in every way. Let's give her a small sample of what she'll be experiencing later. Then we need to feed her. She had just woken up when I heard the security system clear you, and she's going to be expending a lot of energy later." Colt's last words were laced with humor, but Mitch could feel Jenna's mind beginning to lose its focus as their hands continued to run over her sensitized skin. She hadn't even been able to fully process the words they were speaking.

"Please…" Jenna's soft plea confirmed what Mitch had sensed a few seconds earlier. She was already starting to float in a fog of desire that hinted at a completion just beyond her reach.

"Please what, pet?" Colt leaned forward and spoke so close he was sure she'd felt his lips brushing the curve of her ear. "Please stop? Please continue? Please touch you?

Please fuck you? Please push my long fingers in your sweet ass? You'll need to be specific in your requests, my love, otherwise, you may not get what you desire. A Dom's job is to provide everything his beloved submissive needs, so until I've had time to learn your body's every nuance, you'll need to be very specific."

Mitch knew they were going to push her, and Colt was taking a number of calculated risks. Hell, his sudden appearance alone had been a huge leap of faith and jumping right into a scene with her was going to be dicey. Colt insisted even if they gave her the mind-blowing orgasm he knew they could so easily provide, her sharp mind would turn back on before they'd even be able to get her out of the bedroom. So, they needed to make sure it was good enough to begin the bonding Colt swore was going to be the only truth she was going to be able to hang onto when they had to return to her family's home.

Chapter 15

C OLT HAD BRIEFED him during their phone call earlier in the day about Jenna submitting with her body, but still holding everything else back, so Mitch wasn't surprised when he felt those thoughts running through her mind. Having the ability to establish a strong empathetic connection with another person was often both a blessing and a curse.

Mitch was usually able to get right inside the mind of another person and feel what they were feeling as well as hear most of their 'self-talk'. Right now, Jenna was barely functioning on a cognitive level, all logic was quickly becoming glossed over and buried under a thick layer of lust. There were faint whispers of "distance" and "remember last time" he found really disturbing, and those were the thoughts he tried to focus on.

It was as if she was trying to remind herself of some previous experience where she'd allowed herself to care for someone who'd then abused that trust. He didn't see how she could possibly compare the horrific experience of being raped and beaten by Ted Scott to the pleasures he and Colt could provide, but he knew better than most how truly complex and mystifying the human mind could really be.

Grayson looked up over Jenna's shoulder at Colt and gave a barely perceptible nod to let him know he would be able to 'read' Jenna. There were those very rare people who were able to instinctively block an empath from getting in as Mitch liked to think of it. But as a natural submissive, Jenna valued other people's opinion of her, and her desire to please Colt, even though a part of her was fighting their connection, left the door wide open for Mitch.

"Colt, please, I need you to touch me," Jenna's words were barely audible.

"I am touching you, pet. Tell me exactly what you need." Colt was trying to teach Jenna to equate her feelings of need with the pleasures he could and would provide. Mitch knew the sooner she craved Colt's touch, the sooner she'd accept he wasn't ever going to let her go.

"Jenna, you are so passionate and responsive. I will give you exactly what you need. Talk to me, sweetness." Mitch watched as Colt slowly mastered Jenna's body. He'd known Colt had been planning this scene for years and each and every move had been carefully choreographed.

"Please… I need you…" Jenna's pleas were airy and desperate, but Mitch knew Colt was holding out until she told them exactly what it was she needed. He knelt in front of her and separated her folds, exposing her swollen, throbbing clit. When he blew a small puff of air directly on it, she screamed and started to shake. It was enough to push her closer, but not near enough to bring on the orgasm she was chasing.

They wouldn't send her over until she told them exactly what her body wanted. Mitch could sense the battle raging between her mind and body; she was adrift in a sea of passion and desire without a life preserver. As she fought the waves of her own passion, the ability to express her need in words was drifting further and further away.

"Oh God, please, I need to come. I'm begging you, please."

"What do you think, Grayson? Close enough or shall we hold out for more detail?" Even though there was a teasing tone in Colt's voice, Mitch could tell she still wanted to strangle him.

"Damn, man, I don't know. I love how she's creaming all over my hand. How about I take a lick or two over her little clit and see how that works out? Maybe you'd like to push into her rosette and see how she likes that." Mitch had leaned over so his words created a soft breeze that caressed the swollen tissues, and he smiled when she shuddered.

Colt lifted her leg onto the chair she was standing next to and began running his finger through her soaking center. When it was coated with her sweet syrup, he massaged the slick syrup into the tender tissues surrounding her rear hole. Mitch was only able to catch bits and pieces of the chaotic thoughts racing through her mind, but he knew she was caught between loving the touch and feeling as though she should fight it.

Colt nodded just as he pushed the tip of his finger through the tight ring of anal muscles of her anus. Mitch matched the stimulation by fluttering his tongue over her clit, then bit down gently on the throbbing bundle of nerves. Jenna exploded in an orgasm so strong, Mitch got a brief glimpse of what she was seeing. Watching her hurtle through space, surrounded by brilliant colors swirling as if she was falling through a vortex of electric light was one of the most erotic things he'd ever experienced while connecting with another person.

She sagged against the arm Colt had wrapped around her torso, shaking violently. Alarm was practically radiating from her, and Mitch shook his head as he stood to caress the side of her face.

"Don't worry, sweetness, your exhausted muscles are simply paying us the highest of compliments." As she started to come back to herself, Mitch could hear her scrambling for a way to reestablish the distance she felt compelled to maintain.

Mitch gave her an indulgent smile as she started to slip closer and closer to letting go. There was a part of her that knew it was too late—she'd already fallen in love with Colt—but there was a part of her terrified of losing him. What Mitch didn't understand was why she felt so insecure about Colt staying with her.

It was one thing to never know exactly what you were missing, it was another to have experienced it then have it jerked away. That was the last thought he heard float through her mind before she slipped into a blissful sleep.

"CHRIST, MATTHEWS, SHE is fucking unbelievable. You are a lucky bastard. I don't know what you did to deserve her, but I'm sure it must have been a long-assed time ago because you sure as shit haven't been that good since I've known your sorry ass," Mitch chuckled as he watched Colt gently lay Jenna on the bed. Retrieving a warm cloth from the bathroom, Mitch handed it to Colt so he could take care of his woman and looked on in longing. He sent a prayer out to the universe that one day soon, he and Bryant would be caring for Rissa with the similar captivated expressions.

"I am humbled by your appreciation of my worthiness,

you pompous ass. Now go on downstairs and start dinner. I'll take care of Jenna and then be down." Colt's expression was one of brotherly affection even if his words didn't reflect the warmth. He gently cleaned her tender skin then patted the area dry.

COLT MARVELED THAT Jenna was even more than he'd dreamed she would be. He stood and watched her sleep for a few moments before moving away from the bed. She was absolute perfection in his eyes. In sleep, she looked so much younger than he knew she was. All the tension and stress of pretending to be strong and in control faded away and her youthful countenance shone through.

Smoothing her dark hair back from her face in a gesture more affection than necessity, he smiled at his own actions. *Oh yeah, you are so fucked, Matthews!* Laughing at his own self-mocking, he turned and made his way downstairs.

Chapter 16

"**T**ALK TO ME." Colt's cryptic greeting didn't surprise Mitch. Hell, they'd been friends way too long for anything about Colt Matthews to surprise him. Mitch had already started putting their dinner in the oven when Colt walked into the room. Selita had started cooking and freezing dinners for them the year before when they'd spent all their spare hours building the cabin, and she'd continued even after they had a fully functioning kitchen.

The Lamont's sweet cook sent boxes full of meals with them several times a month, so their freezer was always well stocked. They were always grateful and made sure she always got large cash gifts for every holiday, birthday, hell, they'd even given her money for National Peach Lover's Day last year. She'd always insisted they not pay her, but gifts for 'occasions' seemed to be okay. They'd laughed while they'd searched the Internet for an *occasion* the last time they'd felt it was time for another gift.

Leaning back against the counter, Mitch crossed his arms over his chest and looked at his friend. "You're right, she's holding back. I didn't get it all; her thoughts don't exactly track perfectly when she's balancing on the edge, man. She's afraid of getting hurt. She trusted someone before, someone she thought she loved or at least wanted her, but she got hurt. Whether or not that was Ted Scott, I don't know yet, but I'll get it. I need to be able to spend an hour alone with her."

Seeing the look on his friend's face, he smiled. "Christ, Matthews, lighten the fuck up, will you...I mean, I just want to be able to sit and talk with her. I'll steer the conversation and get exactly what you need to know even though I'm fairly certain we already know the gist of it."

Mitch Grayson wasn't opposed to using his gifts to help others, but he was judicious about allowing anyone outside of a very small circle of close friends knowing exactly how effective his skills were. There were a lot of people on both sides who would take great pleasure in using his talents for ill-gotten gains. Hell, he'd made certain no one outside of their immediate team had been aware. He'd spent time with their upper command and knew exactly which of those pricks would sell him out for thirty pieces of silver.

"Tell me what you got, specifically. Stop dicking around, damn it."

Mitch could sense how tired Colt was and he, too, was frustrated with his inability to get through the walls Jenna had built around her heart. He had to have known pulling Grayson in was using an unfair advantage, but this was a battle he obviously didn't intend to lose.

"Now that I've found out the truth about Ted Scott, I'm going to backtrack to those responsible for his placement in our unit; something about it just doesn't jive.

"Okay, Jesus, Matthews, get a grip already. She just kept chanting to herself *remember last time* and then *keep distance*. But, the clincher was at the very end, just as she was falling asleep, she wondered how she was ever going to protect her heart, then admitted to herself she'd already lost it to you a long time ago. Also, you're everything she dreamt you'd be, and she dreads the devastation she'll face when it's all taken away from her. And before you ask, no, I don't know exactly why she thinks it will be taken away. My guess is because Ted Scott ripped her innocence and her faith in love from her at a very young age, she has decided love can't be trusted." Then chuckling softly, he added, "But be careful, that's a mix of psychology and hocus pocus... always a dangerous combination."

"SPEND SOME TIME with her tomorrow morning. See if you can get any more. I have some calls to make. I'm going to light a fire under Franklin's ass again. That little prick aide of his didn't seem all that interested in passing along my message earlier today. I'll go over our dear former general's happy ass if I have to. This is personal. He isn't going to play this smoke-and-mirrors game with me for long. You get anything on that weasel assistant?"

Colt had been trying to warn their former commander for over a year that his disabled 'war hero' aide was a dick of the first order. Hell, General Franklin's ass-hat assistant had his head so far up his boss's posterior, they were both probably having trouble figuring out where one of them ended and the other started. Colt, Alex, Zach, and Mitch were all of the same opinion, all had bad feelings about the guy, and they'd even discussed cutting off contracting with Uncle Sam until the situation was safer. They'd had a couple of missions go south in a big way after he'd joined Franklin's staff, and it seemed just a bit too coincidental for a team who'd been trained to *never* trust a coincidence.

"No and that really bothers me for a lot of reasons, not the least of which is his past record is so perfect, it red flags.

Nobody has a record that squeaky-clean and watertight, and his reeks of manufactured bull shit." Grayson was a born skeptic with a finely tuned sixth-sense and amazing computer skills, and if he red-flagged it, Colt knew they had better sit up and pay attention.

"Manufactured? How could Franklin not notice that?" Colt had known General Franklin for years. It wasn't like him to be taken in by a fraud.

"No fucking clue, but he *is* getting older, and I know the last time I spoke with his wife, she made a couple of comments about things he'd 'forgotten' and hinted about her concern for his physical and mental health. I think she was trying to hedge about Alzheimer's, so it may just be that he isn't as sharp as he once was."

"If that's the case, Mr. Big-Shot Aide could be essentially running the show under the guise of protecting his boss' reputation. Any chance he's on the take?" Colt knew he was going to have to call in a few favors and have the aide checked out. Hell, he was seriously considering sending Grayson to DC for a little personal meet and greet with the guy.

"Fuck, what's the little wart on Franklin's ass called, anyway? I never can remember the prick's name," Grayson growled.

"Theodore James," Colt answered. Colt was the only member of the team who had actually met the guy face-to-face. He hadn't been impressed. The guy had obviously had a lot of plastic surgery after being in a landmine explosion in Afghanistan. He'd also lost a leg, but seemed like he got around well on his prosthesis. They hadn't exactly hit it off that day in Franklin's office, and things had remained chilly, at best, ever since.

"I'M GOING TO run his name against Ted Scott's, see if there is any reason to believe they might be connected in some way." The hair on the back of Mitch's neck had stood straight up when Colt had said his name, and that was a warning sign it was never a good idea to ignore. "I have to tell you, something just feels every kind of wrong about this guy. Something tells me there is more to this whole situation than meets the eye."

"Agreed. Now, I'm going to go check to see if Jenna is ready for some dinner. That smells fantastic, and I'm starving." Colt started to move from the room when Grayson stopped him with a hand on his shoulder.

"Keep this one, Colt, she's really special. There is an innate goodness in her that goes bone deep. She loves you, but she's terrified she'll be hurt again. If you aren't in this for the long haul, walk away now. She's too fragile to weather your rejection if she invests another minute in her love for you." Mitch didn't like giving unsolicited advice, but it was important his friend to understood how truly special Jenna was, and he'd been watching Colt casually fuck, then toss women aside for years.

They'd all teased him that he seemed like he was "holding auditions and test driving every woman he met" and then when he found the least little excuse as to why they didn't "measure up," he tossed them aside. Mitch had felt Jenna's vulnerability and knew she'd never fully recover if Colt walked away from her if this went on any longer.

Colt looked directly into his friend's eyes for several

seconds before speaking. "I appreciate your concern, but I'll assure you—only once—it's unfounded. Jenna is the woman I've been searching for my entire life. I have no intention of *ever* letting her go. Now, if you're done being a fucking Boy Scout, I'm going to get my woman."

As Colt stomped up the stairs, Mitch smiled to himself. *Oh, the Mighty Colt Matthews has fallen. Yes, indeed, Mr. Love and Leave 'Em is officially off the market. More the better for me!* The sad thing was, he didn't want more women, he just wanted the one who kept running. After this mess with Jenna was resolved, it was going to be time for a full-court press on his target. *Rissa, you can't run forever.*

Chapter 17

THEODORE JAMES SAT at his desk just outside his boss's office and listened as the feeble-minded bastard talked to Colt Matthews for the second time in three days. What the fuck was Matthews's problem? Hell, he never called unless it was mission-related, and James had managed to steer work away from him and the Lamonts more and more often as Franklin had fallen further and further under the effects of memory loss that was James' own creation. Well, that wasn't exactly right; after General Franklin had started taking heart and cholesterol medication, he'd asked his new aide to research possible side effects. What newly promoted Staff Sergeant Theodore James found proved to be very valuable information indeed.

It seemed the good doctors at Bethesda had prescribed drugs which tended to have a profound effect on memory in certain patients, his boss included, it seemed. So, when the old man started forgetting whether or not he'd taken his medication, his new aide had been diligent in making sure he took it… sometimes three to four times more often than necessary. It was like feeding candy to a baby. He'd laughed and was totally dismayed by how easy it was to manipulate the situation.

Hell, James had originally joined the old bastard's staff with the single-minded goal of destroying the team of men who had treated him like an outcast and had left him in that hell-hole cave in fucking Afghanistan. Sure, they'd thought the damned thing was caved in, and he'd heard them trying to get to him before another explosion had sent everyone scrambling topside. But it didn't matter, he'd found another way out and spent months recovering in a little god-forsaken hospital on the dark side of the planet.

With his command of the local language and its specific dialect, along with his dark coloring thanks to a Middle Eastern mother, he'd been able to fool the locals into believing he was a fallen brother. Once he'd been well enough to work, he'd managed to get computer access and in a few short weeks, Theodore James had been born, injured, and recovered along a road. He'd been *discovered* as a confused but recovering victim of a mine explosion which had occurred several months earlier. Hell, his heartwarming story of courage had earned him accolades and a fucking Purple Heart. *It should have earned me a fucking Nobel Prize for Fiction!*

And now, the convenient memory lapses of his boss were an opportunity that was simply too good to pass up. Hell, he'd been practically running the special teams who contracted with Uncle Sam for the past year. The old man sat in his office staring out the window from the time he shuffled into work until his loyal aide led him out the door at quitting time.

Sure, James knew this gravy train wasn't going to last forever, but he'd almost gotten enough money stashed so he'd be able to disappear during the night and live the good life courtesy of all those hefty deposits which had been made to his Grand Cayman bank account. Information was a valuable commodity, and it seemed knowledge was indeed power and pretty damned profitable to boot.

But now, Colt Matthews was beginning to be a problem. James eased closer to the door so he could hear his boss's end of their phone conversation.

"I've told you everything I know about Ted Scott, Matthews. What's bringing this up again now? Well, I can make some inquiries, but I'm not going to promise I'll come up with anything new... Okay, I'll get back to you ASAP... You tell those other yahoos you work with the Old Man sent them all a kick in the ass." Franklin laughed at something Matthews said before saying goodbye.

Well fuck, this could easily to go to shit in a heartbeat if it's not nipped in the bud right away. Time for another trip to ShadowDance. I wonder if the Lamont brothers' hot little sister, Jenna, wants another round? Hell, what was it I called her? Oh, right, Genevieve. Yeah, she was a whole lot of fun the last time I was there. Might be time for a repeat performance. I love it when they fight it, fuck, what a turn-on. I'll bet she's still a hot little piece of ass and popping her cherry was icing on the cake last time. Yes, indeed, think I should do the General a favor and go out to be his eyes and ears. God, the old fart loves that annoying expression. I'll fuck that hot little cunt, take care of the other problems, and be back before the end of the week.

ShadowDance Mountain

COLT STAYED IN his office most of the morning to give Grayson plenty of time to get a bead on what sort of blocks he was going to come up against with Jenna. He thought it was likely she had put all those defenses in place to protect her heart from the trauma she'd experienced at the hands of Ted Scott. Fuck, it made Colt almost physically ill to think of what she'd had to endure and at the hands of one of their own teammates, no less. And then to not be able to seek medical care or have the emotional support she'd needed because she'd been trying to protect her two older brothers? *Un-fucking-believable.* Christ, what a mess.

For just a minute, he wondered if he was up to the task of helping her heal, but he quickly brushed the doubt aside. It wasn't like he had a choice—he loved her and would do anything he could to make sure she was happy and healthy for the rest of his life.

Grayson's help was critical to making everything come together because Colt didn't have the luxury of weeks and months to muddle through this kind of emotional minefield. He only had this week. He had to not only help her heal in that short time, but he had to bind her to him, body and soul. *Yeah, you're not asking for much are ya? Remember our team's motto… Whatever it takes!*

Shortly before lunch, General Franklin called back to say he was sending his aide to ShadowDance to personally assist with their investigation of Ted Scott. Their former Commanding Officer thought the combination of his aide's clearance and their team's technology, they might be able to find the answers they were looking for.

When Colt had pointed out each member of the team actually had higher level clearance, Franklin said James had insisted on acting as his liaison and would be arriving the next afternoon. Sometimes, it just didn't pay to argue with a bureaucrat. The team had teased Franklin for years about losing sight of how things really worked when he'd become a pencil pusher at the Pentagon. They'd just have to endure a couple of days of the little weasel, and besides, it would give Grayson a chance to read the little piece of shit. *Yeah, this might work out all right after all.*

Pushing out of his chair, Colt headed to the door that would take him to the front deck where Grayson and Jenna sat in loungers, talking quietly. Pausing before stepping outside, Colt looked out at her and sighed. God, she was so fucking amazing. He'd count himself the luckiest man on the planet if she agreed to be his permanently. He wanted it all... marriage, a hot collaring ceremony at The Club, kids, soccer games, Little League, damn, even birthday parties with those stupid piñatas everybody made YouTube videos of. *Christ, what kind of idiot gives a blindfolded six-year-old a bat, then stands to the side while the sugar craving demon attempts to knock down a candy-filled papier mâché horse?*

Suddenly, he realized that while he wanted that and more with Jenna, if she wasn't a part of the picture, the entire image faded to a dull gray. He'd tried to put her out of his mind a thousand times and had never gotten close. He slowly turned away from the door and made his way to the kitchen. He'd get lunch started and then join them.

He had big plans for his little submissive-in-training this afternoon. Christ, he was going to give himself the hard-on from hell if he started thinking about all the things he wanted to show her and all the experiences he wanted to share with her. *Brilliant work there, horndog, it's going to be a laugh riot fixing lunch around that bad boy.* Laughing to himself, he got to work. The sooner he got everybody fed, the sooner he'd have her naked and his afternoon agenda set into motion.

Chapter 18

J ENNA WAS TOO quiet during lunch, and she didn't know why all the sudden she was feeling overwhelmed and intimidated by Colt. After all the time she had known him and all they had shared the last couple of days, it didn't make any sense. But she had told him things she'd never told another person, and now, she was feeling particularly vulnerable.

Mitch was watching Jenna intently and listening as she wrestled with her discomfort and feelings of vulnerability. *Ah, sweet Jenna, welcome to the mindset of a submissive. Hang in there, sweetheart, you'll work through those troubling feelings and find a freedom in submitting you never imagined possible.*

"You know, Jenna, a large part of any successful Dominant-submissive relationship is communication. Remember, we talked about trust this morning, but the only way to build trust is to communicate with your partner exactly what you're feeling. For example, if you're feeling frightened by something you know is coming up in a scene, it's important for you to express that to your Dom. Or if you are feeling particularly vulnerable that is equally important for your Dom to know. A little apprehension is good, it tends to enhance sensation, but fear—whether it's of something physical or emotional—is counterproductive because it's limiting." Mitch had tried to include a broad enough range of information, so she wouldn't accuse him of mind reading. He'd learned long ago women were extremely leery of that particular skill, but he also wanted to get the message across to her.

Colt seamlessly picked up the conversation track, just as Mitch had known he would. "Jenna, if you have concerns, I will always want to hear them. You are very new to this lifestyle, and I want you to enjoy it. That means you need to feel safe and confident enough to ask questions and express your concerns. As you learn and become more familiar with how things work, I won't always entertain those questions because as Grayson mentioned, apprehension is often a precursor to a good scene. I'm also very aware of the trauma you experienced at the hands of a sexual predator. Because of that experience, I'm going to be paying particular attention to any fears or feelings of extreme vulnerability until you are comfortable with everything you're experiencing. Do you understand?"

Mitch and Colt had learned a long time ago it wasn't enough to just give a sub information when they were in training, it was equally important to make sure they were processing everything being thrown at them, because, often, processing was heavily clouded by lust. When mentoring Doms, they'd likened the processing challenge to trying to steer a boat through Jell-O and the visual was damned accurate.

JENNA SLOWLY NODDED her head. "Yes, I understand. But at the same time, it's really hard to tell you what's going on inside my head when I don't even really understand it."

Colt had to smile because that was probably one of the most honest and insightful responses he'd ever heard a sub give to the information they'd just told her. *Yep, whip-smart as always.* Colt reached for her hand, enclosing her small, dainty fingers in his much larger one before kissing the back of her hand.

"Good enough, pet. Just remember, it's important you use your safe words. I know Grayson covered that with you this morning, but I want you to tell me what they are and when you should use them."

Taking a deep breath, Jenna glanced at Mitch then looked back at Colt. "I'm to say 'red' if what we are doing is just too much—either physically or emotionally—for me to endure any longer. Then everything stops, and after we've had a chance to move apart and have a small break, we'll talk and figure out what went wrong and where we go from there. But everything is over for the rest of that day at least. I'm supposed to say 'yellow' if I'm getting into something I am unsure of or I'm getting close to saying 'red.' If I say 'yellow,' then we stop temporarily and talk, then you decided whether or not we proceed."

Colt wondered how on earth she had said that all so fast and without pausing to breathe. *Damn, woman, it's not a quiz, I just wanted to check your comprehension and comfort level. Comprehension is great, comfort not so much.*

"Okay, we're going to have another lesson this afternoon, Mitch and I will both be involved, and we'll be taking you to our playroom. Are you ready?" Colt spoke as he stood and pulled her to her feet. He watched her eyes widen and could see her pulse had already started to pick up. They had let her wear shorts and a T-shirt all morning and through lunch because they'd wanted to keep her as comfortable as possible while Grayson 'read her', but it was time to get things back into D/s mode.

Grayson also stood up, and as Colt let go of her hand and took a step back, they both crossed their arms over broad chests and widened out their stances. It was the body-language equivalent of announcing the scene had started.

"Strip, pet." Colt's order was spoken in a Dom tone, firm but not loud.

Jenna's eyes looked like solid black discs surrounded by a thin green ring, they were so dilated. Her breathing was faster, and her eyes bright with yearning rather than fear. She slowly kicked off her sandals and reached for the bottom of her T-shirt, drawing it slowly over her head.

"When you are told to strip, you will always fold everything neatly and lay it just to your right on the floor." Jenna carefully folded the shirt and placed it gently on the floor exactly as he'd instructed. She then, with slow deliberation, unzipped her jean shorts and let them fall to the floor before bending at the waist to pick them up. *Aha, my sweet sub wants to tease a bit, well, baby, bring it on.*

Colt was thrilled she felt comfortable enough to perform that little *take a look at my great ass, boys move*, but he needed to remain in character.

"Be very careful with your teasing, pet. We can tease, too. We could easily keep you right on the edge of release for hours. Bringing you right up to the cusp time and again, but always denying the orgasm your body craves, no matter how much you begged for it." Colt watched her eyes widen and heard her soft gasp. *Oh yeah, you gotta love that reaction. I'd bet my interest in The Club, she just soaked that lacy thong she's wearing.*

MITCH STIFLED A laugh as he heard her questioning how she was she supposed to keep from coming? Knowing she'd almost come just from Colt's warning was perfect. She knew there wasn't going to be any way to deny how aroused she was when she peeled her thong down her legs and they got a look at how drenched it was—and she was right.

Jenna unhooked the front clasp of her all-lace bra and let the straps fall off her shoulders. He was getting harder than hell watching her innocent attempt at a striptease. *Turns out the warrior fairy has a sensual side.* She had neatly folded each item and laid everything on top of her shoes, and the only thing left was her soaking-wet thong. As she slowly moved the small triangle of material down her legs, she heard them both hiss.

"Damn, Matthews, seems your little sub was aroused by that warning. I can't wait to get her into the playroom and see how she responds to the scene." Even though he wasn't interested in owning Jenna, Mitch had no problem appreciating a beautiful woman and enjoying the gift of her trust and submission. Jenna Lamont was as natural a sub as he'd ever seen.

"She's amazing, isn't she? Smart, interesting, challenging, and the gifts of her submission and trust humble me." Colt's words of praise caused her to flush, and Mitch could see pride lighting her eyes. "I know she's new to the lifestyle, but she stands before us and waits for her next instruction like a well-trained sub."

COLT STEPPED CLOSER and ran his fingers lightly around the dusky rose areola of her breasts, and when her nipples peaked, he pinched them slightly, and she felt shivers race up, then back down her spine. Her nipples were very sensitive, so they responded to even the slightest touch.

"I can't wait to clamp these gorgeous nipples, pet. That bite of pain is going to bring you so much pleasure. Spread your feet a bit farther than shoulder-width apart and clasp your hands behind your back."

Jenna moved her feet apart, and as she clasped her hands behind her back, she realized how her breasts were thrust forward as if she were offering them to Colt. Mitch reached around her from behind and pinched her tight nipples as he pulled them, so they extended even farther. Colt trailed his fingers through her soaking folds from her rear entrance to her clit and then back again. When she felt herself starting to tremble as she neared release, they both stepped back, and she moaned aloud at the loss their touch.

Mitch was the first to speak. "We had better move to the playroom before we take her right here in the kitchen." His voice was so rough with arousal, it told Jenna they weren't as unaffected and in control as they wanted her to believe.

"Let's go, pet. Time to play." With those words, Colt turned and walked to a door she hadn't even noticed. The door was well-camouflaged in the wall of the hallway. She would bet most people walked right past it without noticing the security keypad incorporated into a small picture.

Mitch was right behind her, and as Colt stopped to press a series of numbers and letters into the concealed keypad, Mitch's warm hands massaged her ass as he spoke over her shoulder. He was so close, she felt his warm breath wafting over the sensitive spot behind her ear that always caused her to flood her pussy with cream.

"We are going to prepare this beautiful ass so you'll be able to have us both inside you at the same time, sweet Jenna. It'll give you an orgasm you'll never forget, I promise you. But, your virgin asshole is so tight, we'll need to use a series of plugs over the next couple of days so you're ready. Oh, baby, you just creamed all over my fingers, and I can smell your arousal, all musky woman. Christ, what a turn-on for a Dom to know he can elicit that response in a sub."

When they passed through the doorway, Jenna was startled by the sound of the door closing and the lock clicking into place behind them.

"Don't worry, pet, the lock is to keep others out, not to keep you in. The playroom can also be used as a safe room. We'll give you a code, so if you should ever need it, you can lock yourself in here and know only Grayson, Davis, your brothers, or I can access the security system. There's also a backup escape route we'll show you later."

The room was so dark, Jenna could barely see anything, the only light from what looked like airplane aisle emergency lighting which encircled the space.

"But right now, we have a few things to teach you. Welcome to our playroom, pet. Lights fifty percent." Suddenly, the lights came up, well, such as they were. The room looked like something straight out of a medieval castle dungeon.

Jenna's gasp was audible, and she saw Colt and Mitch both struggle to suppress satisfied smiles. Her eyes had gone wide, and her mouth dropped open. They watched silently as she took in the torch-like lights mounted to the natural rock walls. They'd even left a dripping natural spring to run down the wall and fill a small, round natural hole in the rock floor. The pool was about four feet deep and six feet in diameter, and it looked like they'd carved and smoothed out various heights of benches and installed hidden colored lights and whirlpool jets.

Mitch must have seen the question in her eyes, because he gave her an knowing look and explained. "The water temperature can be warmed for a relaxing soak in the whirlpool or we can leave it cool as a punishment for a sub who needed something other than our itching palms warming her ass or the sting of a leather paddle. Neither Colt nor I are big fans of a single-tail whips or canes as a punishment. While we do use them on occasion and stay in practice with both implements, we really aren't the Doms for a submissive who consistently needs that sharp edge of pain to reach their completion."

JENNA TOOK IN the large number of paddles, belts, straps, canes, and whips lining the walls, and swallowing the large lump that had formed in her throat, took an unconscious step back and hit the solid wall of Mitch's chest.

"Um, I don't think, well, I don't want… shit, I can't do this. Please, don't hurt me with those th–things." He might not be an empath, but Colt didn't have any trouble knowing how quickly Jenna was slipping into panic. Fear was coming off of her in waves, and Colt knew he had to rein her in, or they'd lose her before they ever got started.

Chapter 19

C OLT STEPPED FORWARD immediately and lifted her chin so he was looking directly at her as he spoke. "Pet, look at me." When her eyes continued to dart from side to side frantically, he deepened his voice and sharpened his tone. "Jenna, look at me, now!"

When her eyes finally met his, he paused several seconds before continuing. "Stay with me, princess, you are to look at me and only at me while I'm speaking to you. Do you honestly believe either Mitch or I would ever truly harm you?"

Waiting for her answer, he saw the dark cloud of fear start to recede, only to be replaced by desire and curiosity. She pulled in a deep breath and shook her head.

"No, I trust you. I just got scared when I saw all those, those, um, things that are used to hurt people. I haven't ever been spanked with anything but a small paddle and your hand, and I'm afraid of those... implements. They look so wicked." He saw the shudder even though she'd tried to hide it. *God, so beautiful and so brave, standing here facing her fears. She is so much more than I deserve.*

"Everything in this room can be used for pain or pleasure, pet, but I want you to remember we are here for pleasure. While in this room, Club protocol is to be observed at all times. You'll only be allowed to speak when asked a direct question, and any hesitation will be treated as a refused order and will be punished. You'll address both Mitch and me as Sir or Master.

"When at The Club, you will be required to keep your eyes lowered unless instructed otherwise. Looking a Dom directly in the eyes or looking at his or her submissive can be seen as an act of disrespect, and the Dom has the right to punish you or demand your Master punish you in his or her presence. Most wouldn't request a public punishment for a newbie, but there are some who will, so those are rules you'll want to remember. But for the purposes of our training, we will allow, actually we'll encourage your eye contact, so we know how you are reacting to what is happening. Is this clear, pet?" When Jenna only nodded numbly, Mitch landed a stinging swat on her right ass cheek.

"Jenna, I believe you were asked a direct question that requires a verbal response." Mitch's voice was stern, and Colt knew her skin had to be stinging although the flush moving over her told him she'd was aroused as well.

"Yes, I understand." Another sharp slap to her left ass cheek got her focus, and she quickly amended. "Yes, I understand, Master." Even though her voice was airy with desire, it was clear, and both Colt and Mitch noted the huskiness of need in her response.

"Good girl, now, we want to show you around the room a bit, but you will only look at what we are showing you, you'll listen to what you're being told rather than losing yourself in fear and gazing at things you haven't been shown yet." Colt could see her mind struggling to track what he'd said. Her mind was probably racing a thousand miles per hour and in about forty different directions.

Colt remembered hearing Jenna's brothers talk about how they frequently had to give Katarina a spanking at the beginning of a scene to get the first orgasm out of the way, so she was better able to focus during the rest of the scene. He wondered if Jenna wasn't going to need that same thing. Looking up at Mitch, he knew the man had heard every word he'd just thought and agreed, his barely perceptible nod confirming his assent.

"Notice the large bed in the middle of the room, its use is obvious. We'll enjoy fucking you there. We do not make love in this room, pet. I'll make love to you in our bed, and I will be the only man to ever make love to you, now or in the future. But in this room, I may allow others to touch what belongs to me as is my right."

He drew his fingers through her soft pussy lips and said, "This is all mine. Everything. Your ass, your mouth, your pussy, it all belongs to me. And if I decide to share it, then you will obey or use your safe word. Notice the rings in the bed; we'll be using various forms of bondage to restrain you. We'll try different things to determine your comfort level and what types of restraints you respond to with the most pleasure. I'll always push your boundaries and be humbled that you trust me to know when you have had enough. Do you understand, pet?"

JENNA FELT LIKE Colt's voice was casting a spell over her, and she'd almost missed his question. When she realized silence surrounded her, she snapped to awareness and answered quickly, "Yes, Master."

Moving to the left, Colt stopped in front of a strange-looking, padded, leather-covered bench which seemed to have two kneeling boards with straps. She was trying to figure what exactly it would be used for, but she just couldn't seem to get her brain to cooperate. *God, what is wrong with me? They're going to think I'm some kind of cretin if I don't get my head back in this.* She could have sworn she heard a snort of laughter from Mitch before he seemed to get himself back under control and his 'Dom face' slid back in place.

She was coming to recognize the expression and posture he and Colt both adopted when they were playing and knew *the look* was used to mask all emotion. Now that she thought about it, she'd seen that same expression on both her brothers' faces too many times to count, but had never known exactly how to label it. And God only knew how often she'd seen them use it, not always successfully, on her best friend and new sister-in-law, Kat.

"Are we boring you, Jenna?" Mitch asked her. *Damn, what's with this guy, he must be some kind of fucking mind reader. That's definitely something to remember because that'll be mighty damned unhandy. Just what I need, a Dom tip-toeing through the tulips of my mind.*

MITCH HAD TO bite the insides of his mouth so hard to keep from laughing out loud. If he bit any harder, he was going to draw fucking blood. God, she was so amazing. Even though she was struggling to keep her head above water in an ocean of lust, she was still functioning cognitively enough to take note of his ability to know what she was thinking.

Reaching around her, Mitch pinched her nipples just hard enough to make her squeak before she answered, "No, I'm not bored, Sir, just trying to take it all in." Since he knew her answer was completely honest, he stroked her clit softly for a few seconds as a reward.

"Such an honest subbie, you please us, sweetheart. Now, we're going to use this particular piece of equipment first. This is called a spanking bench. It can be used for either punishment or erotic spankings. We're going to give you an erotic spanking now, both as a reward and to let you take the edge off, so you'll be able to focus better during the rest of the scene." While Mitch knew Jenna had heard his words, he was fairly certain she didn't fully understand exactly how a spanking could be a reward.

"I can see you don't understand how a spanking can be a reward, but let me assure you it very much is. This will be your first real test of trust, pet, now step forward and bend over the bench at the waist." The smell of well-cared-for leather was predominant in the entire room, and Mitch heard her soft inhalation as she knelt on the bench, bringing the scent even closer.

The softly padded bench she was kneeling on was built to allow unlimited access to the submissive restrained on it. As Jenna knelt on the padded kneeboards and leaned forward, Colt moved to the front and Mitch stayed behind her. It was a good thing she couldn't see his smile as he listened to her self-talk.

Oh yeah, Jenna, you're flashing him with everything, damn, nothing embarrassing about this position. And being so wet, it's practically running down the insides of my legs isn't gonna tell him a thing, damn body, it's like it's connected to my ears, but not my damned brain!

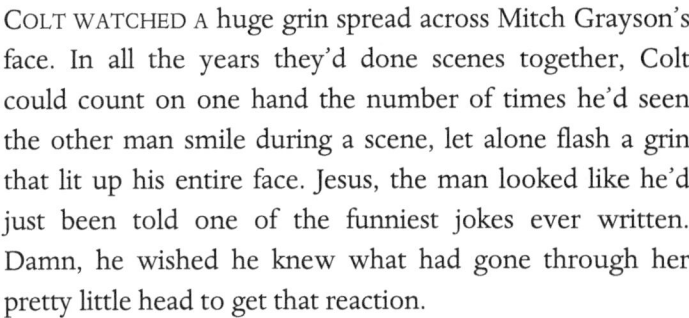

COLT WATCHED A huge grin spread across Mitch Grayson's face. In all the years they'd done scenes together, Colt could count on one hand the number of times he'd seen the other man smile during a scene, let alone flash a grin that lit up his entire face. Jesus, the man looked like he'd just been told one of the funniest jokes ever written. Damn, he wished he knew what had gone through her pretty little head to get that reaction.

Returning his focus to the beauty before him, Colt instructed, "Grab the legs of the bench here." When she did as he'd instructed, he continued, "Now, since you're new to this, we'll be using breakaway restraints. They'll give you the feel of restraint, which adds a lot to the pleasure of the experience, I assure you. You'll also have the confidence of knowing you can get out if you feel panic start to overtake you. Now, I've secured your wrists, so I want you to pull away with a fast, strong motion. It's important you see how this type of strap works."

Jenna pulled hard with both hands and felt the straps release. "Thank you, Master." Jenna's voice was laced with relief and sincerity. He was glad to have given her an added layer of security. Colt and Grayson had talked extensively about how the idea of being truly restrained might send her into a flashback or panic attack as they were certain the asshole who had raped her had no doubt used restraints or she'd have run from him. It hadn't escaped his notice she was referring to him as Master and to Grayson as Sir, and it filled him with pride she'd already made the distinction in her mind. She might not fully understand the significance of it, but she would soon.

"Master Mitch—that is how you will address Doms at The Club—is going to be strapping down your legs at both the knees and ankles; this will keep you in position and protect you from injury. Those straps are not breakaways because the legs are typically so much stronger, and if we provide you with the experience we have planned, you'll be using those strong muscles a lot in response to the pleasure."

Smiling down at her, he gently brushed her hair off to the side, so that it fell over one shoulder. They needed to be able to see her face, so they could gauge her reactions as accurately as possible. Even though Grayson was an extremely strong empath, he'd explained lust and desire were like static to the connection, so using body language and facial expressions were essential to make sure she was responding positively to her spanking. The goal was to give just enough pain to arouse, then send her cartwheeling into orgasm, not to cause anything she'd interpret as *real* pain.

As they finished strapping her in and Grayson moved to get the large paddle and flogger they'd planned to use, Colt continued speaking directly in front of her, cupping her small, delicate face between his large palms, providing support so she was able to look up at him without straining her neck muscles.

"When you are in The ShadowDance Club, you will be expected to address every Dom as Master Mitch, Master Ethan, etcetera, and any Domme as Mistress Rachel, etcetera. Beware of her by the way, she is wicked with a crop and a cane and will use one on any sub she can find the least fault with. Now, the only man you are allowed to refer to simply as Master is the man you belong to. I am the only man you will ever call Master, Jenna. Are we clear?"

Jenna searched his face for any hint of deception but saw only sincere passion. "Yes, Master."

She gave him a small smile, and his heart melted into a mushy puddle. *You are so gone, Matthews. Christ, who knew love would feel so much like handing over your heart to the woman. Any man who thinks he's the one in control is lying to himself. She fucking owns me.* And surprisingly, he didn't mind that revelation at all; as a matter of fact, something about it was completely satisfying.

As MITCH LISTENED to his friend's thoughts, he couldn't help the pang of jealousy that shot through him. He promised himself he'd renew his efforts with Rissa immediately upon returning to The Club, he was tired of waiting for her to come around. It was time for a strategy session with Bryant, Alex, Zach, and Colt; it was obvious bringing her around was going to be a cooperative effort.

Mitch was damned tired of Rissa stalling them to "think about things." No, her *thinking period* had officially ended. It was now time for action. But right now, it was time to work a little magic on this sweet sub's ass. Smiling to himself, he moved to the side and ran his hand down the length of Jenna's spine in a caress so light, she shivered. God, she was so very responsive. She was as sensual a woman as he'd ever seen, and he hoped Rissa would be the same.

"Turn off your mind, Jenna," Mitch spoke in a soft, but firm voice. "Let the sensations wash over you like the waves of the ocean as it pushes over the shore. Consider how you feel when you are floating on an air mattress in the water, drifting wherever the waves take you, knowing you're safe and can simply bask in the warm embrace of the security being provided by the Doms you have entrusted with your body and pleasure. Remember, everything is for your pleasure and enjoyment. Our pleasure will come from yours."

His first swat landed solidly on her left ass cheek, and he held his hand over the spot, ensuring the heat soaked into her skin to enhance the effect. He'd seen her tense, then heard her soft groan as she let the small sting morph into pleasure. The change in the sensation as it moved to her clit sent a rush of moisture to her sex, and the smell of her musk began to swirl around the room. He looked up at Colt and smiled; Jenna was going to enjoy this spanking a lot.

Mitch gave her several more swats with his open palm, varying the placement, intensity, and timing. Keeping her off-balance would be a key factor in keeping her on the edge long enough to build an orgasm strong enough to wipe all other thoughts from her head and keep her focused for the rest of their time in the playroom. Running his fingers through her drenched folds, he lifted them for Colt to see.

"I think someone is enjoying her spanking, what do you think, Master Colt?"

Mitch and Colt moved to change places, and when she lifted her half-lidded eyes to him, Mitch sucked his fingers into his mouth.

"Christ, you are so fucking sweet, I love the taste of you, sweetheart." Jenna watched as he painted his lips with her juices before sucking his fingers into his mouth, humming with pleasure.

"Now Master Colt is going to give you a chance to experience a couple of other implements we are both fond of using."

At Mitch's words, Colt lightly drew the flogger up and then back down her back and over both ass cheeks before flicking her softly with its soft strips of leather. The contrast of sensations, a soft tickle to a slow buildup to a low-burning sting was enough to cause Jenna to moan out loud.

"Oh God, that feels amazing, what is it?" She immediately gasped as she received a hard swat to her upper thighs that really hurt. Her eyes flew wide open, and she cried out at the sharp blow.

COLT WAS PLEASED with her reaction, he'd needed a reason to bring her back from the edge, and she'd delivered it exactly as he'd expected. Jenna had become so lost in the feelings she was experiencing, Colt knew she likely hadn't even realized she'd spoken out loud. "Did you have permission to speak, pet?"

"Oh, no, I'm sorry," she belatedly added, "Master," just as he gave her another sharp slap directly on the crease between her ass and thighs. It was a very sensitive spot, and she'd certainly be remembering that one for a couple of days, he thought with a small smile.

"Keep quiet until you're given permission to come or asked a question. When you are finally allowed to come, pet, we want to hear your cries of pleasure."

Every Dom knew this was a sticking point for almost every new sub. Keeping their pleasure quiet was very, very difficult, and few were ever able to master it completely. No Dom really wanted a sub to remain totally silent. A lot of the Dom's pleasure was driven by watching and hearing his partner lost in the wonders of sensation he was giving her, so being denied the satisfaction of hearing her reactions was not something most true Dominants strived for. But it was important to keep the sub immersed enough they didn't formulate questions, thus his harsh swats, a bit of negative reinforcement.

Colt returned to using the flogger to deliver dual sensations of pleasure followed by bites of pain designed to sink his sweet sub down into pleasure without sending her over into orgasm. He wanted her floating as much as possible in subspace before he started using the leather-covered paddle, knowing it was going to deliver hard swats which would, hopefully, send electric pulses of pleasure coursing through her body and ending in every erogenous zone like heat being applied directly from the inside out. With a few more passes of the flogger, he saw Grayson's nod, took the paddle into his hand, and stepped back so he'd be able to swing it straight and keep the board parallel to her already-bright-pink ass.

Her bottom was going to be a nice cherry red when he finally let her come, but she wouldn't have any lasting marks. She'd feel those two punishment swats for a day or two, but he was sure he hadn't hit her hard enough to give her a deep tissue bruise. He'd enjoy checking her later tonight and a few times tomorrow. Smiling, he brought the paddle down for a resounding first swat.

MITCH HAD TO hold back his grin as Jenna's voice rang through his mind. *Holy fuck, that hurt! Oh, my God... I hope*

he does it again. That was amazing, how can something hurt so much and then change so quickly into such a deep pleasure? Even though Mitch couldn't get it all, he'd gotten enough to give Colt the go-ahead.

Mitch held her face in his hands and watched her eyes glaze over. "Amazing isn't it, Jenna? Pain that morphs into pleasure almost before your body has a chance to register the difference between the two. Remember, the mind interprets pain and pleasure in similar ways, so it can easily be confused by the two, particularly when it's in a sexual context. Let go, sweetheart."

He could feel her muscles tighten, and after the fourth strike, Colt dropped the paddle and pushed two thick fingers into her swollen, dripping pussy and leaned over her.

"Come for us, pet. Let us hear how much you enjoy the pleasure." The words had barely left his lips when she erupted with her release. She'd gone over as much as a result of Colt's whispered permission as from the erotic spanking itself.

It was easy to see how proud Colt was of Jenna. Hell, she'd been more responsive than either of them had expected. Knowing her mind was responding instinctively to Colt as the Master of her body had to be very gratifying. Mitch sent up a silent prayer that Rissa was as perfect for him and Brandt as Jenna was for Colt. He watched his friend continue to finger fuck her until he knew he'd squeezed every ounce of sweet surrender out of the orgasm that had clearly taken her breath away. Now, on to bigger and better things as soon as they provided a bit of aftercare for the amazing sub they were now working to remove from the bench. She was limp as a wet, over-cooked noodle. *You have to love that response. Christ, but she is perfect.*

JENNA HAD HEARD Colt tell her to come and then everything was lost in a wash of color so amazing, she was sure she'd been launched into some kind of H. G. Wells time machine or something equally sci-fi. She felt like her body and mind had actually separated for a few seconds, and it was the most amazing feeling she'd ever experienced.

As she was trying to figure out how to make her neck muscles work—damn, her arms and legs weren't responding either—she felt a warm, wet cloth smoothing over her inner thighs. She instinctively recognized Colt's tender touch and through the fog still clouding her mind, wondered how she'd come to know the difference so quickly.

Colt also dried her, then carried her to a sofa she hadn't even noticed earlier. Settling her on his lap after wrapping her in a fluffy blanket that smelled like a summer morning, she pressed her face into the side of his neck and smiled at his masculine scent. His sweet words of praise brought her back to the moment. When she looked up into his eyes, they were filled with warmth and affection… and what looked like pride.

"You handled that beautifully, pet. I am so proud of you. How are you feeling?"

"Surprisingly good except for my sore tush." She smiled and felt her cheeks heat… dammit, that meant she was flushing bright red. "Um, but what about you and Mitch?" She knew they hadn't found their release, she could feel the steely evidence beneath her.

"Well, pet, we aren't finished playing with you yet.

Now that you're back with us, let's get back into the scene." Colt's words were meant to convey she was to observe protocol, and she had understood the message.

"Yes, Master." Jenna's words were softly spoken against the side of Colt's neck. *Christ, the taste of salt on his skin makes me want to lick him all over.*

Colt stood her on her feet, keeping a hand on her to make sure she was steady before he stood up. Mitch had moved over to what looked oddly like the exam table in her gynecologist's office. *Oh shit, I'm not sure about this. There are a lot of straps on that thing.*

Her steps slowed, and Colt didn't miss her hesitance. "Come along, pet, none of that. We want to play with you, not have to punish you." His words were followed by a smart swat to her tender ass, causing her breath to catch. "Master Mitch and I want to explore you and begin preparing you to take both of us. There are a number of pieces of equipment in this room we could use to do that, but we felt this one would be the most comfortable for you. Now, up you go."

He lifted her effortlessly onto the table and both men chuckled at her hiss when her heated ass touched the cool leather. "Lie down—that's right. Now, scoot down so that beautiful ass is hanging almost entirely off the end. Let's get your feet up into these stirrups. Notice these are nicely padded. I'll bet the ones in your doctor's office aren't, are they?"

Jenna knew he was talking to her in his Dom voice, but it was also threaded with enough compassion, she was sure he was trying to keep her as calm and distracted from the fact they were strapping her down and they hadn't mentioned breakaways this time. Jenna felt herself begin to breathe really fast, and her rapidly beating heart was about to pound right out of her chest.

Mitch stepped into her line of vision just then and started gently massaging her arm, rubbing from her tense shoulders all the way to her tingling fingertips in strong, sure strokes. Looking into her eyes, he spoke softly. "I'm going to strap down your arms for two reasons, sweetness. First, I don't want you flailing around and dropping your arm off the table, it's too easy to dislocate a shoulder or injure yourself by hitting parts of the table you'll see make an appearance from time to time during this scene." Smiling, he added, "Oh yes, this table had features your ob-gyn's table doesn't have. Second, you have us both so close to the edge, if you touch us in any way we can't completely control, this scene will be over way too soon. And we want to play with this sweet body for a while before we come."

Mitch leaned forward and kissed her right on the tip of her nose, then moved the wings of the table out and proceeded to strap her arms just above the elbows and at the wrists. Jenna noticed he checked the straps to make sure they weren't too tight by running his little finger around the inside of each of the cuffs.

Colt ran his callused palm down the center of her chest, over her flat stomach, and continued until it rested at the top of her pelvic bone, causing her to shift her attention to him.

"Pet, it's important you remember to let either Master Mitch or myself know immediately if you start to notice any numbness or tingling; that indicates impaired circula-tion, do you understand?" Colt's voice was full of concern, and she appreciated that they seemed to be making her safety a priority.

"Yes, Master, I understand." Her voice sounded more convincing than she felt, and she was glad when she saw

Colt subtly readjusting his thick cock.

"Well then, pet, we're going to begin." Colt's smile was somehow sweet while still hinting at devilment; that contrast caused Jenna's channel to flood with cream.

Oh shit, what have I gotten myself into? Why am I so turned on by being strapped down spread-eagle for God and anyone else to see everything between my legs, hell, everything ought not to be public? Wonder how many Hail Mary's Father Mike would have given me for this? For some reason, Jenna's disjointed little self-talk seemed to calm her.

Colt had noticed Mitch go still, always an indicator he was 'listening', so Colt watched his friend's expression closely. When Colt saw Mitch working to suppress a smile, he knew they were good to go.

Chapter 20

A LEX HAD JUST gotten off the phone with General Franklin's dick-wad aide who'd announced he'd be arriving at ShadowDance day after tomorrow "at 0900, that's 9:00 a.m.," the jackass had explained to him. *No fucking shit, you little twerp*. He'd never met the guy face-to-face, but Colt had, and his impression was the guy wasn't to be trusted. And when Colt described him as a pompous ass and smarmy, Alex had immediately taken a dislike to the man. Now, the question was what had Colt Matthews said to Franklin that had prompted the old man to send a liaison to ShadowDance? Reaching for his phone, he typed a message to Colt: *Call me ASAP on secure line* and hit send.

Zach walked in and sat down with a heavy sigh. "So, what's got you looking like somebody kicked your new puppy, bro?" Alex filled him in on their impending visitor, and they decided they'd put the man up in a small guesthouse on the property. It was heavily monitored with technology the guy likely wouldn't be familiar with, so they'd be able to keep him away from Katarina while also keeping a close watch on him. Something just wasn't right about this guy, but they neither one could put their finger on it.

Changing subjects, Zach asked, "Have you heard from Dylan? Any luck finding Melita?"

"I have a call into him now, but no, I haven't heard anything yet. I know he was able to contact his former boss, but I haven't heard the outcome of their conversation yet." Turning to gaze out the window that looked into the gardens, Alex spoke, almost as if thinking aloud. "I wonder if Robertson had already picked her up? What if he'd left her with some of his cronies? Where would they have stashed her? Would it be possible she was somewhere close since he planned to come here? Damn, is that possible?"

Alex spun around and zeroed in on his brother as if he'd just had an inspiration. "Call everybody you can think of within a hundred-mile radius. See if they saw anyone matching Cal Robertson's and Melita's descriptions. If Robertson was close, then whoever was with him, babysitting the hostage, took off with her after Katarina killed Robertson. And if so, maybe we can track them from here. It's a long shot, but I don't know how else to help at this point."

Zach rose from the sofa he'd been lounging on and moved quickly to his desk on the other side of the room. He was reaching for his phone before he'd even sat down. Alex shook his head, hoping he hadn't just sent his brother on a wild goose chase. It wasn't much, but it was action, and they'd both grown antsy over the last few weeks worrying about finding the brave woman who'd taken such a big risk to help a stranger in a dungeon club.

Helping Kat escape Robertson had been a risk, not only to Melita's personal safety, but also to the undercover case she had invested two years of her life building. Zach knew Melita had likely paid a high price for doing the right thing, and that price would have been both personal and professional. Had it not been for her courage, Kat would have likely died that night. Then, learning that courageous woman was the ex of a close friend, a woman they both knew and genuinely liked, well, finding her had become an even larger priority.

Before he got caught up in his own calls, Alex asked, "Where is Katarina? I haven't seen her in a couple of hours." They didn't let their pregnant wife out of their sight for very long because she was something of a trouble magnet. They tried to make sure at least one of them was close to her at all times.

"She has gone to town with Rissa for new shoes. She said, and I quote, 'If I have to be as round as a hippo and waddle like a duck, I should at least have great shoes.' I wisely didn't comment, it sounded like a setup to me." Zach's goofy smile reflected just how smitten he was with his little 'kitten'. She really seemed to be coming into her own.

Both he and Alex were proud of the changes in her over the past couple of months. She was no longer the shy, insecure woman who had first returned to ShadowDance Mountain. Her confidence had grown by leaps and bounds. They'd seen it happen with women before. As subs became secure in their submission and learned to trust their Dom, they flourished in other areas of their lives as well, and that was exactly what they were seeing in Kat.

They were thrilled to see her blossom under their love and nurturing, but at the same time, she was getting to be a handful, at times. Katarina was racking up so many punishments, they'd likely have to paddle her pert little ass daily for their child's first two years! Zach smiled to himself. *I can think of a lot worse ways to pass the time!*

DYLAN MARSHALL HUNG up the phone after listening to Alex Lamont's idea. He agreed it was a long shot, but he was out of other ideas. He'd get his deputies on it right away. The downside of living in a small, rural community was everybody was up in your business all the time. But the good thing was they were in everybody else's business, too, so if there had been strangers around, someone was bound to remember. Now, if the trail wasn't completely cold, they might just have a prayer of finding Melita, and God knew, alive and well would sure be a welcome bonus.

He'd been saying every kind of prayer he knew. *Damn, but my granny would be proud. Although, she'd be even more pleased if you'd find the only woman you've ever loved.* Jesus, he was even talking to himself now. He kept turning it over in his mind like a rock tumbler polishing the stones; he was hoping continually rotating the ideas would shine them until something stood out to him.

The one thing her supervisor had said that kept coming back to him was that he'd had a call from Mia a couple of days ago, and he felt she was still undercover, but she'd tried to relay a message he hadn't been able to unravel. *"Tell Matt to come to the ball, but no Cat Woman this year."* He knew the message was meant for him; she had nicknamed him Matt because it was a play on his name, Dylan Marshall. Marshall Dillon's first name in the *Gunsmoke* series had been Matt.

Dylan sat staring at the wall, rubbing a pencil slowly back and forth between his thumb and forefinger when it was like he'd been hit over the head with it… *Oh my fucking*

God, it couldn't be that simple, could it? Christ almighty, the ShadowDance Annual Submissives' Masquerade Ball was this coming weekend. And "no Cat Woman" was obviously a warning that Katarina Lamont should not attend. He grabbed the phone and called Alex. If he was right, he needed to see The Club's invited guests list, immediately.

Chapter 21

J ENNA WAS CONVINCED she'd never felt more vulnerable in her entire life, yet somehow, she still felt safe. She decided to figure out the puzzle of that later because right now something was brushing the inside of the arch of her left foot. The soft tickle of a feather slowly worked its way up and around her ankle. The touch was so light if she hadn't been attuned to what was happening, anticipating each and every touch, she might have missed it.

Just as she was starting to register the sensation, it stopped, and Mitch leaned into her field of vision. "Jenna, I'm going to blindfold you for the first part of the sensation play, so you'll be more focused on feeling. When one of the senses is taken away, the others are enhanced. Now, close those beautiful, inquisitive eyes for me."

Jenna closed her eyes, and she felt him place something soft and silky over her eyes, securing it behind her head before speaking to her again.

"Do you know what your Master was using on your foot before, sweetness?"

"Yes, Master Mitch, it was a feather." Jenna knew her voice was breathless. She was starting to recognize that tone in herself; when she sounded like that, she was beginning to sink into 'the zone'. She smiled at her own ridiculous observation. She felt a small slap directly on top of her already-sensitive pussy lips which caused her to gasp and her juices begin flowing in a rush she was afraid would be literally running out of her.

Christ, how embarrassing would that be? Get yourself together, Jenna, you'd better pull your head out of your ass and enjoy this moment before it's gone and there isn't another to replace it. God, but it was going to be hard to let Colt go. She was starting to see herself in the role of 'his', but she knew he'd never want her forever. Well, hell, even a bastard like Ted Scott had only wanted her for an evening.

Jenna had resigned herself long ago that she was going to be a terrific aunt someday, but she'd probably never find a man willing to deal long-term with the baggage she carried. What man would want someone who had been so weak, they couldn't even fight off the sexual advances of an injured man?

Once she'd recovered enough and her brothers had been home long enough to teach her some self-defense moves, she'd vowed she would never be a victim again, but no amount of preparation or training would ever be able to erase the past. She'd never been able to recover the truly fun-loving, free spirit she'd been before it had all been taken away. For years, her fear every time her brothers had gone on a mission had been almost debilitating. She'd been left wondering if this was the time Ted Scott would make good on his threat and kill them? Would he kill one of them as a warning to her? She'd known if he killed one, the other would be as good as dead because they were twins, and *that* bond was soul deep.

COLT HAD STOPPED moving at Grayson's hand gesture. One of the great things about having been teammates for so long was they didn't need words to communicate. Colt knew the other man was listening to the thoughts he knew had to be racing through Jenna's mind. Damn, he could almost hear the gears grinding in that beautiful little head.

He'd placed a pad and paper in one of the table's many drawers earlier after they'd decided they would blindfold her during this portion of the scene. They'd known it would enhance her responses, what Grayson had told her about that was the truth. But it would also enable Grayson to give Colt some information directly as to what Jenna was thinking.

Mitch grabbed the pen and paper and started to write words and brief phrases, and what Colt read did not make him happy at all. *She feels unworthy? What the fuck? How is that possible? She's fucking perfect!* At his puzzled expression, Grayson signed, *Remember, no victim counseling.*

Mitch Grayson had volunteered at a women's shelter during college, and he had spent a lot of time trying to explain to his friends how the minds of women in general and victims in particular worked, but most of the time he'd end up throwing his hands into the air in frustration and telling them he doubted any of them would ever find a woman willing to put up with their dimwitted, Neanderthal selves. Of course, a lot of the time, they were just fucking with him, but then again, often they truly had no clue what he was trying to tell them.

Deciding he'd let Grayson make some additional notes so he'd be able to remember everything later, Colt started moving the feather slowly up and back down the inside of Jenna's thighs. He drew it softly through her swollen petals and saw the muscles draw together and then relax. It was the same muscle response he'd felt when he'd had his dick deep inside her and slowly started to withdraw—it had felt like she was trying to hold him inside with her tight squeeze. God, her pussy was already so wet, he could literally feel the heat of her radiating clear through his jeans.

"Now, pet, I'm going to let Master Mitch work on those beautiful nipples. We're going to see what types of sensations you respond to. And while he's doing that, I'm going to be loosening up this beautiful ass, so you're prepared for the most amazing experience you'll ever have in a ménage." Colt heard her small gasp as he'd spoken the straightforward words to her. He'd known she'd like hearing what was going to happen as much to ease her fears as she seemed to enjoy the erotic words being spoken to her.

Over the years, he'd known a few Doms who liked to use humiliation during scenes, calling their subs whores or worse, but he'd never seen any value in the practice. None of the Doms he was friends with had found that arousing, either. As a matter of fact, he was certain if that took place in a public scene at ShadowDance, Alex or Zach would be having a heart-to-heart with the Dom before they'd be allowed to leave that evening. Biting back a smile, Colt decided to give her just a bit more blow by blow, so to speak.

"Oh, my sweet pet likes it when I talk dirty, doesn't she? She wants to hear how I plan to use lube on the plug, get it all slicked up before sliding it up into her sweet ass. But since you, my precious pet, are soaking wet, I think we'll use your sweet cream as a lubricant instead. Listen to the delicious noises your beautiful cunt makes when I finger fuck you." Colt moved his fingers in and out, making sure to curve them just right so they not only brushed against her G-spot, but so they'd also make loud sucking sounds. He knew he'd been right about her response when he felt her first flutters and then the pulsing of her impending orgasm. He immediately pulled his fingers out and gave her a slap.

"Oh no you don't, you are not allowed to come until we give you permission. We both want to be inside you before you are allowed your release. Don't forget my love, your orgasms belong to me. Do you understand, pet?" He waited for her response, knowing when a sub was lost in sensation and trying to stave off the rush of orgasm, it often took an extra second or two for them to respond.

"Y–y–yes, M–Master, I, ugh, yes, I understand." Jenna was clearly struggling to speak, but she had managed to get the words out.

"Good girl, now, let's see what we can do about stretching this little rosette." Colt started slowly moving the plug through her folds while he pushed a single finger into the tight ring surrounding her anus and felt her clench her sphincter muscles. Holy shit, she was going to squeeze his cock like a dream. Well, she'd be hugging him tight if he ever managed to get inside. He watched as Grayson used small chips of ice to get Jenna's nipples to rock-solid peaks, then pulled them using his teeth until he'd lengthened them to their max.

"Master Mitch has some new jewelry for you, pet. He's going to place them on you now. You are not allowed to speak unless you're asked a question. And you are not allowed to orgasm. Don't forget that, princess." Just as he'd finished speaking, Mitch set both nipple clamps in place at the same time. They'd already adjusted them, so they knew they would be tight enough to sting, but wouldn't truly hurt her. To a new sub unaccustomed to nipple clamping, this would be a big step. The bite of pain would either bring a flood of cream or a safe word. Which would it be for Jenna?

JENNA'S GASP MADE Mitch grin. *Holy shit that hurts! Oh God, oh God, oh God! How am I supposed to not talk or scream? Breathe, yeah that's it. I'll breathe through it. Pretend it's a panic attack… breathe through it.*

Mitch frowned and scribbled on the pad he'd been using for notes, then leaned over Jenna and spoke close to her ear.

"Sweetness, you handled that so well. You breathed through the pain, much like Katarina is learning in her birthing classes. It's a skill soldiers learn during their training. Anyone coping with pain learns the value of deep breathing and focusing. But the added benefit for those experiencing erotic pain is it allows your body time to change the pain to pleasure. Do you feel how your body is responding? It's incredible, isn't it?"

"Oh yes, Master Mitch, it's so much, but not enough, either." Colt and Grayson looked at each other; damn, but that was a perfect sub response if he'd ever heard one. Jenna truly was a born submissive. If she allowed herself to embrace the lifestyle, she'd find emotional and physical pleasures beyond anything she'd ever imagined.

Mitch started lightly licking the very tips of her nipples which were left exposed by the clips he'd attached to her. Her soft moan was exactly the response he'd hoped for.

"Oh, sweetness, you are such a good subbie. Master

Colt and I are going to give you exactly what you need. Patience is a virtue, you know?" Jenna moaned again, and Mitch noticed she was starting to move against the restraints.

Mitch sat on the edge, waiting as Colt removed her restraints and moved her over to stand in front of him. Colt spoke to her in a soft voice Mitch recognized as the one he used when he was trying very hard to maintain some semblance of control. Bringing his hand up, Mitch brushed Jenna's cheek with the back of his fingers.

"Do you trust us, Jenna? Will you let us show you just how freeing submission can be?"

He didn't have any doubt Jenna was ready for this next step, and he hoped like hell he and Colt would be able to hold on as long as it would take to stretch her enough, so mind-altering pleasure was all she would feel. Jenna nodded her head, but when Mitch raised an eyebrow, she remembered she was required to answer with words and quickly said.

"Yes, I trust you both. I'm not going to lie, I am scared. You're both big, and the only time I had anal sex… well, it didn't go so well." Mitch actually saw flashes of the scene as she was speaking. He rarely got information that way, but considering Jenna's own insightful gifts, he didn't suppose he should be surprised. Hell, her ability to visualize was one of the reasons she'd been so successful in the business world.

Working hard to keep his rage hidden, Mitch cradled her face and spoke to her in soothing tones, "Jenna, this is all about your pleasure and showing you just how good it can be. Your Master and I are honored you are placing your trust in us, and we promise we won't let you down." Mitch saw the flash of recognition in Jenna's eyes when he'd referred to Colt as *her* Master and the fact she hadn't corrected him was also telling.

Colt led her the short distance to the bed, then stepped up behind her and began rubbing his hands up and down her arms. Mitch smiled as he watched she leaned back, relaxing into Colt's embrace. After a few seconds, Colt took the condoms Mitch handed to him and handed them to Jenna. "Sheath Mitch and then me, Pet." Mitch didn't even try to hold back his moan of pleasure as her soft fingers brushed over the sensitive skin of his cock when she rolled the condom down his hard length. After Colt's condom was in place, Mitch watched as he turned her back to face him.

Mitch laid back as Colt instructed Jenna to climb up on to the bed and straddle his lap. Mitch's breath hitched as her pussy brushed over his cock. Even through the latex, the heat of her body slammed into him like a freight train. Damn, his dick was so hard, it was a wonder it didn't burst. He couldn't remember the last time he'd been so hard, it had actually been painful. Mitch started rubbing the head of his cock through her swollen pussy lips.

Oh damn, this is one of the reasons I fucking love a waxed pussy. You can't hide a thing from me, Jenna, I see how your labia is beautifully swollen, the lips almost purple, they're so engorged with blood. Your body is just waiting for me to slip inside your soaking-wet, pulsing heat.

Jenna felt Mitch moving against her aching pussy, and Mitch smiled at her. "That's right, sweetness, I want you to take me inside your hot little pussy. I want to see the pink petals of your sex wrapped around my cock. And after I've had a chance to feel your heat surrounding me and squeezing my cock, you're going to lay on my chest while Master Colt sinks his cock deep inside your beautiful ass."

Mitch watched her closely for any signs of resistance or fear, and when he didn't see either, he continued playing. "As he fucks your ass, I'm going to fuck your pussy. Your body is ours to use, and we're going to use it well. Now raise up, I want you to slide down slowly. Take me into your sweet cunt."

Jenna opened her mouth and ran her tongue along her lips in a move Mitch knew had not been calculated to seduce, but it had been one of the hottest things he had ever seen. Mitch watched Jenna's expression go from tense when she started lowering herself onto his cock to white-hot desire as she felt her tissues begin to stretch. He loved seeing her expression fill with heated anticipation. Her look told him she was ready, so he started fucking her with long strokes. He raised her up until just the tip of his cock was still nestled inside her heat before pulling her down quickly until he could feel his cock bump against her cervix. After several strokes, Mitch pulled her against his chest and held her tightly, so Colt could replace the small plug with a generous amount of lube and his thick fingers. They needed to stretch her, so there was only a bite of pain before the waves of pleasure crashed over her.

The thin membrane barrier between them did nothing to hide the feeling of Colt's fingers pressing into her anus as he worked the lube into the tight passage. After several minutes of his friend's fingers scissoring in her depths, Mitch heard the snap of the lube's lid. Relief washed over him because Colt's addition of more lube meant he was going to begin pressing his cock into Jeanna's tight ass. Mitch knew she was nearing the point of no return, so he signaled Colt to still his movements.

"PET, REMEMBER, YOU do not have permission to come." When Jenna's response was little more than a tortured groan, Colt gave her a couple of stinging swats to each ass cheek. "Pet, I'm warning you, do not come. You will wait until I get myself balls deep in this sweet ass and give you permission. Do you understand?"

"Yes, Master," Jenna answered in a barely audible voice, "I understand, and I'm trying. But it feels so good... I don't know how much longer I can hold it back." Colt was thrilled she'd called him Master rather than Master Colt, proving she was accepting him on a deeper level.

Leaning over her back so he could speak right into her ear, Colt whispered. "Pet, as I start in, I want you to push back against me. That's it—no, not too much. Let me control the speed. Oh, fuck me, you're so damned tight. You feel like a hot vice squeezing me from every angle. Grayson, you better be close. She is so fucking perfect, I can't hold off long. Go!"

They set a pounding pace, thrusting in and out in opposition to each other, so one of them was always seated as deep as possible inside her. When Colt felt her beginning to ripple around him, he knew her body had finally overridden her mind and she couldn't possibly hold her orgasm at bay.

"Come now, pet!"

As she screamed and convulsed under him, Colt felt Mitch continue several more strokes, pressing against the thin membrane separating them before he stilled, his eyes rolling back and his shout of release filling the air around them. Colt's entire body felt electrified, his balls seized by the lightning racing up his spine before he heard his own shout as ecstasy exploded in his brain, and he fell over into a deep chasm of pleasure.

Colt worried his muscles were no longer going to hold him up, so he gingerly pulled out of her ass even as he was still vibrating from her trembling aftershocks. Hell, he wondered if his legs were going to carry him to the bathroom to dispose of the condom. He was forced to lean against the bathroom vanity for long seconds while he wet a soft cloth with warm water.

When he finally returned to Jenna, she was in exactly the same position she'd been in when he left the room, sprawled over Mitch's chest with her hair a riot of black silk lying in a curtain all around her. When he started to clean her she protested, but Mitch's arm was clamped around her preventing her from moving away from his ministrations.

"Shhh. Let me clean you, it's my privilege and respon-sibility." He gently lifted her off Grayson and watched as his friend made a quick exit to the bathroom to dispose of his condom.

Tenderly wrapping Jenna in his arms and pulling her tight against his chest, Colt watched Mitch slip out of the bathroom and then quietly out of the bedroom to give him privacy with Jenna. Colt knew Mitch was planning to make his move on Rissa soon, and he hoped his friend would find the same happiness and contentment with his tiny auburn-haired beauty as Colt had found with Jenna.

Rolling Jenna to her back and moving over her in one smooth motion, Colt pushed himself deep inside her pussy in one quick thrust. He smiled when her eyes came fully open before losing their focus once again as she tumbled over into lust. Taking his time, he pulled almost all the way out of her before thrusting in to the hilt again. Over and over, long, slow strokes that he knew would build her trust and bind her even further to his heart. Colt knew on some level Jenna already accepted him as her Master, but he wanted her heart as well. He wouldn't settle for anything less than everything she had.

All too soon, his own orgasm was nearing, and he didn't plan to go over alone.

"Jenna, I want you to come with me." When she seemed lost in the sensations, he reached between them and pinched her clit as he whispered, "Now! Come now, pet!"

Jenna screamed his name at the same time he shouted hers. The orgasm had been every bit as earth-shattering as the one before, but in an entirely different way. This had been all about making love to the person he intended to spend the rest of his life with and giving their souls a chance to join in a dance as old as mankind. He filled her with his seed and was basking in the primal feeling of satisfaction of knowing his seed was so deep inside her, he knew it had splashed against her womb—tempting fate.

Colt kissed her softly, speaking words of praise close to her ear, and when her gaze returned to him, her eyes were still clouded and half-lidded with her lingering lust, and the small, sweet smile she gave him touched his heart.

"You are the most amazing woman I've ever known, and I can barely think for wanting you, princess." He withdrew from her and watched in wonder as his seed leaked from her body. He heard his own deep growl and saw her tense. "Watching my seed slide from your beautiful body fulfills something so deep inside me, I'm not sure how to put it into words. As much as I'd like to leave it there, so you'd remember this moment when you awaken tomorrow morning, I'm going to clean it from you for your comfort." When she started to protest yet again, he leaned over her and pressed his lips lightly to hers in a tender kiss before speaking. "Remember, it's my privilege and duty to care for you, to provide for your every need. Please don't deny me what is mine." *Mine!* The word had been growing louder in his mind with each passing day.

Chapter 22

J ENNA KNEW WHEN she woke up alone in Colt's large bed something had changed. There was a tension in the air making the hair on the back of her neck tingle. She showered and dressed quickly before making her way to the kitchen to find both Colt and Mitch sitting at the table. They were speaking in low tones, and it was obvious they were not pleased with whatever had roused them so early. Both men looked up as she entered the room with Colt being the first to speak.

"Good morning, princess. How did you sleep?"

"Um, fine, thank you." Jenna knew her voice gave away her growing concern. "What's happened? What's wrong? Are my brothers and sister-in-law all right? Oh God, are my parents both okay?" By the time she'd finished, she was starting to tremble.

"Jenna, breathe, please! Christ, you look ready to pass out. Everyone is fine, but there are some things we need to talk to you about. There have been some developments related to the search for the woman who helped Katarina escape in Las Vegas. Also, our Pentagon contact has sent a liaison here, and he isn't someone any of us are particularly comfortable with, so we need to return to ShadowDance later today." Motioning her to sit at the table, he squeezed her hand before moving into the kitchen.

"Now, please, let's get you something to eat." They hadn't intended to blurt it all out so suddenly, but her panic had made it necessary.

After filling her plate with a mountain of scrambled eggs, sausage links, and toast, they'd given her a glass of orange juice and set them in front of her at the table. Colt moved his chair closer to hers, and slowly rubbed the back of her neck and shoulders, easing the tension she hadn't even realized had been slowly squeezing her muscles. She ate as much as she could and assured them she was full to the gills. Colt took her hand, lifting it to his lips and pressing a kiss on the back before pulling her to her feet.

"Let's go out on the deck and talk, shall we? Everything is always better in the warm sunshine." Okay, now she was starting to worry again. What needed to be better?

COLT DIDN'T NEED Grayson's gift of empathic hearing to know Jenna was strung tight. Holy Mother of God but her muscles felt like they were being stretched to the max, and her body language was radiating anxiety. He'd sat her in a cushioned chair and pulled another chair up so close in front of her, their knees touched when he took his seat. He gathered her hands in his as Mitch sat nearby.

"Sweetheart, after we found out what happened with Ted Scott, we contacted our former commander, who is now our contact for the contract work we do for Uncle Sam. General Franklin is having some memory and health issues, so he's sending his aide out for a few days." His words were calm and measured, but he could see from her wary expression, he wasn't saying anything to ease her gut instinct something was very wrong.

"I am the only one who has personally met Theodore James, that's the aide's name, but we have all talked to him and agree there is something about the man that is just off, and I'd feel better if Grayson and I were back at the mansion while he's on-site. I understand we were supposed to be here until the end of the week, and I feel as if I'm letting you down by insisting we return."

And wasn't that a mammoth understatement? This couldn't have come at a worse time. Jenna already assumed anyone claiming to care about her would eventually walk away. She expected to be hurt, physically or emotionally— or God forbid, both. She'd already been worried he would abandon her, and now, he was walking away from the time he'd promised her. He felt like he was doing a lot worse than just letting her down.

"It's all right." Jenna seemed to relax fractionally, but the small smile she gave him didn't reach her eyes. "Yes, I'm disappointed our time has been cut short, but I under-stand this takes precedence. Please don't feel bad, I'll just go to my room and gather my things." While her words sounded like she was fine, the fact she wouldn't look him directly in the eyes screamed she had just put him in the category with everyone else who had ever walked away when she'd needed them. A quick glance at Grayson confirmed his fears. The set of Grayson's jaw and the spark of anger in his eyes was all Colt needed to know she was putting on a brave front to hide her pain.

Goddamn it to hell why fucking now? Things were going so well, and now I'm just like the rest. I can practically see her locking me out. She stood and made her way to the door, glancing back once before turning and going back inside. The emotional mask was fully in place, but it wasn't fooling either of them.

Colt let out a breath he hadn't realized he was holding. "She's shutting down, isn't she? Fuck, why am I even asking? I can see it, it's written all over her. Christ, why now?"

"Yeah, she's closed herself back in the safe place she built after the rape. We'll get her back, but it's not going to be easy. The key is going to be keeping her from bolting the minute she hits the mansion." Grayson's words confirmed Colt's worst fears.

Colt had already alerted Alex and Zach they'd be returning early and asked they find some mechanical reason to have her car moved to their maintenance department which had been dubbed 'the garage'. The mechanic they employed was a master at deception, so he'd be able to concoct some reason her car needed some of his TLC before it was roadworthy again. Colt knew keeping her physically located at ShadowDance was only a small portion of the battle. Getting her to let him back into her heart was going to be the real challenge.

JENNA WALKED NUMBLY down the hall. Why was she so disappointed? *God, you are being a first-class, selfish bitch, Jenna Lamont. Your brothers and best friend, not to mention your niece or nephew, shouldn't have to deal with this asshole aide person alone.* She knew she should trust Colt. If they felt there was something off about the guy, then, of course, the head of the security team and the head of their IT department needed to be on-site. But the sudden heaviness in her chest wasn't easing with any of her logical arguments.

Jesus, Jenna, you knew this was going to happen. Just because it's earlier than you'd expected doesn't mean you should feel disappointed. Take the memories you've been given and count your blessings instead of acting like a spoiled toddler whose favorite toy has just been pulled out of her grasp. She quickly repacked the few things she'd brought along, grabbed her small case, and walked back into the living room.

Colt watched her closely as she moved quietly back into the main part of the house. She tried to shutter her expression, but if the regretful look in his eyes was any indication, she wasn't doing a very good job. The drive back to ShadowDance seemed even longer today. The tension was thick and hung heavily in the truck. Rather than resting as Colt had suggested, Jenna just sat and stared blankly out the window, working hard to retain her neutral expression. One of her college roommates had referred to it as her ghost walk… no words, no real presence.

Jenna felt like she was drowning in the emotional tension. All she wanted was to get back the house, check on her family, pack, and disappear for a few weeks. She would plan to be back before the baby was born, but she didn't want to be home for Christmas.

It was always especially hard to come home during the holidays. She felt like she was on the outside looking in, like a small orphan watching a family celebrate Christmas through the windows of their home. She could see everything, hear it all, even smell all the delicious food being shared by one and all, but in the end, she still didn't belong there.

When the first tear slipped over the edge of her watery eyes and slid down her cheek, she tried to quickly brush it aside before Colt noticed. But when he drove into the next driveway and stopped, she knew she'd been too late.

Turning toward her, he just held his arms opened wide, and she didn't even hesitate. She unfastened her safety belt and almost leapt across the seat into his embrace.

"Talk to me, princess. It breaks my heart to see you hurting and know you're locking yourself away again. Please don't do that to either of us. Tell me what you're thinking. Just because we're returning early, doesn't mean I don't want you. It just means I want to protect you and your family, and I know ShadowDance is the best place to put those plans in place." Colt's sincere words seemed to relax her a bit, but he continued to hold her tightly against his chest and rub his hands soothingly over her taut back muscles.

AFTER LONG MOMENTS, she finally pulled back far enough to look into his eyes. The sadness was still there, but it seemed some of the distance might have faded.

"I just thought you had found a convenient way to set me aside. I don't really blame you. Every time I've tried to have a normal relationship since, well, since the night everything changed, I end up pushing away any guy who tries to get close. Every single time. I think my heart believes it's just easier than being hurt again. I've never told another soul about Ted Scott, but each man I've ever dated has told me in some way or another that I'm just too damaged to keep around. One was even cruel enough to tell me he'd only gone out with me because of my parents' money, and even that wasn't enough to merit dealing with such 'damaged goods'."

Colt felt the low growl rumble through his chest and knew Jenna had seen the flash of cold anger he'd let surface before he'd been able to mask it. He needed to make sure she knew his anger wasn't directed at her, but at the ass who had fed her that bullshit.

"Never, ever believe that nonsense. There is so much about you that is perfect, it should have humbled any man just to have you agree to spend time with him. The beauty of who you are—both inside and out—brings me to my knees, princess. Please believe returning to the mansion is in no way a reflection on where I want our relationship to go. If I wasn't concerned about the safety of your family, we'd still be at the cabin." And then with a waggle of his eyebrows and a devilish grin, he added, "And I'd be as deep inside your hot, slick channel as I could get."

His words seemed to have had their desired effect; she finally smiled a bit even though tears still shone in her dark-green eyes. Colt had noticed the shade of her eyes depended on her mood, and right now, she seemed too lost in the moment to even speak. She hugged him for a long moment, then brushed a soft kiss over his lips before sliding back to her side of the truck and refastening her safety belt.

KAT WAS ANXIOUS for Jenna and Colt to return. She felt bad their little adventure had been cut short, but she couldn't wait to hear each and every detail of their time at the cabin. *Oh yeah... girls gab session tonight, for sure. Woohoo!* Kat loved living at ShadowDance, but there were times she really missed having a girlfriend to chat with. One of the great things she'd discovered about having two husbands was at least one of them was usually available if she needed a helping hand or a shoulder to cry on, but there was nothing like girl talk to restore the soul.

She'd been pacing in the living room for an hour when Alex stepped into the doorway, leaning a shoulder against the jamb in that too-sexy-for-my-own-good way he had.

"Love, they will be here soon enough, please sit down before you wear yourself out." When she stuck her tongue out at him, he raised a brow. "Hmmm, do we need to have a little focus-Katarina session, love? You know I'll be happy to lend you a hand." His smile told her the play on words was deliberate. Damn the man, he knew full well the effect he had on her. Her pussy was soaking her silk panties, the rat bastard. *Damn him, I'm going to have to go upstairs and change if he doesn't knock it off.*

She glanced out the window and let out a high-pitched squeal and took off for the door before Alex bellowed, "Katarina, stop!" She froze and looked at him, clearly puzzled. After all, she was just going to let in his sister and their security chief. *What on earth is eating him?* Alex answered her unasked question.

"Until this mess is all settled, you will not just throw open the door, exposing yourself and our sweet child to potential danger."

Yep, total rat bastard. He knows exactly how to get me to comply with his damned edicts about my safety. He plays that "Our sweet child" card, and I'm toast. Damn, damn, and double damn!

Stepping around Katarina and using a gentle hand pressed against the small of her back to move her to the side, he opened the door and greeted his sister and Colt. Grayson was already in the crow's nest, having arrived a few minutes earlier.

"Welcome home. I'm sorry we've cut into your time, and I promise we'll make it up to you both." Jenna smiled, but Kat could see the strain around her eyes. Kat pulled her friend into a fierce hug. Alex actually chuckled as he watched Jenna try to hug her around her rounded belly. Jenna had heard he and Zach betting on twins, but they hadn't said anything to her about it yet. Kat was operating on the ostrich theory... if she didn't think about it, it wasn't real. Alex's voice brought her back to the moment.

"Ladies, if you'd like to move up to the suite, I'll ask Selita to bring you up a tray while Colt and I have a sit-rep."

Katarina just rolled her eyes. "Don't go all soldier boy on me, husband mine, and yes, we would appreciate whatever Selita has available. We'll be having a great time without you, so don't you skimp on that 'sit-rep' on our account." She gave him a smirk she knew would earn her at least a couple of playful swats later, or at least she sure hoped so.

God, I miss our wild sexual antics. And double damn those stupid pregnancy books those two read like they were the guiding texts of the universe or something. Waiting until after the baby gets here to get the good stuff totally sucks!

THE GIRLS WERE already chattering like magpies as they made their way up the stairs. Alex and Colt stood watching them like a couple of lovesick fools.

"I don't know how she does it. I swear to you, if another sub talked to me like that, she'd have punishments stacked up through next summer. I know she does it to get to me, but I just can't seem to work up any real steam about it." Alex chuckled to himself and then added, "Zach is even worse with her than I am. Christ, at least I pretend to scold her." At that, Colt laughed out loud.

"Never thought I'd live to see the day, but damned if I'm not right there with you. But that's another problem altogether. I'll be enlisting your help to keep your sweet sister here when this other mess is put to rest." Colt looked at his friend and smiled. "She is everything I've always wanted. I've been in love with her for years, but you already know that. I won't let her go. I just want you to know that up front."

Now it was Alex's turn to laugh. "Damn, Zach just won the bet. I figured you'd at least wait until the end of sit-rep to tell me, and he said you'd blurt it out first thing through the front door. God, there'll be no living with him for months now. And you just cost me five thousand dollars to the charity of his choice."

Alex's laughter and slap to Colt's back told him it was all in good fun, but Colt had to smile to himself. These men were going to be his brothers-in-law as soon as he could convince Jenna to marry him and damn if having his best friends as brothers wasn't about the second sweetest thing about his whole plan.

Chapter 23

ALEX AND ZACH had assembled the entire security team, along with Dylan and his deputies, so their office was standing room only. Selita was in seventh heaven, she had "her girls" upstairs to pamper, and a houseful of guests to feed and hover over. She was in full mother hen mode. Alex and Zach just shook their heads and smiled at the way their former teammates answered to her as if she were their own mothers.

"Hard to believe the same men we've gone into fire-fights all over the world with and never worried about having our six are all 'Yes, ma'am,' 'No, ma'am,' 'Thank you, ma'am' with our tiny tornado of a housekeeper." Alex agreed with Zach's observation, the woman was a force to be reckoned with, and God save the person who dared attempt harming one of "her chicks."

After briefing everyone about the message Dylan had received and their interpretation, they ran various scenarios, responses, and troubleshot for a couple of hours. They had also let everyone know as much as they could about the General sending his aide to visit without giving out every detail of Jenna's trauma and their reluctance to have a stranger near her. There were some details the entire team didn't need to know.

Although they were spared the minutia, they all had

mutinous looks which said they understood exactly what had happened and shared Colt and her brothers' anger over a team member attacking a family member. Hell, they all believed no woman should ever be attacked, but for a teammate to attack the sister of a buddy was a whole new level of low. Everyone was on point about Staff Sgt. James. It was common knowledge if Colt didn't like him, he was a bogie, it was that simple. Everyone wanted Grayson to have first crack at the man because if he could get a solid read, they'd all breathe easier.

KATARINA AND JENNA lay sprawled on the bed, enjoying each other's company and the snacks Selita had sent up. After Kat had been shot in the suite, and then later shot the man who had terrorized her when he broke into the same room, Alex and Zach had remodeled the entire end of the second floor of the mansion. The newly revamped suite was gorgeous, but it was the new safety features which made it truly amazing. It was a virtual fortress when activated as a safe room.

There were various activation devices in each room in addition to a voice-prompt system which engaged if Kat spoke a specific phrase aloud. If any of those systems were triggered, not only did the suite's bulletproof glass windows immediately cover with thick drapes, all doors and windows locked automatically and the room came alive with video and audio access ordinarily not active due to privacy concerns. But in the case of an emergency, every corner of each room was visible from monitors hidden in her husbands' office as well as the crow's nest.

With a simple slap of her hand against what looked like a child's handprint framed on the wall, Katarina could lock down the entire house. No one was coming in or going out until the all clear was sounded by the security team. The entire place was state-of-the-art. Mitch Grayson had enjoyed his carte blanche and had even created some features he hadn't found on the open market. Those inventions were making him a very rich man though one would never know it to talk to him.

Kat loved all the enhancements, or at least, she had before she'd had to endure drill after drill until she had wanted to snatch them—Alex, Zach, Colt, and Mitch—bald headed. When she'd finally dissolved into tears of pure frustration and fatigue, they'd given in and called her training complete. She had even managed to finagle a great foot massage and some off-the-chart sex as a reward for her "cooperation and patience." *Boy, sometimes smart men sure can be dim.*

After Kat had shown all the features to Jenna, she told her best friend and sister-in-law similar features had been added to her smaller suite down the hall. In her case, it was her huge walk-in closet and dressing room which was sealed off and secured. Kat knew the men would have to train Jenna themselves, but she'd told her the basics.

Jenna was impressed with the security upgrades, but sorry they'd been necessary. "You have had such a rough patch in your life for the past few years, hell, forever. I hope things settle down for you soon. But considering you're carrying a little Lamont, I suspect things are going to be a circus for a while longer." Chuckling, she reached over and touched Kat's rounded tummy. "When are you due?" Jenna didn't claim to know anything about pregnancy, but her friend seemed awfully round for only being about four months along.

"Damn," Kat sighed, "I know, I know…at this rate I'm going to be as big as a house when this baby is born. I have an appointment for a sonogram this next week. I'm so excited, the doctor promised me we'd find out the baby's sex and even get to see a 3-D picture of him or her. Do you want to go along? It would be wonderful to have you there." Kat looked hopefully at Jenna, and though she suspected her friend was planning to escape at the first possible opening, maybe, just maybe, the niece or nephew card would help.

"Don't you want to be there to get a first look at your very first niece or nephew? It would really mean a lot to me." Okay, so maybe she was milking it a little… well, a lot, but she didn't care, it was for a good cause. *Right, you are being selfish, and you're trying to say you're doing it for others, remember you had always sworn to be honest with yourself, Kat McKay, um… Katarina Lamont.* Boy, it was hard to remember she was an old married woman now. She suppressed her inner smile all the while giving Jenna her most sincere doe-eyed look.

JENNA LOOKED AT Kat and shook her head. "Damn it, Kat, that's totally not fair. And knock it off with the innocent look, it might work on those lovesick fool brothers of mine, but you're not pulling that shit with me."

Kat's face flushed with guilt even though she was giggling like she always did when Jenna called her out. They'd been friends too long for either of them to pull the wool over the other's eyes.

"Okay, I really would like to stay for the sonogram, but I get to gloat to Gramps and Grammy Lamont that's just part of the deal, understand? I kind of wanted to go to the Masquerade at The Club this weekend, anyway, I've never been. Since you aren't going, I'll be your spy." They collapsed into a fit of giggles and spent the rest of their time gossiping about all things baby, Colt, and Club. *God, it's good to be home, I've missed the mountains, my brothers, the joy of Kat's nearness, and the peace it all brings me.*

"It really sucks that I don't get to go to the party, I had a great costume and everything. But after the risk Mia took for me, I don't want to do anything that might jeopardize the guys helping her." Giggling, she looked at Jenna with a conspiratorial look. "I'll be really glad to have a spy on the inside, maybe you can text me from there, keep me updated, maybe pictures… no that would probably get us both in a lot of trouble, but then again, spankings are usually worth working for." This time they both fell over, roaring with the shared inside joke, and that's how the men found them when they stepped through the doors.

ALEX, ZACH, AND Colt all walked through the door to the master suite and stood stunned to see the women lounging back on the massive bed, nearly hysterical with laughter.

"What the hell?" Colt's stunned response had Alex and Zach both smiling.

"Oh, brother, this is so very typical of these two. I wish I had a dollar for every time I've seen them just like this, well, maybe not since Kat is pregnant, but you get the idea." Zach was grinning ear to ear. "They have been friends since they first started school, I don't remember them ever even having a disagreement. But I promise you if you think either of them is a handful separately, together they are a hot mess. We didn't call them Lucy and Ethel for no reason, I assure you."

When Kat looked up and saw them all standing nearby, it was Alex's indulgent smile that warmed her heart. God, but she loved them both so much. Zach was more straightforward with his affections, Alex's were more reserved, but the passion in Alex's eyes was always scorching.

"Hello, my husbands, Colt. What brings you to our little girls' night in?" Kat had known they wouldn't be alone long, hell, she was rarely alone any length of time at all. She'd also been certain Colt would be anxious to get Jenna back into his arms as soon as possible.

"Well, love, we've missed you, and I do believe Colt has some things he needs to discuss with Jenna. How about we let him have some time with her, and you can try to convince Zach and I why we shouldn't paddle your sweet ass for trying to get pictures sent out of The Club? Hmmm?" Uh oh, Kat knew that tone and that steely look. Fracking cameras, she should have known Spies 'R' Us would be on duty tonight. She turned to Alex and flashed him her sweetest smile.

"I knew those darned cameras would be on, and I just couldn't wait to get you both back into my bed, so what better method than to send up a challenge flare? And see how well my plan worked? Here you both are, all beefy muscles and pent-up sexual energy, just the way I love you." All this was said as she crawled across the bed toward her men like a sleek—well, round sleek—cat.

As Jenna watched the show, she was amazed at the changes in her friend. *I am watching a pro here. Cripes, Kat's, playing them like a fucking song. And look at those two chumps, this is better than HBO. Holy hell, I should be taking notes.*

Kat heard Zach's gasp as she watched Alex's eyes widen and then darken into pools of dark promise.

Colt stepped forward and held out his hand to Jenna.

"Come here, pet, I want to talk to you about your plans for the Masquerade party on Saturday." Even though his voice sounded stern, the look of tenderness and desire in his expression told Jenna she wasn't in any real trouble. She placed her small hand in his larger one, let him pull her to her feet, and followed him from the room. *Damn, Kat may have this D/s thing all figured out after all.* Jenna had always been the Lucy to Kat's Ethel, but something told Jenna she had a lot of catching up to do. *Well, game on, sister!*

Chapter 24

A S SOON AS they entered Jenna's small suite, Colt turned and reached for her, kicking the door closed as he pushed her up against the wall. Before Jenna could blink, Colt had both of her wrists locked above her head held by one of his large hands. His other hand held her chin, so she was looking up into his fierce expression.

"First of all, my precious pet, we need to discuss your plan to spy for your friend, Ethel. You'll never take a cell phone, camera, or any other bit of technology into The Club, is that clear? There are very few exceptions to this rule. Law enforcement officials, firefighters, and a couple of doctors are permitted to wear their pagers, but that's because they're all considered first responders. There are only four cell phones allowed inside and those belong to Alex, Zach, Grayson, and myself. Anyone else caught with one on their person loses their membership for a year for the first offense and for life if it happens again."

Jenna was trembling in his hold, and he could tell she didn't understand why she was so turned on by his force-fulness. She was likely puzzled about why she wasn't frightened when ordinarily, he knew she'd have been fighting against a man's hold with everything she had in her. *Because your heart trusts me, even if your head isn't quite there yet, pet.*

Colt had stopped speaking and watched her expressions move from startled to remorseful to full-on arousal. "Do I make myself clear, pet? No Lucy or Ethel antics allowed at The Club, period. If you violate that rule, your punishment won't be up for discussion, it's just a part of The ShadowDance Club Charter." Colt waited for her answer. "Pet, I asked you a question."

JENNA WAS LOST in a thick mist of desire making rational thought all but impossible. What had he asked her? Finally, her brain seemed to catch up with the conversation.

"Yes, M–Master, I understand, no Lucy or Ethel or cells or cameras or anything techy." Even she could hear the huskiness of her own voice. As soon as the words left her mouth, his lips descended on hers in a punishing kiss that felt like he was trying to steal her soul. She had never been that fond of kissing, and now she understood why; she had just never kissed anyone who could make it a sexual experience in itself. *Holy Mother of God, this man's kiss is worthy of an Olympic gold medal and the Nobel Peace Prize, at the same time.*

Colt's eyes cleared a bit and Jenna watched in fascination as his inner Dom finally came up for air. He slowly put a bit of space between them and eased his hold in fractional increments. Stepping back slowly, he lowered her arms and released her wrists.

"Strip."

His one-word command let her know he wasn't in the mood for arguments or discussions. This is what she'd always labeled in the business world as *a make or break moment.* Taking a deep breath, she toed off her shoes and pushed them aside with her foot. Without taking her eyes off Colt's face, she slowly unfastened the snap, then lowered the zipper of her jeans before hooking her thumbs over the waistband and pushing them down her well-toned legs. She loved the way his eyes flared, then darkened when he realized she was wearing panties. He hadn't tried to hide his displeasure, his jaw tightening as his lips thinned into a taut line.

"THAT'S TWO, PET." Colt made certain his tone was icy cold and watched as Jenna shivered in response. She didn't have to ask what he meant, she knew full well this was his way of letting her know the no-panty rule was still in effect, and her disregard for it had just added another punishment to what she'd already earned for the spying plan. He could smell her arousal and knew her pussy was flooding with her sweet cream. Colt watched as her hands trembled when she reached down and drew her tight T-shirt over her head.

Colt watched in silent judgment as she stood for just a moment in her sheer pink bra and panties. He didn't take his eyes off hers as her gaze traveled to the bulge in his jeans. The heat in her eyes made his cock grow even larger right before her eyes—and he saw more than heard her soft gasp. Waiting patiently, he saw her take a deep breath before slipping the tips of her slender fingers beneath the barely-there elastic on her hips. With a sensual caress to her own thighs, she teased him by slowly sliding the small triangle of fabric down until it was a pool of wet pink silk between her feet.

Colt knew she was deliberately baiting him, but he was enjoying her striptease and even more, he was thrilled she was coming into her own with enough confidence to even attempt it. For a woman so petite, she had very long legs, and holy mother of all things beautiful, they were fucking amazing to look at. And finally… there she stood with her nipples peeking out from under a bra that barely covered the dusky-rose-colored areolas he could see clearly through the transparent bit of pink covering them.

If she thought those panties had covered up any secrets, he had big news for her. God, the woman's body was stunning. Her athletic grace showed in every movement she made, every shift of balance, each motion so fluid it seemed to have been choreographed in a dance to music only she could hear. She unhooked the front clasp of her bra and let it fall off her shoulders to the floor.

After Jenna had removed the last bit of material from her body, she neatly folded everything and set it just to her right side as he'd instructed her to do. Then she just looked at Colt with big, luminous eyes and waited. He let several heartbeats pass before he spoke.

"You won't be able to wear shoes in The Club, so you should just as well begin getting used to that now. Move over to the side of the bed and stand with your legs apart, so when you bend at the waist, you're at the right height to be supported by the bed." When she complied, he moved to her dresser and picked up a large wooden-handled hairbrush. *It will make a very nice paddle, yes, indeed it's perfect.*

Stepping behind her, Colt ran his free hand in slow circles over her lower back and over both of her ass cheeks. He could smell her arousal, so when he drew his fingers through the swollen petals of her pussy, he wasn't surprised to find her soaking wet.

"Well, my pet, it seems you enjoyed teasing your Dom with that little striptease performance, hmmm?" When he pushed two fingers into her tight pussy, he heard the moan he knew she'd tried to hold back. Stroking his fingers in and out several times before moving to her tight rear hole and pushing two fingers inside quickly. He knew there had to be a sharp bite of pain from the tissues being stretched so suddenly, but he reminded himself, this was punishment. He wasn't making love to her, he was teaching her a valuable less, one which would invoke a much harsher punishment if she attempted to sneak electronics into ShadowDance. But he was still relieved to hear her softly moan his name after her initial yip of pain.

Moving his fingers in and out, fucking her ass with two, then three fingers, he waited until he felt her body gathering her orgasm close around her like a cloak, then he pulled out and left her aching with need.

"Uh-uh, princess, no coming until I give you permission, understand?"

"Yes, Master." Even though she had answered, he was sure it had been by rote memory. She was starting to head into subspace, time to bring her back to this moment.

"I will be giving you three swats for the plan you and Ethel were cooking up and five for the panties. Know this, pet, each time you wear panties without permission to do so, the penalty will double, so it isn't something you'll want to forget often. I have a pathological dislike for them, you see. I will also be helping you shop for new clothing. I'll want unfettered access to what belongs to me, and that means I want to be able to slide my tongue, my fingers, or my aching cock into your sweet, wet pussy at any time and at any place of my choosing."

Colt knew full well the effect his voice was having on his sweet sub. She was turning to mush right before his eyes, and he would only have to speak the words, and she'd shoot off like a rocket. God, but he was looking forward to their first scene together at The Club.

"When we sit at dinner downstairs later, you'll sit with your legs hooked around the outside of the chair legs, so I can finger fuck you at my leisure. When we're alone in a vehicle, you'll pull your dress up so your bare ass is in direct contact with the seat, and your legs will remain spread wide so I can see, smell, and touch what is mine. When we are in public, I will often have you standing in front of me, and when you think I won't possibly attempt it, I'll have my hand between your legs fucking you with my fingers until you are mindlessly begging me to fuck you with my cock. You'll hunger for the feel of its ridges and veins surging in and out of your wet, velvet pussy." Colt could feel her orgasm pulsing just below the surface, so he stepped back and landed the first swat solidly on her ass cheek.

Jenna jumped and yelped, and Colt knew the first blow had to have been a hell of a shock. No doubt her skin felt like it was on fire. Grinning to himself, he held the brush in place for a couple of seconds to keep the searing heat dancing over the surface of her skin, maximizing the sting. He saw her reflexively tighten the muscles in her ass a split second before he landed a blow to her other ass cheek. She probably registered the whoosh of air in time to react, which was exactly what she shouldn't do. "Do not antici-pate the swats or they'll hurt much worse. Relax your muscles." He didn't wait for her to respond, but he knew exactly what she was thinking. Landing the third and fourth swats as solidly as the first two, he leaned over her and spoke against her ear.

"Remember, pet, punishment spankings aren't supposed to be fun. They are meant to serve as reminders in the future about the importance of adhering to the rules. The next time you start to slide a triangle of silk over what is mine, you'll stop and think about this moment, how I set your sweet ass on fire. You might want to turn your focus on how you are going to feel trying to sit comfortably on those hard-oak dining room chairs with your bright-red cheeks still hot with the licking flames from your punishment.

"And the next time you and Katarina start to scheme, I want you to think about whether or not it's going to be worth the price you'll both pay. Because"—*swoosh, slap… swoosh, slap… swoosh, slap*—"I promise you that, despite her performance before we left her suite, she is getting her ass spanked just as you are. Alex and Zach may be over the moon about making her their wife and her pregnancy, but they're still Doms, and they'll always willingly provide her with the discipline they know she craves." No doubt Katarina's spanking would be toned down due to her pregnancy, but if they just stacked them up until the baby is born, she'd be black and blue for the first year of their child's life.

Colt knew Jenna was floating. He could recognize the telltale signs of subspace from across a crowded room. Jenna's pulse had leveled out, her breathing was even, her eyes glazed, her gaze almost trancelike.

"One more, pet, brace yourself and remember, *no fucking panties!*" Colt landed a very stinging blow centered directly over the crease at the top of her thighs, so the vibrations went deep into her channel and all the way to her pulsing clit. Just as the brush hit, he leaned over her and spoke into her ear.

"Come, Jenna."

Jenna screamed as the pain of that blow to her ass and legs hit her brain at the same time a tsunami-strength orgasm washed over her as Colt had known it would. Her knees folded out from under her, but he'd anticipated it and caught her easily around the waist, pushing her farther forward so the bed supported her weight as wave after wave assaulted her, making her shake like a leaf in his arms.

Colt dropped the brush to the carpeted floor, shoved his jeans to his knees, and sank deep into her before she had even finished peaking from the first orgasm. His hard strokes sent her right back up the steep slope of pleasure before she crashed over the top of the mountain, screaming his name. He felt the warm flood of her cream as she came twice more. The wet sound of her body trying to pull him back into her wet cunt was music to his ears. God almighty, he loved the sound and smell of sex with this woman. *Mine!* The word roared in his head. *No other man will ever fuck this sweet pussy... It's all mine!*

Chapter 25

ALEX, ZACH, AND Grayson were sitting in the office with General Franklin's aide, Theodore James, the awkward silence making it obvious to everyone the line of demarcation had been clearly drawn. Grayson was as still as either Alex or Zach had ever seen him. Obviously, he was trying to crawl right inside the man's head. Colt had decided to remain in the crow's nest and let the other three have a clear path to James since he'd already met him. Colt's opinion wasn't going to change—he didn't like or trust the little fucker.

Alex watched the man for long moments; something about the way he moved was vaguely familiar and set off warning alarms, but Alex couldn't place exactly why.

"So, tell me exactly what it is you hope to accomplish during your stay, Mr. James." Alex's deliberate omission of the man's military rank was a slap, and they all knew it. Alex watched as his jaw tensed before he quickly slid his mask of indifference back into place.

"As you know, General Franklin is having some health issues, and he has seemed unhappy after the last few calls from Colt Matthews, something about a former teammate who stayed here while recovering and an *alleged* sexual assault that has only recently come to light. While we aren't saying your sister is *lying*, Mr. Lamont, it does seem unlikely an accusation this serious would just now be an issue, don't you think?" Zach came out of his chair and was looming over the man before he'd even finished his ridiculous statement.

"Let me be perfectly clear, ass wipe. I don't give a flying fuck what you think. Our sister doesn't lie. *Ever.* She would not make up this story. She only shared the story with Colt Matthews after she knew Ted Scott was dead because she has been living in fear for *our* safety since the night she was attacked. Scott threatened *our* lives, using that leverage to silence her. And while we all know that is a classic sexual predator behavior, it doesn't change the fact we are talking about *our sister.* This forever changed her from the open and loving young woman she was into a woman who spent years running from her own pain because she was too afraid she'd bring harm to her brothers if she sought any kind of medical treatment, legal action, or victim's counseling." By the time Zach had finished, his face was beet red, and Theodore James was leaning back, away from the anger pulsing like waves of heat from Zach's core.

Alex spoke next with icy calm. "Let me make this as clear as possible. You will not discredit or in any other way hurt our sister, do you understand? I see no reason for your visit, it was only allowed because it was a personal request from a man we've all worked with for many years, and our entire team holds a deep respect for what he has always stood for. What we want to know is why no one in our unit was made aware of Ted Scott's history of sexual misconduct prior to him joining our team, or at the very least, before he was allowed to spend weeks recovering in the home with a young woman who was an easy target for an experienced sexual perpetrator."

While Alex's anger wasn't as obvious as Zach's, his deadly intent was just as clear. "If you have any questions, you will direct them to either Zach or me. You will not question our sister directly. These points are non-negotiable. Are we clear on each point, Mr. James?" Alex had not moved except to raise an eyebrow at the other man when his answer wasn't forthcoming.

"Yes, Mr. Lamont, crystal clear. But rest assured, at some point, I will need to speak with your sister, and it is entirely likely she won't want you present." James's arrogant attitude was getting very near the deal-breaker point. It was definitely time to show the man the door.

Turning to Grayson, Alex said, "Mitch, if you would please show Mr. James to the guesthouse, we'll have his car moved to the garage and his belongings delivered for him within the hour."

Mitch Grayson nodded as he stood and moved silently toward the door. Alex addressed James. "Grayson will see you to the guesthouse. I believe you'll be very comfortable there, Mr. James. You'll be within a short walking distance of the house for meals, should you choose to join us. Dinner will be at eight p.m. Our housekeeper will be expecting you, dress is casual." And then he turned back to his computer, effectively dismissing the man he'd like nothing more than to *dismiss* off the entire planet. God, the man was a gnat on the ass of humanity.

As Mitch led Theodore James to the back door of the mansion and down the stone path winding through gardens toward the guesthouse, he explained how to access the property's indoor gym and exercise rooms where the garage was located. When James asked about keys, Mitch explained that they didn't use them on-site then handed him a small piece of paper with a code he could use to enter the guesthouse and gym.

"Where is my car being stored?" James' inquiry was telling, and Mitch didn't miss the significance as he explained because there were a lot of other vehicles stored in the same building, James would need to let a member of the security team know when he needed access to his car, and they'd be happy to accompany him. Grayson found it amusing the little toad didn't seem at all happy with that information.

Interesting, what do you have stashed in that car that you want to be able to retrieve when we aren't looking? Or do you plan on slithering out during the middle of the night like the snake that you are? And, just who are you, Mr. James? Because even though I don't know your real name, I'm abso-fucking-lutely sure it is not Theodore James. You may be able to block me now, but you can't keep it up indefinitely, and I'll be waiting. The second those shields come down... I'll have it all.

COLT TRACKED JAMES from the moment they left the mansion until he was alone in the guesthouse and continued to watch as the man obviously searched the building for surveillance equipment. He turned to Alex and Zach who had joined him. They'd decided to meet in the crow's nest because there was no way anyone outside this room was going to overhear their conversation.

"Well, what was your impression? I find it interesting he wanted unfettered access to his vehicle, and the first thing he did was search for surveillance equipment in the guesthouse."

Alex was the first to answer. "I think he's a dick and I

want a reason to send him packing. It doesn't even need to be a good reason." Running his hand through his hair in frustration, he added, "His attempts to discredit Jenna seem—shit, I don't know exactly how to describe it, but almost like a preemptive strike to me, and I can't quite get a bead on that. Zach?" Glancing over at his twin, he saw the cold look Zach had always carried into battle, and Alex remembered that even though everyone always saw Zach as the more gregarious of the two of them, it was actually Zach Lamont who was always stone cold when it came to a mission, and he was clearly in mission mode now.

Zach looked thoughtfully at the monitor, watching and assessing the other man carefully. "There is something familiar about him, his gestures, his movements. I can't place him, but I've seen him before, but I'd remember that name. Did you notice his eyes? He's wearing colored contacts. Why? Why does a man who has been through the bowels of hell with reconstructive surgery, prosthetics, etcetera care about changing his eye color? Something doesn't ring quite right about that to me." After several long moments spent leaning closer to the monitor, he said, "I don't want *any* of the women left alone with him for *any* reason. And I want us all on point tonight during dinner."

"Agreed," Mitch Grayson added as he entered the room.

"Get anything on the little POS?" Colt asked him.

"Well, you've got that right, he's a real piece of shit, top to bottom. He's obviously been warned about me, he's making every attempt to block. He's going to have to be off guard or be drinking for me to get a full read, but I can tell you this—the man has major power and control issues, particularly with women. Basically, he hates them, and he seems to go completely white with rage when Jenna's name is mentioned. Zach is exactly right, we can't leave him alone with any of the women, either here at the house or ShadowDance, but I'm particularly concerned about Jenna and Katarina. I don't know if it's because they belong to you three or if it's them in particular, but their names enrage him. He blocks almost everything, but that emotion is so powerful, it would be impossible for anyone except the most gifted and practiced people to totally block an emotion that strong. And here's the kicker, he plans to be at the Masquerade tomorrow night." All eyes turned to Grayson. He shrugged as if to say, *Hey, don't shoot the messenger!*

The hair on the back of Colt's neck stood straight up as if lightning had struck dead center in the room. He'd had this same experience several times during his years in the Special Forces, and each of those times had been a forewarning everything was about to go FUBAR in a very big way. There was too much riding on the next few days, fucked up beyond all recognition was not an option. "We need to call in everybody for tomorrow night's event. And we need a briefing in a secure location where we know dick weed won't eavesdrop. Suggestions?"

"I'll work on the logistics. Zach, you call in every one of The Club's dungeon monitors and any Dom who might be willing to stand down from playing to help with surveillance. We have two very large potential problems staring us in the face, let's get all the help we can. I don't want to cancel the event and lose this chance to recover Mia. Whoever is holding her needs her to ID Katarina. I'm worried we won't get another opportunity for the snatch and grab.

"Colt, call Dylan and get names of any reserve officers he'd recommend, and call anyone else you can get in here by tomorrow night. I don't know about you all, but I'm fucking tired of always being on the R/R end of things. What do you say we stop being forced to respond and react and get on the proactive side for a change?"

DINNER WAS ALWAYS an exercise in organized chaos at ShadowDance, and tonight was no exception. It was also one of the few times they all sat down together at the same time as the family they considered themselves. The dining room was huge, and the table could seat at least thirty people if it was extended to its full length. Jenna had always loved dinner at ShadowDance, especially after her brothers had returned, and their club became increasingly popular. Family, friends, and various staff members all gathered for food and fun, and as far as Selita was concerned, the more the merrier.

Jenna and Colt entered the dining room just as everyone was sitting down. This was her first time to have a 'boyfriend' at a family dinner, and even though they had both eaten in this room together many times over the years, this felt entirely different to her.

Damn, that could be because you have on a short friggin' skirt and don't have on any panties. Having your hoo-ha in the wind will make any woman skittish, suck it up and deal, Jenna Beth. Taking a second to give herself a pep talk and get her bearings, she noticed a man she hadn't ever seen before. *Must be the guy General Franklin sent out here, damned if he isn't a creepy-looking weasel.* Jenna shivered and unconsciously rubbed her palms up and down her own arms.

Colt felt Jenna shiver next to him. "Cold, pet?"

"Um, no, I was just looking at that man over there, and something about him sets off my 'Danger danger, Will Robinson' radar." She smiled up at him, knowing he'd understand her reference to the old *Lost in Space* show she and Kat had watched for hours when the guys were home on leave. They'd never understood the girls' fascination with the old reruns and had often stayed in the room just to make fun of the shows' ancient special effects and campy storylines. "There is something hauntingly familiar about him, he makes me incredibly uncomfortable."

His gaze returned to James as he spoke to Jenna. "Hmmm, interesting. Your brother, Zach, said the same thing about Staff Sgt. James seeming familiar. If he makes you uncomfortable, you need to trust that instinct, pet... *always*. We'll make sure there is a buffer between you and him at all times."

Sensing her discomfort, Mitch moved to flank her on the other side. Mitch's smile was warm, but Jenna could sense a steely ice in his manner, and she could feel the undercurrent of anger coursing through him.

"Did I do something wrong? Why are you so angry?" Her soft words caused his expression to soften immediately.

"Oh, sweetness, I'm not angry with you. I just saw your expression and knew you were uncomfortable with James, and I don't like anyone having that effect on you. I'd be just as annoyed if it was Katarina or Selita or Ris—" Mitch cut himself off before continuing. "Let's have a seat and enjoy the company of your family and all our friends, what do you say?"

The men were careful to position her between them and down far enough Theodore James didn't have a clear line of sight to her. Jenna began to relax, at least until both men reached for the knee closest to them and pulled her legs so far apart she felt a cool breeze brush over her exposed sex. Colt leaned close and reminded her to hook her feet around the legs of her chair so she was spread open and accessible for his pleasure. She heard her own gasp as he leisurely moved his long, callused fingertips through her wet folds. When she opened her eyes and looked at Kat, her friend's eyes were closed, and she was biting her lower lip as if trying to keep from crying out. Jenna knew from the small smile on Zach's face exactly what he was up to. Kat's small shudder was the only outward sign she'd climaxed sitting at the table surrounded by more twenty people. When Alex leaned over and whispered in Kat's ear, her eyes found Jenna's, and she flushed a deep scarlet.

Jenna marveled at the look on her big brothers' faces. She wasn't surprised at Zach's captivation with Kat, she'd always known he would 'love large and deeply', but Alex had always seemed to have a much harsher edge. Jenna had always worried he wouldn't be able to let go enough to love completely. Oh, how wrong she'd been. The looks of adoration he showered on his wife made Jenna's breath catch.

"Are you all right, pet?" Colt's concerned voice brought Jenna back from her thoughts.

"Oh, um, yes, sorry. I was just watching Alex with Kat, and I'm so happy to see how much he loves her, and he's unafraid to let everyone see it. It's what I'd always hoped for, but always worried he wouldn't allow to happen." Jenna smiled at Colt, hoping she hadn't said too much, knowing how macho the team members all liked to consider themselves.

Colt returned her smile and nodded. "I understand

completely, and I can fully identify with your concern. Thank you for sharing that with me. You weren't the only one who had voiced those same thoughts about Alex. Katarina has brought a lot of light into both Alex and Zach's lives. Hell, she mothers every person who works at ShadowDance. That baby is going to be one lucky little boy or girl."

"Both," Grayson added offhandedly.

Jenna turned to him, startled. "What did you say?

"Oh, sorry, I probably should have waited, but I think she's going to have multiples, at least one of each gender. Please don't tell anyone. Let's just wait and see if I'm right." Smiling, Mitch went back to eating. Jenna narrowed her eyes at them both. She knew there was something she wasn't being told, but she also knew this wasn't the time to pursue it. She wasn't going to let it go, she had questions for these two later.

By the end of dinner, Jenna was so aroused, all she cared about was getting someplace alone with Colt and finding some relief, but it seemed everyone in the room wanted to chat. Colt was standing on her left and had his fingers laced through hers holding her still. She was almost bouncing up and down with excess sexual energy. She was so distracted she didn't notice Theodore James walk up beside her. He paused briefly before walking on. *How odd, it was like he just wanted to make sure I knew he could get close to me.* She had no more than let the thought skate through her mind when Mitch closed in on her right side. He stood so close their arms were brushing.

"Did he say anything to you, sweetness?" Mitch's words were soft, but his voice held an edge that screamed protector.

"No, but it was very odd. He just came up from behind

me and paused before moving on. I don't know... but it was like he just wanted to let me know he *could*. I know that sounds very strange, but that was the feeling I got." When a shudder moved over her, Colt turned immediately, studying her closely. She barely caught Mitch's small sideways nod, and they both started moving her from the room without stopping to talk to those who tried to get their attention. No matter who tried to delay them or how confused the person looked, they merely nodded and moved along. The movement must have drawn her brothers' notice, as they'd flanked Kat and were hustling her from the room with the same urgency.

When Jenna and Kat were both safely ensconced in Alex and Zach's office, Mitch and Colt left to find Rissa, who had also been enjoying the after-dinner socializing. Jenna turned to Alex and bristled when he tried to act engrossed in a paper on his desk.

"Oh no you don't, big brother, you're not going all 'big bad Dom has important shit to do' on me... I have some questions for you." Jenna marched herself right over in front of his desk and was standing with her hands on her hips ready to do battle when the office door swung open and Rissa was escorted in to join them. Colt looked at Jenna and burst out laughing which made her bristle. "And what do you think you are laughing at, Colt Matthews?" Jenna had turned to look at him, eyes narrowed, and lips thinned in frustration.

"Well, sorry, darlin', but you look like a warrior pixie, all tough-girl stance, taking on her bigger, hell, much bigger brother. And I have to say, he doesn't look any too anxious to tangle with you either." Colt's chuckle brought a smile to everyone's face.

Even Jenna had to admit it had probably made for a

pretty funny picture. She had never shied away from confronting her brothers, holy hell, if she ever had even blinked, they would have steamrolled her even more than they already had her entire life.

"I'm wanting some answers about that yo-yo at dinner. You guys know more than you're telling, now out with it, or I'm calling for backup." She eyed both of her brothers speculatively. Yes indeed, they knew exactly who she'd call. She saw them both pale a bit—oh the power of a threat to call Catherine Lamont. Smiling to herself, she just stood with her arms crossed under her breasts and waited. She knew they'd fold. It was just a matter of waiting for them to note her resolve.

Zach was the one to step forward to try to talk his sister down. "Damn it, Jenna, you know we have enough on our plates right now, we don't need Mom coming in here guns blazing. If we're busy answering to her, we can't do our jobs this weekend. And right now, keeping you three off James's radar and getting Melita back is taking just about every bit of focus and manpower we can pull together." He had always had more luck distracting her than Alex. Everybody in the room knew throwing Alex at a flaming Jenna was like dousing a fire with gasoline, expecting to put it out.

Batting her eyes at him, oozing fake sweetness, Jenna spoke from under her lashes. "Well then, big brother, perhaps you should try leveling with me instead of blowing smoke up my dress, eh?" She was working up to a real good mad, and every man in the room knew it. Hell, even Rissa and Kat had taken steps back. When she noticed Colt start to step forward, she halted him with a hand. "Don't. Just don't get into this. *This*" she waved her hand between the three of them, "is between my adoring brothers and me."

Turning her focus back to Alex and Zach, she leaned forward, her fingers steepled on the glossy top of Alex's desk. "So, what's it gonna be, you two knuckleheads? I'll call her, you know I will, and hell hath no fury like Catherine Lamont when she thinks her sons are getting too big for their britches. And a few well-timed tears from me and Dad will be standing by to finish off anything left after Mom is done with the two of you." She had them by the short and curlies, and everyone knew it.

Sighing, Alex leaned back in his seat and looked at Mitch Grayson. "You know we can't do this without your permission, right?" Damn, but Alex hated putting him in this position, especially with the woman his friend had been trying to get into his bed for over a year standing at the other side of the room. Alex had no idea how Rissa would deal with the news of Mitch Grayson's gifts. Mitch had often said most women who even *suspected* were more than a little unnerved by the thought a man could actually hear their thoughts. Jenna looked at Mitch, confusion written on her face, and then suddenly she understood. In the time it took her to blink everything fell into place.

"You're gifted, aren't you?" Jenna's question was directed at Mitch, her focus having shifted the moment Alex had sought his permission. "You're an empath, right? Oh shit, that explains so much." She hadn't even waited for his response, but stood looking at him with a mixture of wonder and amusement. "Holy shit, that is amazing. Tell me everything." She was like a kid with a new piece of a mystery, and she wanted to know it all.

Kat finally found her voice. "Hold up here, somebody want to catch me up? I'm not tracking this very well. Gifted? Explain that to me. *Exactly* what does that mean?"

"Yeah, I'm kind of interested in that answer myself. And I notice none of the men seem particularly confused by this information." Rissa's raised eyebrow let them know she wasn't really enjoying being out of the loop.

MITCH GRAYSON DROPPED his chin to his chest and shook his head. *Talk about your total clusterfuck, damn.* He hadn't even picked up on Jenna's own gifts until now. While she clearly wasn't as gifted as he was, she wasn't without some abilities of her own. Mitch had met many people of the years they'd instantly recognized as gifted, and he'd always marveled at their ability to chalk those gifts up to "common sense" or just knowing what "any reasonable person would know." Shit, no wonder she'd known what James had been up to when he'd approached her a few minutes ago. There wouldn't be any getting out of this one unscathed, might as well just walk into the fire like a man and nurse the burns later. Looking up at Alex, he just nodded his okay and let the other man take the lead to tell Mitch's story.

Chapter 26

JENNA LAY GAZING out the window next to her bed, thinking about how much everything had changed in the past week. Her life had been so filled with career goals for the past seven to eight years, her own identity had certainly taken a backseat. And maybe that single-minded focus had been her saving grace; if she hadn't been distracted from what happened to her the night her innocence had been stolen, she'd have certainly been a prime candidate for the cracker factory.

Smiling to herself, she remembered that phrase had always been one of Selita's favorites. It had been years before Jenna and Kat had figured out Selita had somehow gotten the expression "going crackers" changed into "going to the cracker factory." Rolling over to her back, Jenna thought about all the things which had been revealed last night and the look of horror on Rissa's face when she'd discovered Mitch was often able to hear the thoughts of people he was near. She didn't know much about Rissa's background, but there was clearly something she was terrified Mitch might learn.

Jenna vowed that if Colt wanted her to stay at ShadowDance for a while, she'd try to help Rissa work through whatever it was she'd survived. After all the trauma she'd had to endure at Ted Scott's hands, Jenna felt she'd likely have a unique perspective and could always, at the very least, lend a shoulder to cry on. Wondering, not for the first time, if it wasn't time for a change of her personal direction, she let her mind wander to the possibilities before her. Maybe it was time to stop doing a job she'd only kept because she seemed to be good at it. Maybe it was time to do something she actually felt passionate about. She'd send that idea out to the Universe and see what came back.

She'd long believed God put people in the right place at the right time if they were just willing to open their hearts and listen. Well… listen and follow directions. Laughing to herself, she decided it was time to get up and make some phone calls. Perhaps if things started falling into place, she'd know she was on the right track. Besides, if she was going to be going to The Club tonight, she needed to do some major primping. It was time to call in the big guns, and fortunately, she had Kat and Rissa on speed dial.

THEODORE JAMES HAD been frustrated by the men's quick hustle of the women out of the dining room last night. Fucking hell, he still hadn't figured out exactly what had set *that* off. Earlier today he'd been sitting in a small, shaded alcove in the gardens watching the house when Jenna and Katarina had been escorted to The Club right after lunch. He had wondered what they could possibly have been up to until he'd returned to the guesthouse and checked out The ShadowDance Club website and noted the property had an on-site spa called Rissa's. Evidently, the third woman they had hurried out last night was the spa's only technician.

It appeared the clientele of The ShadowDance Club didn't want the pampering related to their peculiar predilections being broadcast throughout their small community. "You want your sub's pussy bald as a billiard ball?" No need to advertise that preference with the local gossips.

James was certain the Lamonts' notorious BDSM club had an ironclad nondisclosure agreement that ensured what happened inside its walls stayed there. Which had also meant Jenna Lamont was right at this moment probably laying stark naked, having hot wax smeared on her teasing little slut cunt, and having the hair yanked out by the roots.

Damn, bitch, I'd have been happy to provide that pain and have done it free of charge, all you'd have to do was ask. I'm all about getting another chance to make you scream, baby. You think your nightmare ended when Ted Scott was lost in that fucking explosion, don't you? That's one body those bastards who'd called themselves teammates are going to wish like hell they'd tried a lot harder to recover.

Making his way toward The Club, James decided he'd take a little walk around and 'interview' some of the other former Special Forces guys, letting them know the General was always interested in how they were coping with civilian life. Oh yeah, it was the perfect excuse for being around and getting a lay of the land before tonight's festivities. He had every intention of getting his pound of flesh, so to speak, from Jenna Lamont before he eliminated her. She was a loose end he couldn't afford to risk. She was the only one who might ever be able to identify him, there was just something about her that told him she was a huge liability. He was so close to closing this whole sham out and disappearing with all the cash he'd been stashing, he wasn't going to let some hot little piece of ass he'd conquered almost a decade ago scuttle years of meticulous planning and clandestine work.

Hell, he'd been selling information to the highest bidder since he'd graduated from boot camp. He had no intentions of abandoning all that time and effort just because one bitch finally pulled her head out of the sand long enough to figure out Ted Scott and Theodore James were actually one and the same.

JENNA WAS ENJOYING a late lunch out on the deck with Kat and Rissa when she looked up into the furious face of Colt Matthews. Uh oh, this didn't bode well for a peaceful afternoon of sun and snoozing before tonight's festivities. Glancing in Kat's direction hoping for her friend's support, all she got was a shrugged "I told you he'd find out." And Rissa looked like she was seriously trying to make herself invisible. No doubt Mitch Grayson isn't far behind and equally livid. *Thanks for throwing me under the bus, Kat, you coward!*

Jenna smiled warmly and sweetly spoke as he stomped closer. "Good afternoon, Colt. Care to join us? I'm sure Selita would be happy to bring you a plate." Geez, she was pretty sure if she looked closely, she could see the steam coming out of his ears. He reminded her of one of those cartoon characters she remembered from Saturday morning television when she was a kid. The steam was looking more possible by the second. Holy crap!

Jenna had asked Rissa to stay behind when Ethan Jantz,

the security assigned to babysit them, had walked Kat back to the mansion, so she could talk to the other woman alone for a moment. Jenna had wanted to apologize for blurting out what she had finally figured out about Mitch's gifts last night in front of the other woman. She felt like she had only added to the tension already sizzling in the air between the two of them. Jenna swore it felt like the two of them were using some kind of electrical current to communicate. She'd planned to apologize to Mitch later this afternoon. Then she'd see what she could do about setting the whole mess to rights; at one time she and Kat had been pretty good matchmakers. Lucy and Ethel could surely cook up some kind of great plan.

After talking to Rissa, they'd been distracted and had just ambled along until they'd found themselves at the door leading out of The Club. Despite Kat's warning to wait for an escort and assurances that yes, indeed, the guys most certainly would find out if they didn't, she and Rissa had decided they were grown women and should be able to walk across the gardens back to the house alone if they wanted to. *Geez, it was only a short distance, hell we didn't see one other single soul the entire time.* But it was obvious from Colt's expression, he was in full pissed-off-boyfriend, ex-soldier-Dom, I-am-the-boss-of-you mode. Time to adopt Catharine Lamont's motto, "The Best Defense is a Good Offense."

Colt's words were calm, but his underlying fury was crystal clear. "Jenna, did you and Rissa walk back to the house unescorted?"

Jenna gave him a considering look. "We walked together, Colt. There was no need to wait for one of your security team to leave something more important to come and walk us that short distance. Perhaps you have forgotten, I am fully trained in self-defense and have been traveling alone in some of the most dangerous parts of the world for several years and never had a single problem. I didn't expect to encounter the boogeyman in the gardens in broad daylight, and my confidence in both my and Rissa's ability to make an adult decision about our own safety turned out to be well-founded, don't you think?" *Way to poke the bear, Jenna, dumb, dumb, dumb.* Jenna just wished Smart Jenna had been at the controls of her mouth instead of Bratty Jenna. Holy shit, he looked about ready to blow a gasket.

"Were you or were you not both told to only leave the spa with an escort? Not just the fucking Club itself, but the spa as well?" Colt's words began to trail off into angry mutterings as he paced back and forth, pushing his hands through his hair in frustration. Wow, looked like a play right out of the Alex Lamont, *Holy Book of Pissed-Off.* He finally stopped in front of the table and speared Jenna with a glare.

"One of the security team will pick you up at your suite at eight p.m. You will wear what is delivered to your suite later this afternoon." Stopping her from speaking by holding up his hand, he continued. "Yes, I know the Submissives' Masquerade doesn't begin until ten o'clock, but the two of you will be paying for this little transgression before we have to focus all of our attention on other matters.

"The men assigned to watch you have been dealt with, they've already paid the piper, and they will be allowed to watch you pay for walking away from them and disobeying very specific, direct orders. Alex and Zach have left this to Grayson and me to deal with, they will be staying with Katarina in the house during your punishments. Don't even think about trying to bolt, Jenna, and that goes for you as well, Rissa. We will find you." And with that, he turned and stomped back down the stairs and disappeared into the gardens.

"Holy shit, you two are really in deep this time. Damn, I'm glad I'm not a part of this." Kat stopped and then sighed deeply. "Shit, I'm turning into an old married robot. I didn't even think of the fun I'd have getting paddled for misbehaving. Crap, I'm turning into a mom already... I'm going to be dull and boring... hell, I'm already dull and boring! This sucks! I've got a reputation to maintain, what will people think if I all of a sudden start doing exactly what those two Neanderthal husbands of mine demand? Damn and double damn!"

Jenna watched Kat with stunned disbelief. The crazy woman had talked herself right into a tizzy fit about not getting into trouble and getting her ass paddled. *What the fuck is that about? Must be the hormones. I've got no other explanation for Kat's insanity.*

Jenna looked beyond Kat to see both Alex's and Zach's smiling faces. No doubt they'd heard Kat's tirade. Her sweet friend had always bemoaned that thinking out loud got her in more trouble than anything she'd actually done deliberately.

Alex stepped up and looked down at his wife. "Katarina? Did I hear you correctly, you wish you had misbehaved earlier today, just so you could maintain your reputation as a problem wife? Hmmm? That doesn't sound quite right to me, what do you think, brother? Perhaps our wife is in need of a reminder about why bratty behavior is to be avoided." Jenna watched Zach work to hide his grin before he stepped forward where Kat could see him.

"I believe you might be just about right, brother. Come

along, kitten. We're going to have a remedial lesson this afternoon." Zach held out his hand, and when Kat placed her hand in his, he pulled his round little wife to her feet. God, it did Jenna's heart good to see the love in her brother's eyes as he looked adoringly at his wife and held his hand over their growing child. Kat had flushed several shades of crimson and was giggling like a school girl at whatever the men were whispering to her as they led her inside.

Rissa looked at Jenna and blinked as if to refocus her eyes. "I've fallen down a damned rabbit hole and landed straight in BDSM hell. Hell no, I couldn't land in Alice's Wonderland, oh no, I went straight past 'Go, do not collect two hundred dollars, into BDSM *hell*. Shit, Jenna, what are we going to do? What do you think they are going to do to us? Damn, I'm so scared, I'm going to throw up!"

"Stop." Jenna reached over and touched the other woman's arm. "Rissa, think about this for a minute. Do you really think my brothers would allow someone to truly harm either of us?" When Rissa slowly shook her head, Jenna asked, "And do you really think any of the security guys who have been charged with protecting us would actually stand by and watch someone hurt us?" Again, she waited for Rissa to shake her head before adding, "And do you honestly believe Colt or Mitch would ever cause either of us true physical harm?"

Rissa let out the breath she hadn't realized she was holding and said, "No, I guess not, but I'm really not sure about this whole punishment thing, ya know? I've got some, well, some kind of bad memories of punishments." Her last words were soft, but her meaning was clear. "I don't know if I can do this, Jenna. What if I fail? What if I let Mitch down? I've been careful to keep him at arm's length because I'm sure I can't be what he needs, well, at least I can't anymore, but damn, I've stepped right into it this time. If I can't do this, I'll have to leave ShadowDance, and I've been happy here…" Her mouthed words *and safe here* weren't audible, but they weren't missed by Mitch, who'd been watching the interplay between the two women from the monitor in the crow's nest.

"DID YOU SEE that? Did you catch it? What does she mean by 'safe'? Did anything in her background check come back hot?" Mitch had already turned to a keyboard and was furiously pounding on the keys before the questions had even stopped sounding in the room. Colt had been damned proud of his performance until he'd seen the stark look of terror in Rissa's eyes. Jenna had held her chin perfectly level to the floor and not even blinked during his tirade. Oh, she was going to be a joy to tame, and Colt was hoping like hell it took him the rest of his life to get it done.

But now, Colt was really worried the scene they'd hurriedly set up for tonight was going to push Rissa too hard. They needed to find out exactly what they were up against with her because no Dom wanted to do physical or psychological harm to *any* sub and particularly, not one he had deep feelings for. One of the basic tenants of Dominant-submissive relationships was to push boundaries, but to never do anything which could cause permanent damage to a person who had given her Dom the ultimate gift of her trust. Every Dom knew his or her biggest responsibility was protection and care of their submissive and that included protecting not only their physical health but their mental health as well.

As Mitch worked his way through the pages of Rissa's background file, Colt picked up the phone and dialed Alex's number. Even though he knew he'd be interrupting his bosses' afternoon delight, he needed to know if either Alex or Zach had information that wouldn't be found in the file. When he was switched immediately to voicemail, Colt hung up and sent a quick text saying, *Call me ASAP*, and turned back to watch the security monitors Grayson had abandoned after Rissa's tear-filled, but silent words.

Chapter 27

JENNA HAD SPENT the rest of the afternoon mentally preparing for whatever Colt had planned. She wasn't just worried about herself, she'd seen the terror in Rissa's eyes and was worried the men would push her too far. Having been a victim herself, she well knew a misspoken comment or overly familiar touch could send her into hiding for weeks and back to having nightmares for months. She'd wondered about talking to her brothers, letting them know her concerns, but had decided she'd see what was planned before making a decision about action. She didn't want to betray Rissa's confidence if that's what anyone would call her vague, mouthed words about safety, but she would if she felt it was in the other woman's best interest.

After she'd made inquiries this afternoon about returning to college to earn her counseling degree, she'd decided she would visit the school and talk to the instructors, but after what had happened earlier and her overwhelming desire to help Rissa work through whatever had happened, well, now she knew for sure this was the direction she wanted to go. There certainly wouldn't be much money in her new career, but the rewards she'd reap helping others would far outweigh the monetary loss. She'd still help out at Lamont Oil when she could, but God knew she'd trained a number of employees who would be fantastic replacements for her, and most would be over the moon for the opportunity.

Jenna had been so lost in thought, she hadn't heard the knock at the door. Mitch stuck his head in the room and saw Jenna pacing back and forth and could hear her muttering something about Lamont Oil and college. *Damn, she must be really distracted to not hear my knock or the door open. Not safe, Jenna, Colt is really going to be pissed if you don't start taking some fucking interest in your personal safety.*

Mitch and Colt had decided to pick up each other's woman because they knew it would add to the women's apprehension and would also allow them to more accurately assess Jenna's and Rissa's states of mind. Emotions could easily cloud a Dom's judgment, and this was too important to take a risk. Both men knew the next couple of hours was going to be a make-or-break moment for both them and the girls. He was praying the adjustments they'd made to their planned scene would be enough. They hadn't been able to get much information about Rissa—seems Sheriff Marshall wasn't all that keen to share what he knew—but Mitch was smart enough to know what they'd gotten was likely just the tip of a very nasty iceberg.

"Jenna, are you ready? Why didn't you answer the door when I knocked?" Mitch had deliberately used his Dom voice, hoping to set the tone for the punishment she was going to receive. Her startled gasp and wide eyes told him he'd startled her. Damn Colt was going to add swats for this, no doubt.

"Shit! You scared me! I didn't hear you. I've been thinking and worrying a bit." She'd started out angry at being startled, but she'd picked up his demeanor and was quickly sliding right into a sub mindset. Perfect! *Should have thought about this before you went prancing out of the spa and Club earlier, sweet cheeks. Now your Dom is going to light that pretty little ass of yours on fire.*

He turned to her and closed the door. "I'm going to inspect you to be sure you are properly attired before we go. Go to the bed and lean over it, move your feet shoulder-width apart." She was wearing the very short and *very* sheer dress Colt had sent up to her room earlier, and God knew, he didn't have any trouble seeing she didn't have on a bra or panties, but the inspection wasn't really about verifying she'd only donned the clothes she was supposed to. This was intended to set the tone and establish power.

Women's bodies were brutally honest even when their words or expressions attempted to camouflage their real feelings. He had a high-tech micro bullet vibrator, a small butt plug, and a tube of lube in his pocket. Jenna was definitely going to get a taste of how it felt to take a stroll through the gardens she loved with her pussy aching with need.

Oh yeah, the remote control in his pocket was going to let him give sweet Jenna a few toe-curling "oh shit" moments on the way to The Club. He would hand it over to Colt when they met in the main room, but until then, Mitch planned to push her to the very edge.

Almost every member of the security team was going to witness her punishment; they were owed this for the reaming they'd taken for letting Jenna and Rissa walk right past them. He and Colt were still steaming mad about their lack of attention. Hell, Alex and Zach had nearly come apart at the seams when they'd heard about the huge lapse in security.

Jenna's brothers had no desire to see their sister stripped naked and punished publicly and had put some significant restrictions in place, but they had ultimately agreed her Dom should be allowed to punish her in a way he thought appropriate. She wouldn't be sitting comfortably for a few days, but then, neither would Rissa.

When Jenna had bent over, he walked over and flipped up her skirt, exposing her bare ass, ran his fingers through her folds and found they were moistening quickly. *Yes, Colt's little warrior pixie is a true submissive.* Reaching into his pocket, he withdrew the lube. After applying a generous amount to both her puckered rear hole and his fingers, he began rimming her with slow circles before steadily pushing in two fingers at the same time. He heard her gasp and watched as she clutched the duvet in her fists. He might have been more concerned he was hurting her if she hadn't moaned and pushed back into his touch.

"You're doing fine, sweetness. I'm going to put a plug in your ass now, relax and press back into it." He felt the rush of moisture from her pussy slide onto his fingers. *God, Colt is a lucky bastard. She is so very responsive.* "Good girl, almost there." He continued to fuck her ass with the plug, gaining ground with each stroke. It was a much larger plug than they'd used on her at the cabin, but it still wasn't a large as Colt's cock. They wanted her stretched, but not so she was completely prepared. That pinch of pain during the scene was going to be a part of her punishment, and she would know it soon enough.

Finally seating the plug all the way, he could visibly see the muscles of her ass flexing as she tried to adjust to the intrusion. He slowly massaged her ass, then slid his fingers between her thighs and pressed the bullet vibrator deep into her vaginal opening using his long, slender middle finger to be sure it was pressed perfectly against her G-spot. *Oh, sweetheart, you are in for a ride.* Laughing to himself, he made sure to school his features into an impassive mask before pulling her back to her feet.

Jenna was unsteady and Mitch listened to her self-talk as she tried to decide whether she'd simply stood upright too quickly or if sensation overload was swamping her. *Holy shit, I'm so full, how on earth am I supposed to walk with these things stuck up... everywhere? Holy crap, what have I gotten myself into? This is just over-the-top. I can't do this.*

When Mitch knew she was ready to throw in the towel, he switched on the devices and watched her eyes glaze over within seconds. She made the most interesting animalistic sound, and Mitch heard the realization the noise had come from her echoing in her mind just as her knees buckled out from under her. He'd been ready and already had his arm wrapped around her waist.

Mitch smiled to himself as she swayed precariously against him. He hadn't been at all surprised when he switched on the bullet and she dropped like a stone. Hell, her eyes had practically rolled back in her head. He'd been listening to her thoughts all the time he'd been in the room, and they had been so scattered, he'd had trouble keeping up. She'd worried about everything from her worries about Rissa to an almost overwhelming fear of letting Colt down in front of his men. She'd briefly wondered if she was brave enough to face the punishment before there'd been a complete whiteout of thought from the sensation. He found it interesting that she hadn't once thought about the pain.

"Whoa, steady now. Take a couple of deep breaths, you're doing fine. Just so you know, that is the lowest setting, and you will be experiencing the higher settings before we're done. Now, let's get moving, your Master is waiting."

He wasn't going to tell her Rissa would not be participating in this scene. He would be meting out her punishment in private. Dylan Marshall had been adamant that even though he wasn't willing to share all the details, public punishment was absolutely not going to happen. He had come clear out of his chair, and the man who was renowned in The Club as being even more detached than Alex Lamont had nearly become a raving lunatic until he realized everyone was simply staring at him, bewildered.

As Mitch started for the door, he pointed at her feet. "Lose the shoes, those weren't delivered to you this afternoon. You'll be getting extra strokes for that infraction as well. Now come along." Jenna quickly toed off her fuck-me stilettos and hurried to walk through the door he was holding open. While he closed the door behind them, she took a deep breath, and he had to suppress a smile when he heard her quoting a children's book he'd read to his four-year-old niece just last week. *I think I can, I think I can, I think I can…*

Chapter 28

I T WAS THE longest walk in history, Jenna knew it had to be true. When had the damned club been moved so far from the house? Holy crap on a cactus, every step she took caused the plug Mitch had shoved up her ass to shift to press on a new sensitive place inside her which in turn moved that blasted bullet vibrator, and he seemed to have developed some unexplained obsession with fondling that stinking remote control... the rat bastard.

Fuck it all, she'd already had to stop several times to take deep breaths, and they hadn't even gotten into The Club's main room where her punishment was supposed to be administered. *Geez, talk about a bunch of damned drama queens. I think they're blowing this all out of proportion... just in case anyone is interested in my opinion.*

Mitch walked beside Jenna trying to not react to her wayward thoughts. God only knew if she remembered his gift, she'd be much more careful, and he didn't want to lose the insight. He almost burst out laughing at the "drama queens" remark. He was going to enjoy mentioning that during the scene, just to remind her he'd been listening in as they'd been making their way to The Club. Sure, their reaction *was* being dramatized for her benefit, but Jenna would understand the reasoning, eventually.

Colt had gone into Rissa's spa to let her know plans had changed, and she would be answering to Master Mitch at a later date. Her surprise had quickly turned to skepticism when she realized she'd be dealing one-on-one with a man she was obviously attracted to, but seemed to fear at the same time. *Because our illustrious Sheriff Marshall went bat-shit crazy when he heard you were going to be punished in front of the security team, but declined to explain why little one.*

Colt directed her to stay in the backroom of her spa until she was given the all-clear. They didn't need her walking in on Jenna's punishment scene until they knew exactly what they were dealing with in her background. They were following a path of extreme caution because they'd agreed it was safer to err on the side of the angels.

When she had started to argue, he shook his head. "I'll be happy to pass along your comments and concerns to Master Mitch." *And let him adjust your punishment according-ly.* He worked hard to suppress his laughter when her eyes went impossibly wide and her mouth gaped open. *Yeah, babe, widen that mouth in front of Mitch and see what he does with it!*

By the time he left, he was relatively sure she'd follow his instructions, but he positioned one of the valets outside her door, just in case.

Walking into the large room known as the main lounge of The ShadowDance Club, Jenna came to a dead stop when she saw at least twelve men sitting in the semi-dark room, facing a small stage lit with soft white and pale-rose-colored spotlights. At the center of the stage was what looked like a huge wooden picture frame with large eyebolts on the inside at each corner. Mitch who'd been close behind her, walked up so his chest pressed against her back. She didn't know if he was making sure she knew she couldn't turn and run, or if he was worried her knees were going to give way again, leaving her little more than a pile at his feet.

Jenna stood rod stiff for a few seconds while the angel on one shoulder battled the devil on the other. *Sure, you two battle it out. By the time you make a blasted decision, I'll be up to my ass in alligators here.* She wasn't sure, but she thought she'd heard Mitch snort with laughter, and when she looked over her shoulder, he seemed to be working hard to hide a smile. *Shit. Shit. Shit. I forgot he can hear my thoughts, damn it all to hell. What all was I stewing over on the way here?*

"Don't worry about it, sweet cheeks. It's too late for that, now. Let's get this over with. Now walk straight to the stage and stand in front of Master Colt with your head lowered, chin to chest. Let's go." *Master Colt? Holy hell, I didn't even see him standing there.* Mitch's voice had been cool and direct... not at all the way he usually sounded and realizing he was putting emotional distance between them made her heart clench.

Jenna's legs felt like they were made of Jell-O. At this point, it was entirely possible she might not be able to walk up the three steps to the stage. When she finally stood in front of Colt, she started to tremble from the intimidation alone. He looked formidable and so hot she fought the urge to fan herself like some Victorian-era maiden.

Standing so close, she could feel the heat of his body seeping into her own. She took in his black leather pants and boots, topped off with a black silk shirt he'd left open to the middle of his massive chest. His feet were planted shoulder-width apart, his hands rested on his slender hips. He looked like a stereotypical Hells Angel, and the sight stole her breath. All he was missing was a tricked-out Harley and a couple of serpent tattoos. *Okay, he's scary, but damn hot, too.* She remembered she wasn't supposed to be looking him up and down like he was a prime piece of steak and quickly ducked her head.

CHRIST ALMIGHTY, COLT would love to know what had been going through her mind. She'd been looking him up and down, her eyes filled with a hunger he'd never seen before. It had been a test of his control to keep from throwing her over his shoulder and stalking from the room with her. He could only hope it wasn't the last time he got to see that particular expression. *Please don't let this punishment send her running from me again.*

When he raised an eyebrow at her, she quickly ducked her head, and fucking Grayson had nearly burst out laughing. Colt had given Grayson a questioning look, but the jerk only grinned from ear to ear and silently gave him the "You're good to go" signal.

Colt gave her a couple of minutes to pull herself together, and when her breathing seemed to finally be approaching normal, he spoke.

"Jenna, look at me." He'd deliberately kept his tone harsh and spoken loud enough for everyone in the room to hear. She flinched and slowly raised her face to his. "Do you know why you are being punished?"

"Yes, Master." Jenna's voice was so soft, he'd barely heard her himself and was sure no one else had.

"Speak up, sub, if you are going to be bold enough to disobey, you should damn well be bold enough to speak up now." Colt wanted to teach her a lesson about disobeying a direct order, but more importantly, he wanted to reinforce the idea her safety would always be his priority. But that had to be balanced against her need to feel confident her submission didn't make her weak. He didn't want to see her become meek and mousey, it wasn't who she was, and that wasn't the woman he'd fallen in love with.

She visibly swallowed, but still hadn't responded so he added, "I want to hear from the Jenna Lamont who keeps Lamont Oil running like a finely tuned machine. I don't want a sub who is afraid of who she is and shrinks away from a punishment she knows she'd earned." He raised an eyebrow in challenge and was pleased when he saw the spark in her eyes.

Jenna would know he'd intentionally challenged her, but she needed to hear his message about admiring her strength. It was important she understood he not only desired her, he admired her as well. He wanted her to know he believed in her, knew she'd be able to handle what was coming. He saw her eyes fill with tears, but he knew they were from relief, not sadness. Her posture straightened before she cleared her throat and spoke clearly.

"I am being punished because I disobeyed my Master's instruction to not leave the spa without a security escort, and by that action, I disrespected not only my Master, but every member of the security team who had been charged with my safety."

In that moment, Colt fought an inner battle, wanting nothing more than to call this whole thing off. Fuck it, she had just given the most perfect answer, hell, if he'd scripted it for her it wouldn't have been any better. He'd watched the expressions of some of the other Doms in the room, and their looks of surprise and then admiration had told him he wasn't the only one with a new level of respect for this woman. Christ, but he loved her. She was absolutely the most amazing woman he'd ever met. He nodded his approval of her answer.

"Strip."

He watched as she pulled in a deep breath and steeled herself for what was to come as she reached for the hem of her short dress and pulled it up and over her head. Mitch took it from her and brought back the padded leather cuffs he'd set on a small table at the side of the stage. When she glanced to the side and noticed the implements on the table, she'd started to tremble again. Colt had deliberately left a whip and a thick cane both in plain sight even though he wasn't planning to use either on her delicate ass.

"Look only at me, Jenna, your eyes are not to leave mine, do you understand?" When she merely nodded her head, he said, "Not good enough, baby, I have to hear the words… let's try again. Do you understand?"

"Yes, Master, I understand," Jenna's words were clear and loud enough he was sure most in the room had been able to hear her.

"Good girl. Now, Master Mitch is going to put cuffs around your ankles and wrists to restrain you during your punishment." Mitch had the cuffs on her almost before Colt had finished explaining. They led her to the frame and secured her, making sure the cuffs weren't cutting off her circulation before stepping back. The frame was set up so it could be rotated either front to back or top to bottom.

Originally, he had planned to do the first half of the strokes with her facing the back and then when her system was flooding with endorphins, he'd make her face the team she'd thrown under the bus this afternoon. His men would be paying for that mistake with extra shifts, punishing workouts, and cash donations to local charities. But now, he wanted all her attention for himself, so he'd be the one facing the audience while Grayson administered the lashes to her ass. Colt wanted to be the one to read her expressions. He knew Mitch would be able to hear her thoughts until she *whitewashed* as he called it. Grayson had said he could read subs until they hit a certain point in a scene when it all became nothing more than radio static or what soldiers called *whitewash*.

The woman standing before him held his heart and soul in the palm of her hand. Anyone thinking he had the power here was a fool. He'd be looking in her eyes during her strapping. He wanted to see every nuance of her facial expressions and body language, so he was assured of her ability to get through this punishment. The last thing he needed was for her to be so overcome, she forgot to safeword out. He'd rarely seen long-term D/s relationships survive that, let alone one as newly minted as theirs.

After she was secured to the frame and he and Grayson were satisfied with her position, he moved to stand directly in front of her again.

"What is your safe word, Jenna?" His words were crisp, but he knew his eyes were conveying his affection and respect for her.

"Um, it's red, Master," she answered clearly, but he could see the apprehension building in her eyes.

"And when are you supposed to use your safe word?" He wanted to make sure she knew and was able to tell him; he'd seen many subs get so caught up in a scene and become so overwhelmed when pain stopped being anything other than just pain, they completely forgot to use their safe word. As a dungeon monitor, he'd stopped several scenes when the sub had been so far in subspace and the Dom so submerged in the role-play, intervention had been all that kept things from becoming physically detrimental to the submissive.

"I should use my safe word if I am so uncomfortable, either physically or emotionally, I cannot continue safely." Jenna clearly understood. It was time to get this over with and get her up to his fourth-floor suite and make sweet love to her before he had to be back in The Club for tonight's Submissives' Masquerade.

"Very good, you are to keep your eyes on me and only on me while Master Mitch administers your punishment. You'll be getting twenty lashes… one for each member of the team you dishonored today and three for the disrespect you showed me. Master Mitch is using my belt as it is something I wear daily. It is important your punishment comes from something personal to me. Since this is your first public scene, I won't ask you to count the lashes. When you have had the last stroke, you'll pleasure me with your mouth before I claim that sweet ass of yours. Having my cock in your ass will be your final act of submission for this punishment." He'd known she would be shocked by the number of lashes, but he was sure she would be able to take them all. The look of determination in her eyes spoke volumes. "Master Mitch, begin."

JENNA HAD NO more than heard the words when she felt a streak of fire across her left ass cheek before she even heard the snap of the belt. *Holy fucking God that hurt! I'm never going to be able to get through nineteen more of those.* Colt had taken her chin in his hand, so she couldn't even drop her head and knew she had tensed up in anticipation of the next stroke.

"Don't tighten your muscles, it'll just hurt worse, baby." Colt's words were spoken so softly, she was sure no one aside from Mitch could have heard him. She tried to relax her muscles just as four more blows landed in quick succession. She noticed he was never hitting her in the same place twice in a row and two had been across her back. As the blows continued to fall, Jenna cried out and let the tears she'd been trying to hold back roll freely down her cheeks.

Jenna had kept her eyes on Colt's face and mouthed the words "I'm so sorry." Through her tears, she saw Colt's eyes soften, and she suddenly felt more vulnerable than she could ever remember. As the last strike landed, her entire body was being flooded with Mother Nature's built-in painkillers, and she was beginning to feel like she was floating. As they released her from the restraints, she heard the security team leave the room.

COLT HAD NEVER intended for her final two acts of submission to be witnessed by anyone other than Grayson. He had never really been into exhibitionism, and his sweet sub's pleasure and orgasms weren't something he was particularly anxious to share with everyone else. Those sexy moans weren't for the entire team's entertainment.

As Grayson helped Jenna kneel, Colt opened his leathers, letting his aching cock spring free. He'd been so close to coming when he'd seen her walk into the room wearing that see-through dress, he'd had to take several deep breaths. Now, he was skating on that same edge again. *Christ, the minute that sweet mouth takes me in, it's gonna be all over.* She looked up at him with such a sad expression, he felt his heart clench.

"Well done, baby, I'm proud of you. You took those strokes beautifully. Now, open up and suck me into that hot, wet, velvet mouth of yours." As he slid past her sweet lips, all puffy and red from where she had bitten down trying to stifle her earlier cries, he thought he was going to die from the pleasure of it.

"Ah, Christ, Jenna, your mouth is so fucking sweet." She began to suck harder as he grasped her face and started moving in and out at a feverish pace. "I'm gonna fuck this sweet mouth and come down your throat, and you are to swallow every drop, don't lose any of it, Jenna. Oh shit... *Fuck!*"

Colt stiffened, white-hot pulses of his seed shot to the back of her throat, and he groaned when she swallowed around the sensitive head. She swallowed every drop, then licked the last remnants from his still-erect cock as he withdrew from her mouth. While she'd still been on her knees, Mitch had been playing with the remote and Colt knew she'd felt the vibrator in her ass moving and the plug in her pussy some to life as well. Colt pulled her to her feet as Mitch pulled the remote for the bullet from his pocket and grinned.

Jenna swayed on her feet when the tempo of the bullet sped up. Colt let his gaze sweep over her and groaned to himself when he saw the glistening moisture coating her inner thighs. Mitch moved a padded bench close to them, and as soon as they had her bent over the bench in position, Colt pulled the plug from her and began pressing the blunt tip of his cock against her tight rosette.

The lubricant he'd hastily smeared over his cock was cool at first touch, and he grinned at her gasp when he drizzled it over her heated rear hole. His cock was so engorged, he prayed he'd be able to maintain the control required to let her body adjust to his intrusion.

She'd gasped in response to the final sharp pinch of pain before her body flushed, letting him know it had quickly morphed into a shot of electric pleasure. *Wait for it, love, it's going to go straight to your clit.* Colt pressed forward and groaned when she pushed out against him, easing him into her heated depths. He started taking long, fast strokes and just as she didn't think she could hold on any longer, he leaned over and whispered.

"Come for me, my love. Let me feel and hear your pleasure."

Colt felt her orgasm gathering around them like a summer electrical storm and as soon as his whispered words of permission registered, she clamped down on his cock like a vise. She shot straight into the heavens and took him with her.

Colt knew the instant Jenna had gone totally into subspace. He'd been surprised the pain of her punishment hadn't put her there. But there was something immensely satisfying in the knowledge she associated pleasure with the blissful feeling rather than pain. She'd started floating while he'd fucked her mouth, and then as he'd fucked her ass, she'd gone so deep, she'd actually passed out at the end of her orgasms.

Grayson handed him warm, damp cloths, and he'd quickly cleaned Jenna, them himself. After he'd righted his leathers, he took the soft subbie blanket from his friend and wrapped her carefully before lifting her to his chest.

"I'm taking her upstairs for her aftercare, I'll be back down before the Masquerade starts. Thanks for your help. I know that was really difficult for you." He paused briefly, trying to gather his emotions before he continued. "You'll never know how close I came to calling it off after her answer at the beginning."

Mitch Grayson was cleaning the equipment, but he stopped to meet Colt's gaze. "I do know. And I wouldn't have blamed you if you had. Hell, there wasn't a man in the room who would have questioned your decision. But she needed this. She craves submission, well, actually, she craves submitting to you. You did the right thing. Now, go make love to your woman. I'll see you in a couple of hours." Colt nodded and smiled as he quickly took the stairs two at a time.

Chapter 29

M IA WATCHED OUT the windows of the sleek black
sedan carrying her up the winding road to the
Lamonts' ShadowDance Club. Being a well-trained DEA
agent and having worked undercover on this case for
almost two years, she knew full well what was at stake. She
also knew it was all going to come down to whether or not
her message had gotten to the man she'd loved enough to
walk away from to keep him safe.

Christ, every time she even thought about that night, it
felt like someone was reaching inside her chest and yanking
her heart out with their bare hands all over again. Even
though she'd known it was imperative to distance herself
from Dylan Marshall for his own safety, seeing the look of
utter disbelief and defeat in his eyes their last night together
had nearly destroyed her. Knowing she'd been responsible
for putting the look of desolation on his face haunted her
still.

Dylan was the only man she'd ever loved, and Mia
knew there would never be another man in her life. No
one else would ever come close to living up to her sweet
memories of their shared hopes, dreams, and passions.
Sighing inwardly, she sent up another a litany of prayers
he'd received and understood the message.

Smiling to herself, she felt a flush of pride when she

realized she had every confidence in his ability, after all, he was a master at puzzles. Dylan had worked as a cipher and code breaker for years. But all of that ability and skill was dependent on him actually having received the message.

Holy Christ, what were the odds the woman she'd helped in Las Vegas would end up at ShadowDance? Damn, talk about karma coming back to bite you in the ass. What was it they always said? Something about no good deed going unpunished... yeah, that about summed it up all right.

Mia just hoped Dylan was still the tenacious investigator she'd always known him to be, and that he still cared enough about her to push for answers. *That's an awful lot of hopes you're betting your life on there, Melita.* Straightening in her seat, she glanced over at Nikolai Petrov. Now, here was a man who was evil to the depths of his soul. How Cal Robertson had ever gotten mixed up with the Russian mob was a mystery to Mia. From the bits and pieces she'd been able to put together, it seemed Robertson had hidden a cache of diamonds in some trinket he'd given to Katarina McKay, then proceeded to whip her so badly during a scene, Mia had feared for the other woman's life and helped her escape.

When Cal had gone to ShadowDance, he'd led with his ego rather than simply attempting to retrieve the diamonds. The egotistical sadist had decided to take Kat as well, and she'd shot him for his trouble. Likely no one had made too much of an effort to save his sorry ass after what he'd put Kat through, and it served the little weasel right in Mia's opinion.

Before his fateful trip to ShadowDance, Cal had stashed Mia in a local hotel room with one of his cronies. As soon as word had come down Cal was on ice at the local morgue, the guy had tossed her in the trunk of a car he'd stolen from the hotel parking lot, and they'd been back in Vegas in a matter of hours.

Mia had been amazed they'd kept her alive until she'd realized she was their ticket into ShadowDance, and she was the only one who knew what Katarina looked like. They were no doubt counting on Alex and Zach allowing Kat to see her friend and welcoming both Mia and her 'date' with open arms. Mia's message to Dylan had been a warning; she wasn't taking any chance her tiny friend would be taken by the sexual predators she'd been tracking for two long years.

As it turned out, the 'Big Boss' himself decided he'd left this particular clusterfuck in the hands of his minions one too many times, and he was personally escorting Mia to the annual Submissives' Masquerade at The ShadowDance Club. Mia was to point out Katarina and engage the other woman in conversation, then finagle an invitation to stay at the mansion for the weekend.

Mia looked down at the dress she was almost wearing. *No shit, calling this sheer piece of fabric I'm barely draped in a garment is a pretty huge fucking leap of the imagination. It would be more accurate to call it a see-through shirt that's been ripped to shreds. Why do Doms think it's cool to dress women in clothes that look like costumes better suited for a Middle Ages slave girl? Well at least my tattoo is plainly visible; can't imagine Dylan missing that since he was there when it was inked.*

Not likely any man in the room was going to miss the deep indigo dragon on her lower back, the dragon's tail wrapped around nearly to her navel, and the fire he was breathing wrapped around from the other side. It really was too distinctive for undercover work, but it had been a gift from Dylan, and she had never been able to bring herself to have it removed.

Petrov didn't seem to know much about the lifestyle of D/s, but he was a ruthless bastard who didn't hesitate a moment to use pain to guarantee a woman's cooperation. As they pulled up to the security gates, he reached over and squeezed her upper thigh so hard, she cried out. His warning had been clear, no talking unless it was directed toward their goal.

We'll see, ass hat, you're about to walk onto a playing field I know a whole lot more about than you do. You think you've got this one all wrapped up? Well, give it your best shot, because it's game on, baby.

As they passed through an ornate gate heavily laden with cameras, it would have looked like any Dom keeping his hand possessively on his submissive's leg. It would seem like one of the most basic forms of restraint to anyone monitoring the security feeds.

What Petrov hadn't seen was her quick hand signal. Now, she hoped her little "Heads up, boys" signal hadn't been missed by Dylan and whoever he'd brought on for tonight's little dance with the devil as she'd been thinking of it for the past several weeks.

DYLAN LEANED BACK against the wall, watching the ShadowDance security team monitor every square inch of the property with military precision from the state-of-the-art office affectionately known as the crow's nest. Mitch Grayson was keeping a close watch on the monitors at the front gate, hoping to give them as much warning as possible that their target was on-site.

"Fuck, Matthews, get over here. I think I've got her, and it looks like she tried to give us a signal. Hang on, I'm running it back." Dylan was behind him in the time it had taken him to blink. *Christ, she's really here?* "Is that your woman?" Mitch had been listening in on the sheriff's thoughts for days and hadn't needed anyone to tell him about the past these two shared.

"Jesus fucking Christ, what's she almost wearing? Yes, that's her, and you'll have a positive the minute she exits the vehicle if she hasn't had her dragon tat removed. Run it back and slow it down, I want to see the signal again."

They watched it replay several times when Dylan leaned back and sighed. "We each had a hand sign for 'I love you'—that was hers to me." God, he felt like he'd been gutted and then re-filled with hope in the blink of an eye. They'd had dozens of hand signals, things they'd worked out during long, boring stakeouts, and of all those, she'd used this one? Damn, was it possible? Was he lucky enough to get another chance with the woman who still held his heart?

"Let the team know we're good to go and find out who that bastard is, he's got his fucking paws on my wife." Dylan had never been able to refer to Melita as his ex-wife, and he sure wasn't going to start now that she'd used her one second of opportunity to say, "I love you" with a flip of her hand she'd known only he would recognize. No, there wasn't a snowball's chance in hell he was going to lose her a second time.

Mitch Grayson gave him a knowing look. "I know who he is. That's Nikolai Petrov, a high-ranking official in the Russian Mafia. Fuck, I have calls to make. Jesus Christ, this thing just got about a thousand times more complicated."

Grayson was typing furiously on the computer and

talking on the phone at the same time, and Dylan watched in utter amazement at how the man could maintain two completely different cognitive lines of processing at the same time and not miss a single beat. Hell, most men he knew couldn't watch a ball game and listen to their wife and know for sure an hour later what she'd said. Every man on the security team was being given a sit-rep via their coms, and the security surrounding Katarina's suite on the second floor of the mansion had just been doubled.

Now that they knew who they were dealing with, they held no illusion the bastard was alone. *When you see one cockroach, you know there are a hundred others lurking in the woodwork.* It wasn't going to be a simple 'snatch back' because it was a given Petrov had spent a small fortune placing people inside. Talking to himself, Mitch's muttered words echoed the thoughts of every former black-op team member working tonight.

"Yep, what we have here is a regular SNAFU, boys. Oh yeah, situation normal, all fucked up!"

Chapter 30

A S MIA WAS escorted through the front doors into The ShadowDance Club, there was no doubt in her mind her message had been received. Holy Mother of God, there were security people everywhere, and each one looked at her, then their eyes went straight to her tat. It was freaking hell trying to keep her eyes downcast and not scan the room for Dylan.

Petrov's grip on her elbow bordered on painful as he pulled her forward and spoke quietly so only she could hear. "Come, slut, you must find the woman Katarina. If we can get the diamonds before needing to stay tonight, we will, and then you will be free to go."

Yeah, right, I'm real sure you're just going to let me waltz away knowing you killed a man two nights ago in the motel in Salt Lake City, you're smuggling a fucking fortune in diamonds out of the country to buy weapons for your little band of merry murderers, and your sex-trade business is quickly becoming the largest network of human traffickers in the world. You're just going to let me out at the nearest gas station, sure you are! Damn, I sure hope I don't look that stupid.

"Yes, Sir," Mia forced herself to whisper in response. She had no intention of playing her hand too soon. "Sir, permission to speak?" Even though Petrov wasn't a trained Dom, he'd learned enough over the past couple of weeks to at least look authentic in the role for a short time. Mia was counting on using his lack of specific knowledge about protocol to her advantage.

"Speak, slut. Christ, this shit is a pain in my ass." Petrov had a total disregard for others and being a sex trader was just one example of his complete disregard for women in particular. He had led Mia into the main bar area, and his eyes had widened when he'd seen a woman tied naked to a St. Andrew's cross while her Dom used a single-tail whip to lay perfect red stripes in a crisscross over her back and ass. The woman was begging her master for more, and Petrov stopped near the small stage, appearing entranced with what he was seeing. Grateful for his distraction, Mia used the opportunity to look quickly around the room, and it only took her a few seconds to lock eyes with Dylan Marshall.

Dear God, he was just as gorgeous as she remembered. She could practically feel his eyes caressing her nearly naked body. He flicked his eyes to the center of her torso, his lips quirking up fractionally in acknowledgment of the tattoo he'd designed and had inked for her on their first wedding anniversary. Mia's knees nearly buckled in relief, and it took every ounce of self-discipline she had to stay rooted in place. She didn't know who else in the room was in Petrov's pocket, but she'd bet her last nickel there were several.

Dropping her eyes back to the floor, she felt Petrov's attention return to her. He'd finally realized she hadn't asked her question.

"What did you want? You asked to speak and then stare at the floor. You are a typical stupid American whore, you want always to talk when you should be silent, then you're silent when told to speak. Why men all over this damned planet want American women for their slaves is a baffle to me." He turned to face her and grabbed her shoulders and gave her a violent shake. "Speak now, or I will give you to one of these perverts and watch as they whip you."

His angry tirade caused spittle to spray her face as he shouted, and she fought the feeling of nausea, fearing she might throw up. The man must not even own a damned toothbrush, and the seafood he'd eaten at lunch didn't smell any better now than it had when he'd eaten three platefuls hours earlier. *Yep, real classy fella, this one. Just have to pretend for a little bit longer, then I'm going to love watching as you're cuffed and stuffed, you piece of shit.*

"Sir, I need to use the restroom. Doms are always served free drinks at these clubs, I'd be happy to bring you something as soon as I return, Sir." Trying to act subservient to Robertson and now Petrov was taxing every bit of reserve Mia possessed. After this mess, she was going on a long, much-deserved vacation. She planned to spend about a month lounging in a hammock on some beach letting cute cabana boys fetch her fruity drinks with little umbrellas, yes, sirree, she had it all planned out.

Just need to get those diamonds and drop a net over this thug. Come into my country and act a fool, we'll just see how you like American women when Special Prosecutor Brianna Davis gets done with you.

Oh, baby, she is locked and loaded, waiting for a chance at you. That sweet little brunette your guys picked up on the University of Texas campus last summer, that was Tiffani Davis, Brianna's younger sister. Oh yes indeed, she is most anxious to have a conversation with your happy Russian ass.

"You think I am so stupid as to let you out of my sight? No, you must wait." Petrov didn't care if she pissed herself, and she fought the urge to roll her eyes at his juvenile attempt to keep from losing track of her. "You would probably just stir up shit, and we do not have time for your reality television idiocy."

She took a deep breath and bit the inside of her mouth to hold back the retort dancing on the tip of her tongue. Just then a tall man in jeans and boots stepped into Mia's limited field of vision. She'd kept her eyes down trying to convince Petrov she honestly believed she had a chance to win her freedom. The man's deep voice was clearly that of an experienced Dom, but there was an underlying warmth Mia didn't miss. "Excuse me, sorry to interfere, but I couldn't help but overhear your little sub there mention needing to use the bathroom. I know how you feel, not wanting to let a pretty little filly like that get away from ya, but the restrooms here are monitored by Doms and dungeon monitors. May I?" He'd obviously asked Petrov's permission to touch her because, at the ass-hat's grunt, the man had placed his finger under her chin and lifted her face to his.

"We don't worry about our little subs' privacy, hell, with this outfit showin' off all her personals, privacy ain't much of an issue, is it, pet?" She was sure he'd just given her a message, likely the monitor in the restroom was one of the security team. He released her chin and quickly returned his gaze to Petrov.

"She'll be safe in there. You tell the Dom on duty to keep an eye on her, and he'll make sure she don't leave his sight for a minute." With that, he turned and walked away, never looking back. Mia had to suppress a smile; damn, that cowboy sure missed his calling. Oh yeah, last year's Oscar winner didn't hold a candle to her new hero.

Petrov grabbed her hand and dragged her through the

crowd toward the direction the cowboy Dom had nodded his head. Mia's heart was racing, she was sending up prayers way faster than she figured even the most benevolent God could fulfill them. *Please, oh please, let there be a contact waiting in the bathroom for me!*

DYLAN HAD HEARD Trace Bartell's conversation about the restroom and had silently praised Alex and Zach Lamont's deep pockets and foresight by placing hidden mics on several of The Club's regular members. They'd met with men they trusted and had known would be mingling through the room, giving them a brief rundown of the situation and asking them to engage the targets if they had the opportunity. The general consensus was the more they talked, the better the team's chance of knowing what was planned. Bartell had played it perfectly. He'd set it up so they would have a chance to speak with Mia, and he'd kept Petrov in the conversation long enough to give someone a chance to get in place.

Dylan had to laugh. Anybody who thought ranchers weren't great businessmen capable of stepping into any situation and make it fly had never met the man known locally as The Gentle Giant. Petrov didn't question the information because he didn't see the *uneducated* cowboy was a threat—big mistake, because the man was one of the smartest men Dylan knew.

Trace Bartell lost his wife a while back when she'd been run off the road by a drunken teenager from a neighboring community. Even though the man had been devastated by the loss, he'd lobbied the prosecutor and judge to impose a sentence requiring the young man to work on his ranch for nothing but room and board for a year and a thousand hours of community service.

The young man had been a problem in his hometown for years. Everybody expected him to fail and damned it if the kid hadn't tried his hardest to prove them all right. But this past year spent on Bartell's ranch had turned the kid around. Trace had taught him values and was even helping fund the kid's college education.

When people had asked him why he'd done it, he'd assured everyone it had been healing for them both. Everybody hoped Trace would find a woman who would appreciate the kind spirit who was still mourning the loss of a great love.

Dylan had seen Alex move into position, so he'd stayed back. It was best to let Alex talk to Melita. Hell, if he got close to her, he was going to wrap her in his arms and never let her go, and that wasn't going to help them tie up this cluster fuck so they could clear both Katarina and Mia of the danger that would continue to haunt them if this didn't end tonight.

Petrov stopped at the entrance of the women's lounge and faced Alex Lamont, who stood with his feet planted shoulder-width apart and his arms crossed over his chest. His leather pants left nothing to the imagination and his black silk shirt was open to the waist, showcasing his massive chest and highlighting the deep bronze skin tone he owed to his Native American lineage.

Alex was in full Dom persona, and Mia had to duck her head so she didn't smile. She'd spent many nights sitting out on the deck drinking beer and laughing at Alex and Zach Lamont's crazy stories about growing up on ShadowDance Mountain, then later their harrowing tales of war and narrow escapes.

Petrov looked at Alex and snarled, "Are you the man watching the women urinate?" Good thing she was standing behind Petrov, she knew her shoulders were shaking with her silent laughter.

ALEX RAISED HIS eyebrow and looked down at the Russian thug. *Jesus Christ, did he really just ask me that?* Alex was sure the men in the crow's nest would be throwing that little ditty in his face for years.

"I'm Alex Lamont, my brother and I own this Club, but we all take shifts monitoring the bathroom the submissives use. No Dom wants his sub coming in here and touching what belongs to him any more than is necessary. We don't need them chatting each other up either. Nothing good comes of them comparing notes if you know what I mean." Petrov was nodding like his neck was made of rubber. *What an idiot.*

"You want me to watch your sub? You think she's going to try to get herself off while she's in here? Maybe ease the tension before you get a chance to play with her? I'll keep an eye on her. Help yourself over there at the bar. Bartender's name is Cort Douglas, tell him Alex said to set you up with some of the good stuff under the bar." Alex hadn't met a Russian criminal yet who didn't love thinking they were getting preferential treatment and the best vodka in the bar. And it didn't look like this asshole was going to be any different.

"Yes, watch the slut for me. She is a slippery one, don't let her out of your sight. You can have some of her if you like, I don't care so much for her, but she has her uses, you know? Cort Douglas, you say? When she leaves, watch her to make sure she returns to me. Thank you." Petrov shoved a twenty into Alex's palm before he walked toward the bar.

Knowing the entire back of the bar was a mirror and Petrov would be watching closely, Alex grasped Mia by the upper arm and roughly dragged her out of sight. "Damn it, Alex, that fucking hurt!" Mia was rubbing her upper arm as soon as Alex had released her.

"Yeah, well, nice to see you, too, Melita, and that piss wad you brought into my Club was watching in the mirror over the bar, so I had to play my part. You owe Trace Bartell a beer, too, by the way." At her puzzled look, he added, "The cowboy who got you in here. Christ the man thinks quick on his feet." Smiling now, he reached over and pulled Melita into a rib-crunching hug.

"Goddamn, Melita, in a million years, Zach and I won't be able to repay you for helping Katarina escape and return to us. I can't wait to reunite you with her, but right now, you need to tell me everything you know about what's going down here tonight."

Mia quickly filled him in on the details she knew. She was sure he was wired, so likely, she'd just told their whole team. *You gotta love rich boys with cool techy toys.*

Chapter 31

W HILE MIA EXPLAINED what she knew and what Petrov was looking for, Alex was fussing with her clothing and securing a plastic bracelet around her wrist. *What the hell, are there fucking carnival rides in here?* "Excuse me, Alex, are you listening to me?" She had stopped talking and was looking at him as if he'd completely lost his mind. "I'm trying to give you some really important information here, and all you care about is straightening my dress, such as it is, and putting a damned 'Ride Free All Day' bracelet on my wrist?"

Alex's eyes glinted with amusement, and she saw the first signs of the fun-loving man she'd known years earlier. "First of all, you have been updating the entire team while you have been speaking to me. Second, I think your dress is lovely, but it lacked the tracking device I have now attached. Third, since I have no guarantee you'll be keeping that lovely frock on all evening, I'm attaching a band that not only tells other members you are a 'newbie', and they must check with a club dungeon monitor before engaging you in play, it also has a tracking device. We want to know where you are at all times, sweetheart.

Make no mistake, Master Dylan is not planning to let you leave ShadowDance with anyone but him." Smiling down indulgently at Mia, he wiped the single tear slowing sliding down her cheek. "Please don't cry, Mia, we'll keep you safe."

Mia took a deep breath and seemed to re-center herself. "I'm not worried about my safety, it's just... well, it wasn't ever supposed to be about a bunch of damned diamonds. I've been working on this case for two years. I gave up the only man I ever loved in my naive belief I could protect him and his friends from being associated with me. Then look what happens. I land right on your doorstep bringing who knows how much danger front and center in your lives."

Dylan was listening, and it was taking every ounce of self-restraint he possessed to stay out of the women's lounge. The only man she'd ever loved? To protect him? What the fuck had she been thinking? She'd broken his heart and nearly taken his soul down in the process. Hell, it had taken him over a year to even eat dinner with another woman, and he was just now attending The Club again on a regular basis. As his dismay faded, his hope blossomed, and smiling for the first time in a long time, he promised himself a long-overdue vacation when this evening was over... and he sure wasn't planning on traveling alone.

BY THE TIME Alex returned Mia to Petrov at the bar, he was already on his second drink and becoming more and more agitated as he listened to those around him speculating about all the extra security in The Club for tonight's festivities. As Alex led Mia closer, Petrov turned, glaring at the two.

"What the fuck took so long? You decided to take her

for a test drive, Mr. Lamont?"

Alex went completely still. Mia felt him tense, but knew the other man wouldn't be watching carefully enough to notice. One thing she'd learned, the more powerful the criminal, the less they cared about others, and that often translated to inattention on their part. Most were so accustomed to having someone else do their dirty work, they rarely saw far enough past their own agendas in social situations to notice subtle changes in the body language of others.

"Not at all, I am happily married, and I do not cheat… *Ever.* I noticed that your sub did not have an identification band as is required of all nonmembers. We wouldn't want her being approached by another Dom, now would we?" Alex heard snorts of laughter coming through his earbud and knew he'd better shelve his sarcasm.

"No, I don't suppose we would. Now, if it's all the same to you, I'd like to talk with the slut privately for a moment." It hadn't escaped Alex's attention the man hadn't referred to Mia as his sub. Maybe he wasn't completely stupid after all. *Nope, asshole, she isn't yours, not even close.*

STANDING IN THE shadows watching Petrov lead *his* woman to a secluded corner, Dylan bit back a curse as the man slid his hand down Mia's back and gripped her ass cheek with enough force to cause her to wince. He growled his rage before turning to see Zach standing next to him. Zach's eyes held a compassion Dylan wasn't used to seeing directed at him.

"Don't worry, we'll keep her safe and get her back to you. Remember, Dylan, this is what we all do best." Slapping Dylan's shoulder, Zach moved through the room.

Petrov pushed Mia so hard her shoulder hit the wall with enough force to have her crying out at the white-hot streak of lightning that shot all the way to her fingertips. "Shut up and tell me if you see Katarina McKay in this room, you stupid bitch. I don't know why Robertson didn't kill you when you helped her escape, but your time is running out if you don't tell me where she is now."

Mia worked her shoulder, trying to ease the pain and hoping the small action bought her a few more seconds to figure out how to tell the man in front of her Kat was not only not in the room at this time, but wouldn't be for several more months, according to Alex.

"I don't see her, but I haven't been anywhere but the bathroom and near the bar. Is there a dance floor? I know she always talked about how much she loved to dance, perhaps we should look there?" She'd tried to make her voice sound light and hopeful, but she could tell by his scowl he wasn't buying her story.

"I hear from other members she is pregnant, and her husbands will not let her come to The Club until after the child is born. What kind of tramp has two husbands? American women must be insane."

Mia had done her homework and knew Petrov's background, so she wasn't surprised by his comment. He'd been raised by a sadistic father who took great joy in regularly sending his wife to the local emergency room, so it wasn't difficult to imagine Petrov not understanding the dynamics of a ménage.

"My men tell me there is cause for concern, we may have been compromised. They have overheard comments about added security. It is time for us to leave." He'd grabbed her upper arm, his hands so large, his fingers more than circled her bicep, and his hold so tight, her fingers were quickly starting to go numb.

"But what about the diamonds? How will we get them? Do you have men in place to search her car? I'll bet it's in the garage, maybe you and I should go look." She knew she was babbling, but she was terrified he would actually get her outside, and that would be a disaster. He would have at least two alternate forms of escape; he'd bragged about how he always had at least two backup plans. At her words about searching the garage, he'd slowed his pace fractionally before moving to the side and speaking with the man who was also acting as their driver for this evening.

Petrov's words were too quiet for her to hear over the blaring music, but suddenly she found herself being dragged along as the other man led them toward a door at the back of the room. Mia prayed the men Alex had assured her were watching her every move had noticed their abrupt change of direction.

As soon as she felt the cool air waft up under her dress, she became all too aware of the fact she was barefoot and outside. There was nothing to protect her from the bitter cold wind heralding the first storm of the coming winter. *Shit!*

Mia remembered the times she and Dylan had visited Climax during the fall and knew the weather could... and often did, change from glorious to deadly in a matter of minutes. The rocks of the gravel drive were cutting the bottoms of her feet as Petrov drug her farther from the lighted path.

"Wait, I can't keep up, the rocks are cutting my feet,

please slow down."

A second man stepped out from the shadows and grasped her other arm. She'd known Petrov would have people already in place in and around The Club, so she wasn't surprised when he'd approached them.

"Do not complain, I am giving you the chance to help us if you have no purpose, perhaps I should just let my friend here end your misery? Eh?"

Petrov's progress was only slightly hindered by staying in the shadows as they moved down the path. Mia only hoped it bought them enough time for Alex to get people in place to save her. She caught a fleeting glimpse of two men who'd been forced to step back to avoid being bumped into by the men dragging her through the darkness. She was grateful they were so focused on hustling her down the rocky path they weren't watching the shifting shadows surrounding them as Alex's men moved into place.

"WHAT THE FUCK do you mean she's gone?" Colt Matthews's voice was icy hot as his temper flared. He did not need this additional complication. Goddamn it to hell, he'd left her sated and sleeping in his suite, with a note saying he had to return to work, and she was to stay put until he returned. What about that was so fucking difficult for her to comprehend?

"Find her—*now!*" Christ the woman was going to be the death of him yet. "Is her car still disabled?" He was having it 'looked at' which was team code for disabled until further notice. He had wanted to be sure she didn't try to take off like she was so well known to do. Grayson's soft chuckle in his earbud was all the answer he needed, but the words were a welcome assurance.

"Oh yeah, that little sports car has been keeping the mechanics entertained; they're itching to put it back together though. I'm sure the test runs are going to be worth buying a ticket to watch."

"It's a given she's headed to the damned garage. Heads up everybody, it seems Jenna has decided on a late-night fucking stroll." Colt was still muttering under his breath about disobedient damned subs and a thrashing she'd never forget when he saw movement out of the corner of his eye.

"What the hell is James doing making his way to the garage? Team, we have another bogie, the son of a bitch is armed, too."

JENNA STAYED OFF the main path as much as possible. Even though the majority of the elaborate garden had been constructed while she was crisscrossing the globe for Lamont Oil, she had still spent hours exploring the paradise her brothers had created. It always amazed her that two ex-Special Forces soldiers could be such visionaries of created beauty. Just as she was about to round the last corner into the garage's security lighting, she heard the scuff of a boot. She stopped, frozen in place as the small hairs on the back of her neck stood straight up. And then she heard the voice she'd heard in her nightmares for years.

"Well, well, if it isn't little Miss Jenna Lamont. Interesting name, Jenna, is it short for Genevieve?" For just a split second, Jenna was afraid she was going to faint as little pinpoints of black clouded her vision, making her light-headed. She'd recognized his voice immediately, but it was his question that had sent all the air out of her lungs.

Jenna knew all about the body's fight-or-flight response system. She'd studied self-defense and was an expert in several disciplines, but she was most proud of her street-fighting skills. She'd begged her brothers to teach her, insisting she needed to be able to defend herself when she moved to college, and they'd reluctantly agreed.

Once she'd gotten them on board, they'd been tough taskmasters, and she still remembered Zach preaching to her that "All that fancy shit is great for the gym and competition, Jenna Beth, but if you want to save your ass, you need to fight dirty." Those words moved through her mind, and she was grateful he and Alex had taught her well.

She'd sparred with both of her brothers and any team member they'd brought home over the years. A small part of her brain was still a victim because she'd never allowed herself the opportunity to process and heal, and that small part of her wanted to scream and run, but the larger part of her wanted to take out the bastard who had caused her years of heartache and loneliness.

Turning slowly toward the man who had stolen her innocence so long ago, she assessed him coolly. "Well, well, Ted Scott is alive and well after all. I was told you'd died in a cave, buried in hell. And to think I'd been so awed by the irony of it, but it seems that wasn't exactly factual intel, now was it?" She paused to gauge his reaction and was pleased to see his jaw tighten. "But, oh my... let's see, it's Theodore James now, isn't it?"

She was face-to-face with the man she'd always dreamed of having a chance to use all her skills to hurt as he'd hurt her. She wanted nothing to do with the man sexually, but a small part of her was relishing the idea of beating him to a bloody pulp. He was a pencil pusher now for some damned ailing General, and she was in top physical condition.

Oh, yes. Just step a bit closer, you piece of shit. I'm going to make certain you never have the urge to hurt another woman again. It's going to take a surgeon a week to find your balls, I'm going to kick them so high and hard.

Deciding to engage the man in conversation until she could maneuver him into a better position, she asked, "So tell me, why all the plastic surgery? Why hide who you really are from everyone?" Taking a step to the side, she continued on without giving him time to respond.

"Tell me about how you survived all alone in one of the most inhospitable places on earth. How did you convince them to help you?" Jenna would have bet her inheritance she already knew the answer, but she was hoping he'd tell her, and at least one of the zillion security feeds which covered every inch of the gardens was trained on him.

His dark laugh sent chills racing up her spine. The man's eyes were not just cold, they were also completely empty. It was as if he had no soul at all. *How do other people look at this man and not sense what is missing?*

"Well, since all my teammates decided it was too much trouble to retrieve my body,"—his voice lowered to a point it sounded like it should belong to Satan himself—"I had to make nice with the locals, and it was just a lucky coincidence I happened to know the local dialect and had enough contacts to drop the right names."

"What do you mean contacts? And I don't believe in coincidences. You'd been working for the enemy all along?" Jenna's voice reflected the total disdain she felt for the traitor she was facing. The idea that this man had served beside her brothers and other dedicated and loyal soldiers almost made her physically ill.

Ted Scott looked at her as if she was nothing more than a bothersome insect. "Don't be such a fucking hypocrite, Jenna. What do you think your family's oil company is doing if they aren't supporting the enemy when they buy oil from Middle East countries secretly funding terrorists? I merely cut out the middlemen. Think of it as furthering their education. I taught them about our planned missions, and they paid me—and oh, did they ever pay me."

Jenna was slowly inching closer, just another few inches and he'd be close enough to land the first kick. After that, it was going to be all her show.

"You see, I'd been stashing money for years and never made a mistake, except for you. You were a temptation. You were the only one I ever let walk away. And now? Well, I'm almost done. There are just a couple of loose ends I need to tie up, then I'll be enjoying the good life in my beachfront villa while your family mourns the loss of their precious little princess."

Jenna was shocked to the depths of her soul. *I was the only one he let walk away? Oh my God, how many other women did he brutalize and then kill?*

Her shock fueled her fury and with a burst of power which even surprised her, she sent a lightning-fast kick to the front of his knee and smiled as she heard the satisfying pop of soft tissue and snap of bone. Scott screamed and drew up a small pistol, but before he could get off a shot, Jenna had kicked the weapon from his hand, spinning around to land another solid blow to the center of his chest. When she heard the whoosh of air leaving his lungs, she knew it was time to rearrange his dick and balls before she rendered him unconscious, she certainly didn't want him to miss out on that fun.

Two lightning fast kicks to his groin were answered with a gasping sound that was somewhere between a howl of a wolf and the screech of an owl. Smiling to herself, she didn't have much time to bask in her victory before they were surrounded by the ShadowDance Club's security team.

When Colt had heard Grayson give Jenna's location and his brief recap of what was taking place, his heart had nearly failed. Theodore James was really Ted Scott? The implications of the man's compromises to not only his own team's safety, but to national security were staggering. Hell, it was going to take years before they really knew the extent of the man's betrayal and the cost of his greed.

Colt ran into the area on the heels of two of the younger men who had been working the perimeter of the property and saw Scott had already been secured. Colt turned and wrapped Jenna in a hold that would have made a grizzly bear proud. All he could do was hold her tightly. Jesus, he'd never been so scared in his entire life. Was this how life with Jenna Lamont would always be, challenge and terror? He wasn't sure his heart could take it. When he finally stepped back far enough to get a good look at her, the first thing he noticed was the look of smug self-satisfaction in her expression, and then he realized his little warrior pixie wasn't even out of breath and the man hog-tied nearby had obviously had his ass handed to him.

"Woman, I have no idea what to do with you. You scared me so badly, I'm pretty sure my brain is scrambled. Why on earth are you out here in the dark, alone? Didn't you read the note I left you giving you very clear instructions to stay right where you were that under no circumstances were you to leave my suite without an escort?"

Colt knew he was almost yelling at her, but given the circumstances, he felt he was handling the adrenaline surge remarkably well. "I'm going to have to think up some whole new level of punishment for this, and when I'm done, your brothers are sure to want their turns."

JENNA NARROWED HER eyes at him and crossed her arms underneath her beautiful breasts and spoke in a tone that was nearly arctic. "Excuse me? Punishment? You must be bat-shit crazy if you think you're going to go all big bad Dom on my ass. No, I don't fucking think so, buster. I brought down a spy who has eluded not only your Special Forces 'Super Troopers', but the US government in general, and I'm the dimwit here? Don't think I want to buy a ticket for this little guilt trip, thanks anyway." Jenna was seeing red, literally. She was beyond pissed off... about everything—having been raped, then convinced to cover it up—Christ, who knew how many other people had suffered because she'd been naïve and so selfish, she'd let him get away with it.

She was mad the man now being led away by deputies had betrayed his team and her country, how dare he? She was thoroughly steamed because, at this moment, all she wanted was to be cuddled, and that alone was enough to make her nearly thermonuclear. Damn, couldn't he just say, "Wow, great job, babe. Way to get the confession and kick the prick's ass in less time than it took my team to run across the gardens"?

Colt recognized the signs of adrenaline crash a split second before Jenna's knees folded. Hell, he'd been so caught up in his own reactions, he hadn't even considered how she was coping. Talk about all those years of training as a Dominant flying right out the window. Fuck! Right now, the only thing even remotely important was listening to his heart and holding the woman who had just single-handedly taken out a rat bastard the rest of them had overlooked. Christ, he was so proud of her, even when his palm itched to paddle her sweet ass until she couldn't sit for a week.

Looking into her sweet face, he was overcome with his love for her. "God, Jenna, I'm so very proud of you. You not only did an amazing job of settling a very old score, but you've done a service to your country few have ever rivaled. Fuck, if I have my way, you'll get your own national holiday!" Smiling down at her he continued, "But I'm still wondering why you're out here? Hmmm? You weren't thinking of running again, were you?"

Looking down at her hands as she twisted them together, she finally let out a big breath before looking up at him through her lashes. "Honestly, I didn't even see a note. I was mad when I woke up alone, but then I remembered everything that was supposed to happen here tonight. I knew I'd left something in my car, and I wanted to make sure I had it in case someone took my baby. Face it, my car would be the fastest and most agile vehicle if you wanted to make a quick escape down the mountain... and well... I got so distracted by well... everything... I forgot about the gifts I'd brought back. And... well, one of them is really valuable, and I didn't want it stolen or destroyed." Her voice had dropped to a near whisper by the time she had finished speaking.

"Jesus, Jenna, what could have possibly been so important you'd risk your life to retrieve it amid all the danger you knew you might face?" He couldn't believe it. Would she really risk her life for a few gifts she'd brought back from Egypt?

"Well, I have always remembered the story you told me about your dad losing a priceless amulet to thieves during one of his archeological digs... and well, one-night years and years ago we were sitting in the kitchen and you drew me a picture of it on a napkin... and..."

She had to stop and re-center her thoughts before continuing. "Well, I saved that napkin. I kept it in my jewelry box for years, and when I started traveling to that part of the world, I always took detailed copies of that picture with me and showed it to everyone, from museum curators to back-alley venders. And this last trip... well, I found it. That's why I missed my original flight back home, I was buying it back for your dad. I know he isn't well, and I was hoping this would help."

Colt was absolutely stunned, nothing she could have said would have surprised him any more than this had. The amulet had been worth hundreds of thousands of dollars at the time it was taken, and his dad had been devastated by its theft. His career as an archeologist had taken a huge hit because of the loss. He'd barely retained his teaching position at the university he'd dedicated his entire career to.

"Jenna, I don't know what to say, this is the most incredible thing I've ever heard. My father will be overjoyed, and I am grateful beyond words, but how on earth can we ever repay you for this?" He knew her family was wealthy, but if it took him the rest of his life, he would repay her.

She smiled shyly. "Well, it turns out the amulet was given to the thief's mother as a gift. The family is still very poor, but had never considered selling the piece because it was the last gift the son gave his mother before he died in a car accident later that year. They kept it all these years, but now, there are grandchildren in the family, and the grand-mother wanted the gift to benefit someone else before she dies. What she wanted most was to know her two young granddaughters would have American educations.

My parents and I arranged for those two young women to come to the US, they will be enrolling at the University of Colorado for this next semester. Mom and Dad are thrilled to have them stay at their condo. The girls are really lovely young ladies, who'll be much safer there; it's kind of a win-win situation for everyone."

"I'm completely speechless. You are the most amazing woman I have ever known. We'll get the amulet later, your car is in a secured section of the garage, its contents are safe, I promise you. Now, we need to get you out of this cold night air before..." Colt's words were cut off by the sounds of gunshots near the backside of the garage. As chaos erupted around them, Colt turned and walked up to what appeared to be a flower-covered trellis. He pressed his palm on a hidden panel, and a door slid open revealing a set of stairs descending to a hallway.

"Go. Follow the hallway straight, don't take any turns, just go straight, and it will lead you to the mansion's wine cellar. Grayson is in the crow's nest. He'll open the door on the other end. Please go straight to Katarina's suite, that place is more secure than fucking Fort Knox." He kissed her once with enough heat to be sure she'd remember it until he could get back to her, then he was gone.

Chapter 32

Rissa stood at the railing of the balcony overlooking the main room of The ShadowDance Club with a mixture of fear, horror, and exhilaration. She loved special events at The Club and always dreamed of attending them with her own Dom rather than standing on the sidelines just watching. She'd been disappointed when no one had asked her to attend with them.

Hell, who am I kidding, I was hoping Mitch Grayson would ask me, but he obviously isn't as interested in me as I am in him. Time to move on, Clarissa Jean... dreamin' don't make it so. She laughed to herself when she realized her self-talk sounded an awfully lot like her sweet Granny.

Growing tired of waiting for someone to walk her to her car, Rissa decided if her bosses got their shorts in a wad, they'd just have to cope. She wasn't staying cooped up all night reading and rereading the same damned magazine articles when she could don the outfit and feathered mask she'd purchased weeks earlier and have a look-see at the action downstairs before making her way to the employee parking lot behind the garage and heading home.

Between the jet-black wig covering her auburn-colored hair and the phony sub collar she'd bought from the Internet, she was confident no one would recognize or approach her. She just wanted to watch for a while without worrying about her mother hen bosses or those other overprotective zealots on their security team.

Sighing to herself, she was lost in thought while gazing out over the crowded main lounge. She knew Mitch would be up in the crow's nest during tonight's event, and dammit all to hell, just thinking about him made her pussy flood with her cream, soaking her panties. Hell, she had finally given in and started keeping spares in her locker at the spa. It was embarrassing, but she'd grown tired of having to work with wet drawers, as her granny had been so fond of referring to women's underwear.

Remembering her sweet granny always made Rissa smile and her heart warm. Damn, but she missed that woman so much. It seemed a whole other lifetime ago she'd been able to sit on Granny's sofa, watching old reruns, eating popcorn, and talking about anything and everything with the woman who had always been the most stable influence in her turbulent life.

Shaking off the melancholy, Rissa descended the stairs and headed for the back door. She passed several of the security staff and even more Club members, and none had recognized her, but several had taken second glances, something which would not have happened if she hadn't concealed her identity.

Damn if Mitch Grayson hadn't made sure not one single man in The Club didn't avoid her like she had the freaking plague. Most wouldn't give her more than a one-word answer to a question about anything besides the weather. She'd evaded his advances for two years, but the man was tenacious, she'd give him that. But she had decided perhaps it was time to at least consider going to dinner with him. She'd even been trying to find out a bit more about him.

The sudden realization her own behavior was bordering on stalking gave her pause. Even if he wasn't interested in anything more than a casual relationship, she knew it was time to move on from her fear of being alone with a man. *I wonder... exactly how you distinguish between a man's tenacity and my stalking? Hmmmm.*

Just as she reached the back door, Rissa felt a firm hand grasp her upper arm, and gasping in surprise, she turned to see Bryant Davis looking at her with curious, brilliant blue eyes. Holy Mother of all things angelic, the man was so beautiful it was almost frightening. His hair was jet black, which made his electric-blue eyes seem like an even bigger anomaly. He was easily six and a half feet tall and moved with the grace of a tiger.

She'd heard Bryant had only recently returned from some bridge project in Japan. He had been gone for almost a year, and every Club member she knew was thrilled he'd finally returned to ShadowDance. From what she'd heard, he was one of those rare people who everyone seemed to like and admire. Rissa knew he and Mitch were known to share women in the past, but she'd never been close enough to speak to him until now. His touch on her arm sent electric tingles zipping through her, and it took her a second to realize he had actually spoken to her.

"Miss, answer me. Where do you think you are going? That collar tells me there is a Dom somewhere in this room who will be looking for you, and I'd like to have an answer to provide. So, I'm going to ask again, where are you going, and where is your escort?"

Oh shit, hadn't thought about this wrinkle. *Damn, stop staring at the man and think, Clarissa Jane.* "Um, well, I wasn't feeling well and asked his permission to just step right outside the back door and get a bit of fresh air. I won't go more than just around the corner, I promise." She didn't think he was buying it, but then someone at the other side of the room called to him, and she knew she'd been saved. He looked at her for a few very long heartbeats.

"I am trusting you to go no farther than just outside the door. You are to stay close, do you understand?"

God, the man really was too yummy for words, and his deep voice resonated low in her abdomen the same way Mitch Grayson's did. She felt like someone had started a small fire inside of her, and with just the right amount of tending, it would quickly become a raging inferno.

Mentally shaking herself back to reality, Rissa nodded her head and slipped out the door as he headed back to the bar. *Yikes, that was close. Time to hightail it to my car and get my happy ass home before he decides to check up on me.*

Walking at a brisk pace, Rissa cursed herself for not wearing a jacket. The wind had picked up and the temperature was dropping fast. She shivered but wasn't sure if it was because of the chill in the air or the encounter she'd just had with Bryant Davis. If anybody in The Club found out she'd just left against orders and lied to a dungeon monitor, holy shit she'd be in deeper trouble than she could dig out of in a month of Sundays.

Hurrying along the walk, deep in thought about how big she'd just messed up, she didn't even see the two men hustling a woman toward the garage until she was right behind them.

"Oh, sorry, I didn't see you. Hey, wait I don't recognize any of you, what are you doing out here? This area is off-limits to everyone except employees. You'll need to go back to The Club's designated play areas and... hey, let go of my arm. Who the hell do you think you are? You can't go manhandling me like that, Christ are you fucking deaf? I said, let go of me!"

The man who appeared to be in charge signaled the other one. "Bring the nosy bitch along and either shut her up or shoot her, I don't particularly care which at the point."

"Do as Mr. Petrov says or I'll happily shoot you so you'll stop yammering."

Shaking the other woman's arm, the man called Petrov, fumed, "What the fuck is wrong with Americans? Can they not stay out of other people's business?"

The brute didn't let go of her arm and continued dragging her down the path behind the guy who was giving the orders. The other woman was obviously not going along voluntarily either. Rissa had always cursed her tendency to chatter when she was nervous. Frack she just couldn't seem to remain quiet even though it would no doubt be prudent to hold her tongue.

"Where do you think you're going? You can't get in the garage, you know, and Grayson will be on you like white on rice when he sees you out here on the monitors."

Speaking loud enough she hoped somebody nearby noticed a problem or the motion- and sound-activated sensors kicked on, she continued even louder. "Oh yeah, Mitch and the other guys are so gonna be pissed big time when they find out you're out here, and I don't think that lady with you looks any happier than I am about suddenly becoming your date for this evening. What do you say, let's all head back up to The Club and get something warm to drink?"

Rissa knew if the men managed to get them around the corner, it was going to be pitch dark, and there was a really steep drop off down to the lower level of the parking area and falling off that in the dark sounded way too painful to her. Time for some distraction.

BRYANT DAVIS'S EARBUD clicked, and Mitch's voice filled his ear "Who was the little sub who walked out the back door just now?"

"Don't know, she said her Master knew she was going for fresh air, and she promised to stay right by the back door, why?" Suddenly Bryant was on alert, something about the little sprite had seemed vaguely familiar, but he just couldn't place her. He'd been gone so long he was having trouble getting reacquainted with The Club's membership. Was she someone he knew? He just wasn't sure.

"Well, she straight-up lied to you. She's headed toward the garage. I'd bet you anything that was Rissa. I had the spa checked, and she isn't there, and that little bit of a thing is the right size and walks just like the woman I've been telling you about for a year. Our target's tracking devices put her right in Rissa's path. I am so going to paddle her ass bright cherry red for this. Fuck! Isn't there a single woman in this club tonight who can follow a blessed instruction?

Head that way. I'm grabbing a com unit, and as soon as I get somebody up here to replace me, I'll be right behind you." And after a brief pause, he added. "Be careful, my friend, we just got you home, don't want you to go getting yourself splattered or anything."

"Thanks, man, your poetic expression of concern touches my heart." Bryant hoped Mitch understood that even though their exchange was all about snark and sarcasm, he really did appreciate the reminder things were not business as usual for tonight's event. Just as Mitch was ready to leave the crow's nest, he heard Rissa's voice loud and clear.

"Mitch and the other guys are so gonna be pissed big time when they find out you're out here…"

Holy shit! She'd just told him Petrov had them both. He quickly set off the alert to every man working in The Club and started giving the team location and intel when he heard a gunshot and then a blood-chilling scream… Rissa!

As RISSA WAS falling backward over the retaining wall, she thought how odd it seemed everything was happening in slow motion. She'd tried to yank her arm free from the big gorilla who was apparently half leech, and just as she felt his grip loosen slightly, the woman had thrown herself at Rissa.

The momentum had sent them both over the edge, and just as they were losing their footing, she'd seen a flash a split second before she'd heard the rapport of a gun. The woman had made a sick grunting sound at the same time Rissa had felt a burning sensation in her shoulder. She'd looked up to see the woman grimace in pain, and then everything went black.

Dylan was the first to round the corner, coming to a dead stop when he remembered the retaining wall. He looked all around and couldn't see anyone. *What the fuck?* He knew this was where the sound had come from, damn it all to hell, four people could not simply vanish into thin air.

Just then, in the distance, he heard what sounded like dirt bikes. *Oh, hell no.* He radioed for the other men to intercept, then called the crow's nest for a location on Mia's tracking devices.

"What do you mean they show she's behind the garage? I'm behind the garage's main building, and there is no one here." He heard what sounded like a soft whine and yelled, "Somebody, get me some damned light back here." In less than a second, the entire area was flooded with enough light to mimic high noon. *Typical Lamont overkill.*

Looking down, his heart dropped to the pit of his stomach. Mia lay atop another woman, and holy fucking hell, she'd been shot!

Dylan hit the alarm on his radio, sending an alert and request for the first responders from The Club as well as a request for ambulances. Running to the stairs, he was beside the women in mere seconds. He could hear Zach telling the team he had grabbed his medic bag and was on his way after he tuned out everything, but his too-still woman lying face down on top of an equally too-still form. He was afraid to move Mia without a backboard, fearing neck and back injuries.

From what he could see, the bullet had gone in through the fleshy part of her shoulder. If it was a through and through shot, likely the other woman would also have a wound. The bullet would have lost enough velocity to be lodged in her upper torso somewhere. Shit, he really was getting mighty tired of women getting hurt in his jurisdiction, and it really tanked that, this time, one of them was his.

Sending up prayers to a God he hadn't been on a first-name basis with for many years, Dylan looked up into the terrified eyes of Mitch Grayson and Bryant Davis. Mitch was white as a sheet.

"Is that Rissa?" was all he managed to ask as he swallowed around what Dylan suspected was a bolder sized lump in his throat.

Dylan looked at him, a frown creasing his forehead as he answered his friend. "I thought she was supposed to be in the spa? This woman has black hair." Reaching down, he slid his fingers along her hairline dislodging the wig enough to see the deep auburn locks beneath before looking up into the terrified expressions of Grayson and Davis. "Shit, it is Rissa. Where the hell is Zach with that damned medic equipment?"

He had no sooner spoken than Zach Lamont and Jamie Creed moved up beside them and motioned him back. Jamie had been a sniper on the Lamonts' team and had joined the ShadowDance contract team a while back. Dylan knew Creed had been stationed in the surrounding evergreen trees, so he wasn't surprised to see the lanky young man had fallen in with Zach as they made their way through the gathering crowd to the injured women.

Someone handed down a couple of backboards which were kept in The Club's small medical ATV. With a flurry of motion both women were secured to the boards and moved into the heated garage for assessment, then transport. Even though the property had a helipad, the coming storm was packing a powerful punch—wind speeds were already picking up quickly—so there was no way anyone would attempt an airlift.

Doc Woods met them at the emergency room entrance, barking instructions as they wheeled both women into a single large examination room with two bays in order for him to better treat them both simultaneously.

"Update me," he bellowed at the EMTs who'd brought

the women in. Listening as he worked, he frowned then asked, "Never regained consciousness during the ride down the mountain? Shit, that's quite a drive, and I know that bus wouldn't be the fastest sled around."

Dylan was thinking the same thing as he leaned with his back against the wall, but he wasn't going to speak up in hopes the elderly doctor would consider him part of the scenery and not order him out of the room.

THE CLUB HAD been cleared quickly. The Masquerade would have to be rescheduled for a later date. Looking around the waiting room, Dylan had to wonder if the annual bash hadn't just been relocated. He shook his head at some of the outfits he'd bet had rarely been worn outside of a fetish club. Thank God some of The Club members were community leaders. Maybe he wouldn't be getting calls about this for the next month after all.

If the situation wasn't so damned dire, he might even find some humor in the fact that most of the town council was sitting around in little more than underwear under their coats and jackets. *God, but I love this town and its crazy, quirky citizens. Well hell, there is never a dull moment, that's for sure.*

Katarina Lamont came bouncing, literally, through the automatic doors and headed toward him like the heat-seeking missile he knew she could be. At least her husbands, Alex and Zach, were on either side of her. Even though they had very little real control over her, they did seem to be able to distract her most of the time. And wonder of blessings, Jenna Lamont was right behind her,

Colt Matthews nearly jogging to keep up with her. *Damn pixies, neither of them is a spit over five feet tall, how the hell can they walk that fast?* Katarina reached him first.

"How are they? Have you seen them yet? Is Doc Woods here? Have they done a CT scan or MRI yet? When will they be moved upstairs? Did they regain consciousness in the ambulance on the way in?"

Dylan stared at her, utterly amazed she hadn't fainted into a heap from lack of oxygen. How did the woman talk and never breathe, anyway? She paused about a half a beat before frowning, crossing her arms over her rounded baby bump and tapping her tiny little foot at him before speaking in that impertinent tone he knew drove her husbands both to distraction.

"Well? Are you just going to stand there looking like I'm speaking Pekinese to you, or are you going to answer me?"

Finally, Alex stepped up and took her elbow. "Love, I think you have overwhelmed Dylan a bit. Perhaps if you ask your questions one at a time, it might be more conducive to a conversation, hmm? How about we all go over there and sit down, and Dylan can update everybody at the same time?"

Leading her toward a chair as she muttered about "Damned bossy men... not made of glass for Christ's sake.... nobody ever tells me anything anymore..." Jenna grabbed her sister-in-law's free hand and helped Alex move her over to a nearby sofa.

Dylan smiled and shook his head, looking over at Zach, who was watching the scene with eyes filled with love even as they danced with mischief.

"Damn if she isn't fun to live with. I swear, we never even have to turn on the television for entertainment anymore, ought to just sell it." He chuckled then turned to Dylan and grasped his shoulder. "She'll be okay, man, you'll see. They're both strong women, and this place has the best equipment available. We've already got a neurologist from Denver on standby in case it's necessary. We're all here for you, don't forget that. Now, why don't you update everybody on what you know so far?"

Dylan turned to face everyone in the room and took a calming breath before speaking in a steady voice. "I really don't know all that much at this time. I spoke with Doc briefly just after we arrived. Melita has a gunshot wound to her shoulder, but it went through clean and didn't hit anything major. She'll need surgery to repair the damage. They've called in a specialist, and he'll be here shortly."

He paused for several seconds before continuing. He was dreading relaying the rest of the news because it was much more difficult. "It appears the gunman was aiming for Rissa and Melita jumped to shield her. Had either of them taken the shot where it was intended... well, it looks like it would have been a clean heart shot." He heard the gasps from those around the room. *You got it, the SOB had intended to kill Rissa, no doubt about that.*

"The bullet appears to still be lodged in Rissa's upper chest. It's likely Melita knocked her just enough off balance, the bullet didn't hit her in the center of the chest. Rissa's gunshot wound isn't a life-threatening injury either, and she'll be having surgery to remove the bullet as soon as they can do it safely."

He paused briefly, looking over at Mitch and Bryant with compassion before he continued. "The overriding concern with both women is their possible head injuries and brain swelling. So far, they don't see any indicators of brain trauma, but those symptoms can take several hours to develop, so both women are being closely monitored."

Dylan paused and simply stood looking out over the heads of the people gathered around him as he tried to rein in his worst fears and remember it hadn't really been that long since they'd been hurt. But the bottom line was, every minute they remained unconscious, the dangers and risks increased.

"WHAT DID DOC Woods say? Have the specialists arrived yet? Alex, Zach have you called our parents yet? Do you have the jet and chopper standing by?" Jenna's voice sounded strained, and she appeared to be as tightly wound as Katarina as she sat on the very edge of her chair.

Colt moved around in front of her, kneeling to wrap his arms around her shaking shoulders, pulling her into his warm embrace.

When she started to hyperventilate, he pulled back until he could see her face. When her eyes didn't come up to his, he spoke quietly to her. "Jenna, look at me." When she still couldn't bring her focus back to him, he spoke more firmly, using the Dom tone he knew she always responded to. "Pet, look at me, right now." Her eyes immediately met his. *Mine, she is mine, all mine. God, but I love this woman with everything in me. I can't wait to collar and marry her.*

"Good girl, now breathe with me, nice and slow." It only took a few seconds for her to settle down. "Very good, now, let's hear the rest of what Dylan has to say, shall we?" With that, he picked her up and sat her on his lap, so her back rested against his chest, and his arms stayed wrapped firmly around her chest, anchoring her with his warmth and support.

"They are both still unconscious," Dylan continued, "and that's not a good sign. But, we're holding on to the hope the combination of fear, being shot, and falling one on top of the other onto a concrete surface... well, hell.... Please, say prayers for them both."

He turned on his heel and walked out into the hall, knowing Mitch Grayson and Bryant Davis were right behind him. Without even looking back, he simply said, "Follow me." His voice was gruff with emotion, but he knew the other men wouldn't be able to settle in the waiting room until they'd seen Rissa for themselves. Mitch had been trying to claim the elusive little redhead for a year or more, and Bryant was drowning in guilt for letting her walk out the door without an escort.

MELITA FELT LIKE she was listening to a conversation from underwater... must be deep beneath the surface, too, judging from the feeling of pressure on her chest. Her head felt like a freight train was rumbling through it. Straining to make out the words, she knew one of the voices made her feel safe while the other didn't sound familiar.

"No, I'm staying here again tonight, I have deputies to cover for me. I'm not leaving her alone. Her cover has been compromised, she isn't safe. Doc doesn't know why she isn't awake yet, I can't even tell you how worried I am about that. Goddamn it, Alex, she was right there, right within my reach and now she may slip through my fingers yet again."

She would recognize Dylan Marshall's voice anywhere,

the low timbre, the rough edge even in his lightest moments teetered on the edge of the role of Dominant he filled so well. God, she had missed him and the lifestyle they had enjoyed together. Her love for him had never been in question.

Vowing if she ever surfaced, she'd tell him what a foolish mistake she'd made, she let herself drift back into the inky blackness.

MITCH AND BRYANT stood on opposite sides of Rissa's bed, staring down at the fragile woman lying too still between them. "Jesus, could they plug her into anything else?" Mitch's exasperated question was rhetorical, but eerily, it echoed Bryant's exact thoughts. Bryant had always been awed by Mitch Grayson's special gift, but he also understood the inherent challenges it presented.

They'd spent many nights on the deck at Pomola, watching the river snaking its way down to the mountain valley below, drinking beer, and talking about anything and everything, including their views on long-term ménages. They had known it would take a very special woman, one who ignited electricity in them both, and without even speaking the words, they knew that woman was laying right between them.

"Letting her walk out that back door alone will haunt me until my last breath, brother." The sadness in Bryant's voice had Mitch looking up at his friend. When Bryant looked up, Mitch's eyes held nothing but compassion.

Bryant Davis had been a geeky college freshman, trying to find his way around a campus larger than his entire

hometown when Mitch Grayson had seemed to material-
ize out of nowhere with answers to questions Bryant
hadn't even had the courage to ask.

Bryant had laughed to himself many times about how
he'd wondered if the other man could read his mind, as it
turned out, that wasn't all that far off from the truth. "Her
beautiful green eyes sucked me right in. God, what a
bonehead mistake! Christ, Mitch, I fucking know the rules.
I knew what all was going down, all the extra security in
place that night." Sighing and running a frustrated hand
through his hair before continuing, "I nearly fell headfirst
into those green pools. All I could think about was how
much I wanted her, and she obviously belonged to someone else. Fuck."

Mitch understood how Rissa could scramble a man's
thinking. Hell, she'd been wreaking havoc with his for
months. His voice was low but strong, his words sounding
more certain than he felt.

"Hang in there, she's going to be fine. The bullet is out.
She'll have to do some rehab on her shoulder, but we'll
have fun helping with that, and the massages afterward will
be their own reward."

Smiling down at Rissa, he was struck by how small she
looked lying there. Her personality was always so large, it
was easy to forget how tiny she was. He knew some of the
staff referred to her as Tink, short for Tinkerbell, and it was
certainly an appropriate nickname.

"I have to tell you though when she's all healed up,
we'll be having a serious session on a spanking bench, she's
racked up some rather significant punishments." His soft
expression and warm voice were a contrast to his words.
Oh, he'd make her pay all right, but it wasn't going to be as
much about punishment as it was about getting his hands

on her sweet body.

Leaning down right near Rissa's ear, Mitch's voice was pitched low and full of authority. "Clarissa, you need to wake up and face the music, sweetheart. You have some serious explaining to do. Master Bryant and I are waiting to hear what you have to say. Alex and Zach are also waiting to hear what you were thinking. If you don't come back soon, I'm going to let Katarina in here, and you don't want that, do you?"

Smiling up at Bryant, he said, "You haven't met Alex and Zach's pregnant tornado yet, have you? She's their wife and sub, well, at least she lets them think she's a sub." He chuckled to himself, then his eyes widened, and his grin spread clear across his face as he watched Rissa's grass-green eyes flutter open and her mouth twitch into a smile.

HER MOUTH FELT like she'd eaten all the stuffing out of a good-sized sofa, blah! She blinked at the bright rays of the setting sun streaming in through the window of her room. Bryant immediately closed the shades and dimmed the room lights. She appreciated the effort because she could already feel the stirrings of a monster headache. *And what the hell is on the back of my damned head? It feels like a rock. And am I laying on a donut pillow?*

"Awww, sweetheart, welcome back. We've been mighty worried about you." Mitch was speaking to her so sweetly, and his knuckles softly caressing her cheek were the most soothing thing she thought she'd ever felt.

"C–can I have a d–drink? My mouth is so dry, and my throat hurts." She felt tears stinging her eyes, damn her throat was so sore, and her head was really beginning to throb. "What happened? Where am I?" She turned her head just slightly, and when she made eye contact with Bryant, she gasped in surprise.

Bryant just stood perfectly still and watched as her mouth formed an *O* and then her face flushed bright red. *Oh yeah, babe, you know exactly who I am, and that you are in big trouble. Oh, little one, this is gonna be a mighty fine ride, indeed.*

WHEN MIA FINALLY opened her eyes, the room was dim, but the first thing she noticed was the very large, toasty warm body lying next to her. God, she would recognize Dylan's unique scent anywhere, all dark musk and clean outdoors. She had no sooner opened her eyes and looked at him than he came instantly wide awake and smiled a lazy smile.

"Well hello, darlin.' Glad to see you finally decided to return to me." His drawled words warmed her heart even though she knew they held a wealth of double meaning, and for the life of her, she couldn't think of a single reason to protest.

"I love you. I've always loved you." She felt the first tear slide over and trace down her temple by the time she continued. "I just couldn't wait another second to tell you. I've made some very selfish decisions, but I never stopped loving you." She searched his face for any thread of hesitation or anger and saw nothing but sincerity and hope for the future reflecting the depth of love she'd walked away from. She'd hurt him so badly, and she had no idea how she was ever going to be able to make it up to him.

"I know, I heard it all, and you aren't slipping away from me again, my sweet love. As soon as you get the all-clear from Doc, we're heading out for some much-needed R & R. I need to know you are safe while some things are wrapped up here, but more than that, I just need you. I'll always need you. Why I let you go so easily is a mystery I'll probably never unravel. Hell, I think I was just so stunned, my brain went into neutral and didn't re-engage for almost a year. And by then, you were so deep undercover, I couldn't get to you."

Dylan was gently stroking her hair back from her face, his touch tender, but his callused fingertips were sending sparks of desire pulsing through her entire body. *Oh boy, some things never change, his touch still sets off a five-alarm panty-drenching heat.*

MIA WAS LOOKING at him as if he held her entire world in his palms. God how he'd missed this sweet woman. Fire and ice—he'd always teased her she was fire in bed and ice on the job, an irresistible combination. There wasn't a single thing he hadn't loved about her. His total devotion and deep love had made her sudden decision to divorce him even more devastating. Had he been able to really step back and analyze the situation, he would have known something was seriously wrong, and he'd have never signed the fucking papers she'd blindsided him with that night.

But the time for looking back was over. He knew he was going to have to tell her Petrov had eluded them and her career with the DEA was all but over, but right at this moment, he just wanted to touch her, to make sure she knew exactly where she belonged... and to whom.

Chapter 33

One week later

"I COULD LIE on this beach forever and never be ready to leave." Mia had been released two days after she'd finally awakened, and it hadn't taken Dylan and the Lamonts long to whisk her to the nearest airstrip and deposit her safely out of harm's way. Oh, she knew she'd have to return sometime soon, that she'd never truly be safe until Petrov was dead or buried so deep in some godforsaken federal prison, he didn't have a prayer of ever seeing the light of day. But for now, she was going to enjoy her time with Dylan.

They'd found a small chapel and remarried quietly the second night after they'd arrived. She'd heard Dylan talking to Alex and Zach's wife, Kat, assuring her that, yes, she could plan and host a reception after their return. Smiling to herself, she thought those few words were about all he'd been able to get in edgewise. She could hardly wait to see Kat again. She felt like she was starting a new life and would have an old friend already waiting in the wings.

"What are you smiling about? You have a cat-that-swallowed-the-canary grin that always worries me," Dylan chuckled and reached over from his lounger next to hers and squeezed her hand.

"I was just thinking about Kat and how glad I am that I'm going to already have a girlfriend when we return to Climax. Kat was always so timid when I'd see her with Cal Robertson, but from what I overheard of your conversation with her, it sounds as if she's come out of her shell." Mia had laughed at Kat's high-pitched scream when Dylan had told her they'd already remarried and his multiple attempts to assure her, she would still get to play hostess.

Dylan returned Mia's smile. "Oh, indeed, Mrs. Katarina Lamont might be small, but she packs a powerful punch. Hell, both Alex and Zach have always been two of the strictest Doms at their Club, but rest assured, that little bit of a woman leads them on a merry chase. And if Grayson is right and she's carrying multiples, oh hell, this is going to be priceless to watch."

They laid back in companionable silence for a long time, enjoying each other's company and the sound of the waves beating against the white sandy beach. The soft breeze carried the sweet scent of orchids and the gentle strains of an acoustic guitar playing in the lounge a few yards up the beach.

They'd spent the past couple of days making sweet love so often, they'd barely made it out of their cottage. There wouldn't be any BDSM play for a while yet, Mia's shoulder was healing nicely, but any strain might well cause a setback Dylan wasn't willing to risk. So, for now, he was perfectly happy to slide his throbbing cock into her wet, velvet pussy and take them both over the edge of ecstasy again and again. They'd have the rest of their lives for scenes, well, at least until he managed to plant his seed deep within her. God, but he couldn't wait to see her round with his child. She was going to be an amazing mother.

Finally, Mia broke the silence. "I've loved being here with you, you've made this time together so perfect. I'm going to spend the rest of my life showing you how much I love you, Dylan Marshall. And as much as I love this lost paradise, I'm ready to go home. I'm ready to go back to Climax and begin our life together."

Dylan squeezed her hand gently before answering. "I can't think of a single thing I'd like more."

Chapter 34

J ENNA WAS LYING alongside the rock-lined stream, trailing her fingers in small circles through the crystal-clear water as it made lazy, bubbling progress on its way down the mountain. She had always known there wasn't any other place on earth she felt as settled as she did on Shadow-Dance Mountain. Everything that had happened since her return home recently had just underscored how empty her life had been without the joy which could only be found with family and friends.

She'd traveled all over the world, met thousands of people, seen everything from the Eiffel Tower to the Great Barrier Reef to the Great Wall of China to the Corcovado in Rio. But deep in her heart, Jenna knew she would trade it all for the chance to experience the type of love and acceptance she saw reflected in the eyes of her brothers and her best friend.

The leaves dancing in the breeze above her were a wash of brilliant gold and vibrant shades of orange. Hell, even their reflection on the water's rippling surface was something to behold.

Jenna knew she would have to make a decision soon, but even after everything they had shared, Jenna wasn't secure enough in her relationship with Colt to make a life-altering decision just on the outside chance he might have really meant all those things he'd said about her belonging to him.

One of the things she had always hated the most about Ted Scott's attack was the self-doubt he'd been able to instill so deeply in her soul, she'd never been able to dig it out. Being beaten and raped had been trauma enough to overcome, but she still struggled with the lingering effects of insecurities born of his actions and words. And if she was really honest with herself, she would admit the only person who had ever been able to reach through all that and see her heart had been Colt Matthews.

COLT STOOD IN the shadows, watching as Jenna lay stretched out on the flat rocks beside the mountain stream. She was a vision surrounded by the fall splendor of the mountains, lost in thought. Colt knew he would never forget the picture of her at this moment. Standing still and watching the play of expressions move over her beautiful face, he etched the moment firmly into his memory, knowing someday he'd be able to tell his grandchildren about how amazing their grandmother had looked as he'd approached her with the most important question he'd ever asked another person. He knew he would have to be honest with those beautiful blessings to come and tell them just how scared he'd been about asking her to become his wife, but he'd also tell them he would have never taken no for an answer either.

Wondering at what she was thinking, he smiled to himself knowing he wouldn't be able to figure out the workings of the female mind if he lived to be five hundred years old, and that was just one of the things about Jenna Lamont that made her the most captivating woman he'd ever known.

Colt realized how lost in thought she was when he walked right up to her and sat down alongside her before she ever registered his presence. The lover in him was thrilled her first reaction to his touch was immediate recognition, but the Dom was much less than thrilled with her lack of awareness of her surroundings. *Looks like we'll be having another discussion about how important I consider your safety won't we, my sweet love? Oh... but I am so looking forward to revisiting that lesson.*

When Jenna started to move to a sitting position, Colt stilled her with a palm to her back. "No, please, stay still for a moment. Seeing you surrounded by the beauty of the mountain, lost in the peace I know you feel here is just about the most amazing thing I have ever seen."

He smiled at the softness he saw in her eyes at his words of praise. *She is so perfect it's as if she was created just for me. As much as I hate to admit it, Grayson is right, I've never done anything that makes me worthy of this gift.*

Colt ran his fingers through the soft length of Jenna's hair as it trailed over her shoulders and down her back, marveling at the silky slide of it through his fingers. Her hair was the same midnight color as her brothers, showing the Native American heritage they all inherited from their father, but her striking beauty was a genetic gift from her mother. Catherine Lamont had been a model before her marriage and was still a beauty even as she was preparing to become a grandmother.

They remained in companionable silence for several minutes before Colt finally leaned over, scooped Jenna up into his arms, and cradled her in his lap. When she leaned into his broad chest and sighed in contentment, he wasn't sure, but thought his heart might well burst right out of his chest.

Jenna finally broke the silence by asking, "What have you been up to this fine afternoon? You disappeared after lunch, and I wasn't sure where you had gone, so I decided to come out here. This was always one of my favorite places to escape and relax. It's just so peaceful here... no matter the season, this must be one of the most beautiful spots in the entire world."

Colt recognized the wistful tone in her words and knew his sweet sub was struggling to find the balance subs missed when they weren't held close enough to their Masters' hearts.

A submissive whose desire to please her Master was as deeply ingrained as Jenna's would always struggle with melancholy moods and a strong sense of disconnection when they felt they were drifting freely without the security of the anchor they found in their Dom. Knowing they were loved and cherished above all else by the man they entrusted their heart to was a magic elixir for their souls.

Colt had always been amazed the truest submissives were usually viewed by the outside world as the most intelligent and independent women. Only the best Doms understood the value of earning the trust and submission of the strongest woman he could find, those were the deepest ties and the most-enduring relationships.

Colt sat Jenna to his side, so she was facing him and took her small hands in his and raised them to his lips, kissing away the last of the cool mountain water.

"Well, my love, I had a very important call to make, and it took me a little while to track down the couple I wanted to talk to. You see, they are busy people and travel a lot, so they are often hard to catch up with."

Smiling at her puzzled expression he continued before she could ask him any of the questions he could see lighting her eyes. "But I finally caught up with them as they were getting ready to board a flight in Paris with a couple of young ladies in tow. They sounded exhausted, but absolutely over the moon about their two new 'adopted' daughters." Colt knew he'd just given her the hints she'd needed to figure out he had talked to her parents.

Daniel and Catherine Lamont had been thrilled when he'd finally connected with them as they made their way back with the young women Jenna had arranged to have stay with them while studying in the United States. Colt had spoken to Catherine first because she had known for years how much he loved her daughter.

He and Catherine had sat at the kitchen table one night over a year ago talking as they'd made short work of a bottle of Daniel's best wine hijacked from the mansion's well-stocked wine cellar. They'd talked long into the night, and she'd finally gotten him to admit to his feelings for Jenna.

Catherine had warned him there was a heart of pure gold in her sweet daughter, but something had changed in her, and neither she nor Jenna's father had ever known exactly what. She'd cautioned Colt timing was going to be paramount. Colt had recalled that late-night conversation with Catherine many times, and it had been months before he'd truly understood the underlying message had been one of acceptance.

Daniel Lamont had gotten on the phone when he'd seen tears racing down his wife's cheeks; even though their relationship wasn't as overtly D/s as their sons, it was still obvious by the stern questions Colt heard coming from his future father-in-law. Daniel had demanded to know exactly what Colt had said to make his sweet wife cry, and Colt hadn't wasted any time in asking him for his daughter's hand in marriage. Daniel had gone completely silent for just enough time to have Colt feeling a bit unsettled when he'd finally sighed and said, "Damn, son, it's about fucking time."

Colt had let out the breath he hadn't even realized he was holding and laughingly agreed. They'd talked briefly about the recent events at ShadowDance before their flight had been called, and they'd all said their goodbyes.

Watching as realization lit Jenna's eyes, he smiled down at her and watched as the sunlight filtered through the trees and danced around her. "You are so beautiful you take my breath away… and your beauty is soul deep, sweet Jenna." Pausing for a few seconds to try to calm his racing heart, he finally continued. "I love you with every beat of my heart, and I can't even imagine living the rest of my life without you as my wife."

Pulling a small velvet box from his pocket, he held it up and flipped open the lid. When he looked up into Jenna's eyes, he nearly drowned in the love he saw filling them. Leaning forward, he kissed away the tears that had started to fall.

"Will you marry me, Jenna? I want to spend the rest of my life showing you what it feels like to be the center of my universe. I want to share every joy and sorrow life brings us and know I've been blessed beyond measure to have the most amazing woman I've ever known love me in return. I want to raise a family with you, and I'd very much like to do that right here on the mountain I know you love because I believe in my heart this is the one place you are the most at peace. But if your heart truly wants to live somewhere else, rest assured, I would follow you to the end of the earth if it meant sharing my life with you."

STARING UP INTO Colt's face, Jenna was lost in the love she felt coming from him like warm waves washing over her soul. For a few seconds, she had to make herself concentrate enough to absorb the words he'd spoken. It was almost too much to take in after all she'd been through. All the years of suffering and struggling in silence, and now, she was being given the very thing she'd always been too afraid to even wish for.

She'd loved Colt for years, but she had never felt worthy until he'd shown her the freedom she could find in submission. Last night, when she hadn't been able to sleep, she'd made her way down to the kitchen and found Zach making hot cocoa for Kat. He'd taken the steaming cup up to his wife then come back downstairs to talk to her. When he'd finally gotten her to open up about what was troubling her, she'd laid her soul bare and asked him to explain the sense of the inconsistency she felt.

Zach had done his best to explain the dynamics of D/s relationship, but it hadn't been until Alex had stepped into the room and wrapped his arms around her from the back in a hug and told her she didn't need to 'slice and dice it'… she should just follow her heart, she'd finally realized sometimes things were just too significant to try to explain.

Jenna didn't realize how lost she'd become in thought until she noticed Colt's intense look just before he spoke. "God how I would love to know where you just went."

Chuckling, he quickly added, "The expression of pure love that washed over your sweet face was something to behold. Care to share? And by the way, I'm still waiting for an answer to my question, pet."

Taking her hands from his, she reached up to cup his face as she spoke. "I spoke with my brothers just last night, asking them questions about the workings of D/s relationships, and amazingly it was Alex whose words had the biggest impact." She gently placed her finger over his lips when he started to speak, silencing him as she continued.

"His words of wisdom were to stop analyzing something that just *is* and to follow my heart. And my heart belongs to you, Colt... I love you more than I ever knew I could love anyone... you have given me so many gifts, but more than anything, you have put joy and meaning back into my life when I believed I'd lost them forever."

Colt pulled the ring from its velvet perch and slipped it onto her finger before leaning down to kiss her hand, running his lips over the ring that now brought their hearts even closer together.

"I can't promise you I'll be a perfect husband, hell, I can guarantee you I'll be way less than perfect as a matter of fact." He looked at her and then leaned forward to brush a light kiss over her lips.

"But I can tell you, I will always love you and cherish you more than you can possibly imagine. You are the light and center of my life. I want to marry you as soon as possible, sweetness. And as soon as we return from our honeymoon, we'll have a collaring ceremony."

Jenna smiled at the mention of a collaring. She'd been almost eighteen before she'd figured out the beautiful diamond choker her mother wore was a collar. When she'd asked about it, her mother had been completely honest with her, explaining in relationships like hers and her father's, a collaring was actually more significant and binding than a marriage ceremony. It had fascinated Jenna, and she smiled now at that memory.

"I spoke with your mother and father, and I can assure you your mom is in full wedding-planner mode already." He smiled and shook his head. "God help your brothers when she hits the gate and starts in on the plans she was texting to me even before their plane had left Paris. I know you have a lot of things going on with deciding about redirecting your career and everything that entails…"

He found himself in novel territory as he blew out a breath and then said, "I'd love to work with your mom on the plans if you don't mind. I want to make this something so special you'll remember it as one of the most beautiful days of your entire life rather than the end of a stressful couple of months of planning and preparation.

I want you to concentrate on getting yourself to a place where you can balance your need to help others with the time I'm going to be taking keeping you naked and shivering in a sexual haze." He was pleased to see her eyes dilate and a small smile move over her lovely face and knew his words had broken some of the tension just as he'd hoped they would.

JENNA COULDN'T BELIEVE it. This man… the one she knew was a Dominant to his core, was offering to work with Typhoon Catherine to plan the wedding of her dreams, so she could concentrate on getting ready to start college after the first of the year? It was enough to make her dizzy. At that moment, she finally looked down at the ring he'd slid onto her finger and gasped.

"Oh my God in heaven, Colt... this is the most amazing ring I've ever seen." The gold band had interlocking swirls of titanium whose focal point was the enormous princess-cut diamond, flanked by a dazzling pair of alexandrite stones. The gem had always been her favorite, she was fascinated by its changing color. Looking up into his eyes, she asked, "How did you know?" in a voice that was little more than a wisp of air.

Wrapping her in his arms, he pulled her into his chest and kissed her temple. "As your Dom and your fiancé, it's my job to know everything about you, my love. Don't think for a minute you will have even the smallest secret... I'll spend the rest of my life uncovering every wonderful little detail that makes you the most intriguing woman I have ever known."

Jenna wrapped her arms around Colt's neck and sighed as she inhaled the woodsy scent of his aftershave. Pulling back, she slowly ran her fingers along the underside of his jaw before raising her eyes to his.

"I want to live here. I want to go back to college and get a degree that will allow me to help other women who have endured and survived the horrors that lurk around every corner. I can do most of that from here, and I want to talk to my brothers about building here on the mountain if you'd like that, I mean, well, I want to live close to my family, and they already love you, and well, I'm going to have to be around a lot if I'm going to be the world's best aunt and then someday when we have a family... oh my God, you do want a family, don't you? Oh geez, you said that, didn't you? And well, I want to continue to learn about D/s, and I love going to The Club, and Kat is my best friend and…"

Colt leaned his head back and laughed out loud. "God, I love you so much. You are just an absolute treasure… you beguile me, and living here with you as my wife, raising our children… which yes, by the way, I want very much, is just about as perfect a life as I can imagine."

Pausing for several seconds while she settled, Colt used very best Dom voice and said, "Now, about the issue of you being out here all alone, and so lost in thought, you didn't even hear my approach. Do you remember our discussion about how serious an issue I consider your safety and how important I consider your attention to each and every detail relating to that? Hmmm?" He almost laughed aloud again as he saw the lust and anticipation flash through her dark eyes.

"Let's just have a little reminder lesson, shall we? Stand up and strip, pet. Lose everything but the ring…" His words were laced with love rather than reproach, and Jenna felt the last pieces of the ice she'd wrapped around her heart so long ago melt away.

BOOKS BY AVERY GALE

The ShadowDance Club
Katarina's Return – Book One
Jenna's Submission – Book Two
Rissa's Recovery – Book Three
Trace & Tori – Book Four
Reborn as Bree – Book Five
Red Clouds Dancing – Book Six
Perfect Picture – Book Seven

Club Isola
Capturing Callie – Book One
Healing Holly – Book Two
Claiming Abby – Book Three

Masters of the Prairie Winds Club
Out of the Storm
Saving Grace
Jen's Journey
Bound Treasure
Punishing for Pleasure
Accidental Trifecta
Missionary Position
Another Second Chance
Star-Crossed Miracles
Dusted Star
Lilly's Choice

The Wolf Pack Series
Mated – Book One
Fated Magic – Book Two
Tempted by Darkness – Book Three

The Knights of the Boardroom
Book One
Book Two
Book Three

The Morgan Brothers of Montana
Coral Hearts – Book One
Dancing with Deception – Book Two
Caged Songbird – Book Three
Game On – Book Four
Well Bred – Book Five

Mountain Mastery
Well Written
Savannah's Sentinel
Sheltering Reagan

Enchanted Holidays
The Christmas Painting

I would love to hear from you!

Website:
www.averygale.com

Facebook:
facebook.com/avery.gale.3

Twitter:
@avery_gale